What the hell just h

She wanted to be friends.

The only kind of "friend" he wanted to be with her had "boy" attached to it. No, that wasn't true. He enjoyed her friendship because he loved talking to her, hearing her opinions, sharing himself with her.

But he was becoming more attracted to her. So far, they'd only kissed, but that one kiss, that unbelievable kiss, haunted him. His lips still burned where they'd touched hers, his insides still turned to jelly when he thought about it. In fact, he'd been hoping there would have been more kissing in her apartment once he'd apologized for his gaffe.

But she'd focused on their arrangement and her overreaction, and here he was pulling away from the curb into rush hour traffic.

She thought he was dating her only to impress his father. If he were one hundred percent honest with himself, he'd acknowledge the partial truth in that statement. But the more time he spent time with her, when he wasn't royally screwing things up with her, the more he wanted to move beyond their arrangement.

His head was another matter. It was still focused on not making a fool of himself, on maintaining the right reputation, on spinning the right message.

But listening to his head was probably what had gotten him into this mess in the first place. As unbelievable as it might sound, it was time to follow his heart.

Learning to Love

by

Jennifer Wilck

Serendipity, Book 3

Learning to Love

COPYRIGHT © 2018 by Jennifer Wilck

Cover Art by *RJMorris*

The Wild Rose Press, Inc.
PO Box 708
Adams Basin, NY 14410-0708
Visit us at www.thewildrosepress.com

Publishing History
First Rose Edition, 2018
Print ISBN 978-1-5092-2312-1
Digital ISBN 978-1-5092-2313-8

Serendipity, Book 3
Published in the United States of America

Dedication

To all the smart girls out there—especially my two—
always let your brilliance shine.

And to everyone at The Wild Rose Press
who helps my books to shine as well. Thank you.

Chapter One

After he read the email from his father, Adam dropped his head in his hands and massaged his temples. Freezing rain pattered against his office window. It made his head pound. Another deadline missed? This was the third time a misfiled motion or missing deadline tanked one of his cases. How the hell had this happened? His stomach turned at the tone of his father's email. He needed to fix this. Now. As he walked the long carpeted hallway to his father's corner office, he glanced at his friends and co-workers. None of them had this problem, or did they? Outside his father's office, he paused to draw a slow, steady breath. He hadn't missed the deadline. His paperwork was complete. It wasn't his fault. His father would have to believe him.

With a nod to his father's secretary, Diane, he knocked on the cherrywood door. A muffled "come in" made him enter. His father didn't look up. Adam sat in the black leather executive side chair across from his father's massive mahogany desk, crossed his arms, and waited for his father to acknowledge him. He stared at the older man's shock of thick, white hair. He'd spent countless hours of his life staring at that proud head. The scratch of the fountain pen on the lined legal pad grated against his eardrums, but he refrained from interrupting him, although he suspected the writing was a stalling tactic. It usually was. Noah Mandel was the best corporate lawyer in the state of New Jersey and forged his reputation carefully. Adam knew better than to mess with him.

From the time Adam was seven years old and his mother walked out, his father made it clear work came above all else. When Noah's wife left, she'd taken whatever affection he'd possessed, even for him. While still physically in their home, Noah had made it clear to Adam that any emotions he might feel disappeared along with his wife. Adam learned at an early age attachments to people only caused pain when they left. Maintain control, protect your reputation, and never let anyone get too close.

Finally, his father laid his pen on the desk and fixed him with his hawk-like gaze. That stare still made Adam want to flinch, even at twenty-nine years old, but he resisted the urge and maintained his outwardly smooth façade. His father hated signs of weakness, perceived or otherwise, even in his son. The two men remained silent, until his father spoke.

"We have a problem."

"We?" Adam asked.

"Don't get cocky."

"I didn't miss the deadline."

Another silence greeted the statement. "That's what you said last time, and the time before." His father slid the letter from the court across his desk. "This letter says otherwise."

Adam frowned as he skimmed it. His gut tightened. The deadline to file the responsive pleading was last Monday at midnight. He'd given his paralegal all the material she needed to file, saw it in her possession, and left the office. But this letter from the adversary stated it never arrived at court. Therefore, their adversary filed a default, requesting the court to issue an order they won the case. In other words, Adam's client lost. "I have no idea what happened, Dad. I gave Ashley the motion and told her to file it. Did anyone ask her about it?"

"Yes, Ashley says you never gave her the final documentation."

"That's insane. I gave her everything she needed in a manila envelope for her to mail."

"Did you see her mail it?"

"No, I left to go out with some people from work."

"So you were drinking." His father's eyebrows raised in disapproval.

"I drank two beers. I wasn't drunk. I never have more than two in social situations. And it was after I gave her the materials." His reputation was too important to him, and too essential for his career, to ever lose control. Two beers with co-workers was his max.

"I'm not accusing you of drinking on the job. No one has ever smelled alcohol on your breath."

Adam refrained from cringing at the comment.

"But your eagerness to go out and party made you sloppy. Again."

One time. He'd rushed through an assignment for a case one time two years ago and his father never let him forget it. He was meticulous ever since, but his father didn't care. "No, Dad, I wasn't sloppy. I made sure everything was in order before I left."

"So what happened?" His father leaned forward, his gaze piercing.

Adam gripped the armrests until his fingers ached. "I have no idea."

"So you don't remember?" His father glared. "I thought you said you only drank two beers."

"I did. Why don't you question Ashley?"

"Because I've already talked to her and she swears you never gave her anything to file. Between missing this deadline on the motion, messing up the deadline for filing the initial complaint on the Bradley case, and your sloppiness on the Hyde case, you're proving your head isn't in this game."

"Dad, Hyde was two years ago and Bradley was a misunderstanding." The excuse sounded lame to his ears, but he wouldn't give away any more information. Not until he figured out why his father was suddenly questioning his cases. "I've been on top of things since then, I swear. Maybe something is fishy with Ashley. She's acted odd around me lately. We should look into her and why she's fabricating this story."

"I didn't raise a son to slough off blame to someone else. This firm has our name on it. That means the buck stops with me. And you. It's dishonorable to try to blame someone else for your mistakes. Do you have proof you gave her the motion? You didn't have one with the Bradley case. Didn't you learn your lesson last time? And why, if you are concerned about doing your job correctly, would you leave before the filing was completed? You don't need me to answer the question for you, do you?"

Adam flexed his fingers as he waited for the barrage of questions to stop. "I'm sure there was someone around who saw me give her the file, Dad. As for leaving before she finished, since when do I have to micromanage a paralegal?"

His father held up a hand. "Adam, enough. Our name is on the door. This is my firm. You, more than anyone, have a standard to live up to, one you are failing at the moment. I won't warn you again."

Adam's eyelid twitched, and he rose and walked toward the door.

"Oh, and Adam? I know you have your eye on the promotion to junior partner, but with this lingering over you…"

Adam gripped the doorknob, willing his tongue to listen to his brain and remain silent. No one who argued with his father ever won.

****

Dina pulled her car out onto the busy Morristown street, her latest pile of library books on the seat beside her. The best part of being a librarian was her access to books—thousands and thousands of vellum-smelling, page-crackling books. She smiled as she came to a traffic light. A weekend of reading would follow tonight's Shabbat services. It was her ideal plan for the coldest weekend of the year.

As she left the town proper toward its outskirts, she drove over one of the many huge potholes the county had yet to fix. Her car veered to the right, the wheel bump-bump-bumped, and she pulled over onto the shoulder. A freezing drizzle fell, and she wrapped her coat tighter. *Great, just what my frizzy hair needs*, she thought as she bent to look at the tire. Flat.

She popped the trunk and rooted around for the jack. With her warning lights flashing, she positioned the jack behind the rear wheel and pumped, watching the car rise. She rubbed her chilled hands together before trying to remove the spare from its compartment. Headlights lit her view of her trunk, and she turned as a car pulled behind her. A man got out of the car, and she fingered her cellphone in her pocket. At rush hour, plenty of other cars traveled on the road, but she backed up a little and reached for a crowbar, also in the trunk.

"You look like you could use some help," the man said as he approached. He wore a wool overcoat, which flapped open to reveal a dark suit and a pressed blue shirt. His hands were stuffed in his pockets. The icy drizzle speckled his shoulders and his tawny hair with a silver halo. Moss green eyes glowed in the dim light from the passing cars. He reminded her of a mountain lion.

"Nope, I'm fine. Thanks."

"Are you sure? It's freezing out here. I can have you on the road in a few minutes." He was a head taller than she was, and he smelled like cloves. Despite his unneeded assistance, Dina fought the warmth of home his smell suggested.

"Fifty percent of women know how to change their tires, and I'm one of them." Dina picked up the crowbar and prepared to change the tire herself.

He backed away, hands up, the vein in his neck pulsing. "I was trying to help. Never mind. I seriously cannot win with women," he muttered.

She swallowed. Maybe she had been too harsh. Before she could soften her tone, or question him further, a police car pulled up and rolled down the driver side window. "Ma'am, is everything okay? Sir, is there a problem?"

"I'm fine, but thanks. It's just a flat," she said to the officer.

"Sir?"

He grinned. "Nothing, officer, I offered to help her change her tire."

The officer nodded but turned to her anyway. "Ma'am, do you need assistance?"

"I'm almost done." Why did no one believe she could do this?

"Are you sure?"

"Officer, I really am fine, and he just wanted to help me."

The officer scanned the other man. "What's your name?"

"Adam Mandel." He stood straighter and thrust his shoulders back.

"Ma'am?"

"Dina Jacobs."

He exited his car and approached them. "Can I see some ID?"

The man named Adam nodded, dug his ID out of an expensive-looking leather wallet, and handed it to the officer. She gave hers as well. The officer scanned them both before returning them. "Okay, I'm going to wait in my patrol car until you two get on your way." He pulled past her car and waited.

Dina looked at the Good Samaritan and her stomach tightened. Chances were he had no other motive than to help her, and now the cop eyed him suspiciously. He strode to his sports car, and she heaved a sigh. "Wait." she called out.

She jogged toward him, trying not to slip on the icy pavement. "I didn't mean to get you in any trouble. I think I over-reacted. I appreciate your attempt to help me."

His stance relaxed, and he smiled, warming her despite the cold weather. "I didn't mean to come on too strong, honestly. Last chance if you want me to help you with the tire, though. You look cold."

She was, even if his green-eyed gaze acted like a heat ray. "That would be great."

He handed her his keys. "Sit in my car and get warm. You can turn on the music if you want. I'll be done in a jiffy."

She climbed into his BMW and turned the ignition key. The motor purred. Heat blasted from the vents and she sighed in delight as she sank into the butter-soft leather seat. The dashboard gleamed, like something you'd see in a fighter jet. She had no idea how to find the controls if she wanted to turn on the radio. Five minutes later, he returned. She got out of the car.

"All fixed," he said.

"I really appreciate your help. Can I buy you a cup of coffee?"

He hesitated. "Nah," he said, "I'm good."

"Are you sure? You look pretty cold…and wet. It's the least I can do."

He rolled his shoulders, the wool of his overcoat glistening from the moisture. "Follow me to the diner?"

She nodded and waved to the cop, who pulled out onto the road behind them. As she drove, she realized she'd never be home in time for Shabbat services. Oh well. She was thanking him for a *mitzvah*. There were worse reasons to miss temple.

****

Adam pulled his Beamer into an empty spot, leaving the one closest to the door and the light, for…dammit, he didn't remember her name. Unlike his lack of memory about Ashley, he could fix this memory lapse. He shook his head and tried to dispel the thought. Well, whatever her name was, she appeared sweet enough, and she shouldn't have to walk through a dark parking lot alone. He took the stairs two at a time and waited for her in the foyer, staring at the team pictures on the walls and the multicolored stacks of business cards in the rack. A moment later, her nondescript car pulled into the spot he'd left for her and she joined him.

"Hey, I realized I don't remember your name," he said. He hid his embarrassment with a rueful grin.

Her round face reddened, but she laughed. It was a beautiful sound. "It's Dina Jacobs." She held her hand out and he clasped it, finding it softer and smaller than he expected.

"Hello, Dina Jacobs. I'm Adam Mandel."

She pulled her hand away and clasped both of them together in front of her. "I know. Shall we sit down?"

She was nervous, he thought as he followed her and the hostess to their booth next to the window. His neck heated. Was she always like this or was it in reaction to him? Did his anger at his father spill over to his actions with her? As he slid into the gold leather booth, he made a concerted effort to relax his muscles and to forget about the accusation—at least for now.

Their booth overlooked the parking lot and the highway, so it didn't provide much of a view. The huge faux-leather menus contained page after vinyl page of everything you could imagine. It was an indecisive person's hell. Luckily, he only wanted coffee.

"You know what you want already?" Her menu was open, and she scanned each page, as if she'd never seen such a plethora of food.

"You invited me for coffee."

She snorted, which he somehow found refreshing and adorable. "Oh, please. It's dinnertime. You can't possibly tell me you're not hungry."

Well, when she put it that way. He studied the burger section.

"So, other than rescuing women on the side of the road, and almost being arrested, what do you do?"

His cheek twitched. "I'm a corporate attorney in Morristown."

"I'm a librarian at the main library in town."

If anyone fit the stereotype, it was Dina. Matching pink sweater set, frizzy black hair pulled away from her face with combs—all she needed were reading glasses hanging around her neck. But she wasn't old enough. She looked around his age.

"Did you always want to be a librarian?"

"I've always been more comfortable in the imaginary worlds found in books, so yes, I did. I suppose you don't get to read books much."

"Why would you assume I don't read?" He worked hard to maintain his image. Between his designer suits, well-groomed appearance, and his law degree, the last thing anyone would ever mistake him for was an idiot.

Her mouth dropped. "Because corporate law practice requires tons of hours, and I'd assume a lot of reading of law materials. You probably don't want to spend what little down time you have reading for pleasure."

He leaned toward her, arms on the table. "You're around books all day, right?"

She nodded.

"Do you read when you go home?"

She nodded again.

"Why would you think otherwise of me?"

She blinked. For the first time he noticed her violet eyes.

"You're right. I made a snap judgment based on your car and your clothes and I don't know what else." She played with her red plastic water glass before she continued. "If I weren't already treating you to dinner, I would now."

He sat back in the booth. "There's always dessert." He winked. He couldn't tell who was more surprised, he or Dina. Because despite her incorrect assumptions about him, he started to enjoy himself.

She ran a hand through her hair, fingers catching tiny knots the rain caused. "So, what do you like to read?"

Her hair intrigued him, and he responded without thought. "Actually, I love reading science fiction and comic books." Dammit, why had he told her? He'd never told anyone about his fondness for those subjects—the people he hung out with wouldn't understand. It didn't exactly fit his image, at least, not the one he projected. He should have said mysteries. Or thrillers. Maybe she'd drop the subject.

"Really? I never would have thought that about you. Superheroes always appealed to me, though."

He should let the subject drop. "My favorite is Captain America. His stories make me nostalgic." *So much for letting it drop.*

"I'll keep you in mind."

At his quizzical look, she continued. "If we get anything interesting in the library. Why does Captain America make you nostalgic?"

Damn. He played with his water glass, suddenly fascinated by the red hue his fingertips took when they gripped the glass. "My mom used to read them to me."

The aroma of sizzling beef accompanied the server carrying their burgers. As he set down the plates, Adam used the time to try to think of a different subject. Any subject to turn the conversation in a different direction. Before he could put together a coherent sentence, Dina spoke again.

"Do you like working at your firm?"

He swallowed. Talk about changing subjects. "It has its challenges. It's my dad's firm. I started there because he expected it of me, and a smaller firm provides great experiences. But everyone watches the son of the lead partner to see how you're treated." *If you screw up, it's worse.* He shrugged, letting his mouth spread in a half-smile. He looked around. God, he wished they served alcohol.

"I'll bet people's attention on you all the time must be difficult. Because even if they don't judge you, you sort of always think they are."

Her tone soothed him. This complete stranger understood. He looked at her over his half-eaten burger. Her eyes really were lovely. Her long lashes made shadows on her creamy skin. Her lips were pretty too.

"It's one of the reasons I want to move to a larger New York City firm. The hours are longer, but the separation would be worth it."

"Do they still make their lawyers work all night? I mean, you're not fresh out of law school anymore, right? My cousin is a lawyer, and he never left the office when he worked for one of those big firms."

"I'm almost four years out and the hours will be a

lot more than here, but no, I shouldn't need to work all night. Especially if I can leave where I am as a junior partner." *Which right now is a crapshoot, especially if I keep screwing up.*

"Do you think you'll make it?"

He couldn't remember the last time he talked to a woman who showed him genuine interest. Most of the ones he associated with wanted a simple hookup or a rich boyfriend. He warmed to her. "I'm not sure, but I'm hopeful."

The bill came, and he whipped out his credit card. They reached for the check at the same time. Their hands touched. A jolt of something ran up his arm. Beneath his fingers, her hand fit perfectly. He wished he could sit longer like this.

"I said I would pay," she said.

Her voice broke whatever spell she'd cast. When she pulled her hand, and the bill, away, she broke the physical bond as well. His hand felt empty. He moved it to his lap, clenching it in a fist.

"It's not necessary. I was happy to help."

"I wasn't very nice, and this is my apology."

He tipped his head in acknowledgement. "Next time, it's on me."

As they walked toward the cashier, past a display of towering desserts, she shrugged. "Did you know about seventy-five percent of men aren't comfortable letting the woman pay the check?"

He looked at her askance. "Can I have your number?" *What the hell?*

She paused, and he thought she would refuse, but she rattled off her number. "You'll probably be a successful New York attorney by the time you think of me again."

Her smile lightened her words, but as he watched her drive away, he couldn't help but wonder. Could there be a next time?

Chapter Two

Dina staggered into the gray stone library Monday with a stack of women's fiction books. As planned, she spent the weekend reading, coming up for air occasionally to eat. She couldn't remember the last time she had a free weekend, and it was just what she needed. A huge grin lit up her face as she approached the circulation desk in the center of the rotunda.

"Whoa, those are all yours, Dina?" Her friend, Tracy Batton, laughed as she reached out to steady the pile on the desk. "How in the world can you read so many?"

"Speed reading. And they were great. Well, most of them. This one," she pulled one from the middle of the pile and jumped to prevent the pile from toppling, "wasn't fabulous."

"Not a bad ratio. Guess I know what you did this weekend."

"In its entirety." Well, except for Friday night.

"I envy you. Joe and I spent the whole weekend home with a sick baby."

Dina's expression grew serious. "Oh, poor thing. But I actually envy you, Tracy. Because you've got your life together and you're the most confident woman I know." She'd give anything to have a life like Tracy's.

"Come on, Dina. You do too. You've got a job you

love, great friends…what's wrong?"

"I'm dreading my high school reunion. I just got the invitation to my tenth."

"So don't go."

"I'm tempted. I'm pretty sure I attended high school with every mean girl on the planet. And they all grew into scary PTA moms, nasty soccer moms, and bitchy executives. To make it worse, I'll be alone."

"Want to borrow Joe?"

Dina burst out laughing. "That would be hilarious. But no. I probably won't go, anyway. Only about twenty to thirty percent of alums actually go. Don't mind me, I'll figure it out."

She took the elevator to her cubicle in the office on the second floor and spent the rest of the morning updating files and cataloguing. Usually she loved her job, but today her mind wandered to her reunion. There was no point in attending if it made her miserable, but a part of her wanted to see how people changed. It was a milestone, and probably the last reunion she'd attend.

Would her high school classmates resemble the women who often came to the library to peruse magazines—long straight hair, slip dresses, phones out? Would the guys she remembered still have their hair, or would they be like the man crouched at the computer this morning, sporting a bald spot and a ring of hair like a monk? How many of the women would already have children? She thought about the woman she passed in the brightly colored children's section, pregnant, with four kids attached to her like accessories, hanging from her arms and her skirt and grabbing her leg, dragging her toward the stuffed chairs. Would her classmates remember her? Her shoulders slumped.

Jim from Inventory knocked on the metal rim of her cubicle and she jumped. "Just got a new shipment of books. Do you have time to start on them?"

"Sure." She loved the new books. Getting them ready to shelve and eventually borrow was sure to improve her mood. Not to mention, give her a preview of what to add to her TBR list. She followed Jim to the acquisitions room lined with tables and settled in among the cartons. The first box held romances and as she assigned them their own Dewey decimal number, she made note of which ones she wanted to read. The next one contained reference books. She had almost finished entering them into the computer when she came across one about the history of comic books. Her heart rate increased as she remembered what Adam said about liking superheroes. He'd find this fascinating. Paging through it, she wondered if she should let him know about it. *He probably has no use for reference books. He's not a researcher.*

However, once Adam entered her mind, she couldn't let him go. She'd had a surprisingly good time with him at the diner. Her first impression of him, after she got over the idea he might be a serial killer, was a playboy—fancy car, nice clothes, platinum credit card. Overall, not someone she'd choose to spend time with.

She wasn't usually attracted to good-looking men. Not as good looking as Adam, anyway. From her experience with them in high school and college, they tended to be shallow and looked for women as gorgeous as them. She'd examined herself too many times in the mirror to believe a guy like Adam would fall for her. Reddish blond hair, green eyes, lanky, and as her mother would say, good bone structure. When he smiled, she'd spotted a dimple in his left cheek and an intriguing divot in his chin. His voice was like aged whiskey and she remembered its timbre had made her stomach flutter.

But Adam was more than his outward appearance. He was smart. During their conversation in the diner, his intelligence came through, turning her initial conclusion about him on its ear. That made him more attractive. He'd obviously studied hard if he was a lawyer and he was interested in topics other than law. And despite their reputation, superheroes were a fairly complex subject, tackling issues like race relations, women's rights, and government, among others. Which brought her to the box of books.

Should she contact him to tell him what she found?

Shaking her head, she moved onto the next box. She would never see him again. And if he wanted to do research, he knew where to start. He didn't need her useless information.

Her shoulders cramped. She stretched. Grabbing her lunch, she took it outside, and sat on a bench beneath a maple tree to watch passersby as she ate. A few moments later, Tracy joined her.

"Perfect day for this," she said.

Dina nodded. "After unpacking books all day, this is exactly what I need." The fresh air and first scents of spring refreshed her.

"Feel better now?"

"Dina?" A husky bass voice vibrated through the air.

She looked up. Her stomach fluttered. "Adam? What are you doing here?"

He walked the flagstone path toward where they

sat, all pressed pants and shiny wingtips, and stopped in front of their bench. He stood with the sun behind him, making her squint.

"I needed to get out of the office for a little while," he said with a shrug, moving until he wasn't backlit. "I thought I'd stop by and say hello."

"I thought of you earlier." Why did she say that?

He beamed. "Is there a problem with your car?"

"My car? Oh, no, my car is fine. But we got this book in I thought you'd be interested in. Or not, since it's a research book. But it made me think of you." *Way to babble, Dina.*

His face tightened in wariness. "Oh?"

"*The History of Superheroes.*" She turned to her friend. "You know the book I mean, right? He loves comics and it would be perfect for him, don't you think?"

He swallowed and stuffed his hands in his coat while eyeing Tracy. "Uh, okay. Most people think of me because of my charming personality." He winked, and Tracy started to laugh.

Dina stiffened. "It's not on the shelves yet but give it about a week and it should be available if you want to take a look at it."

Adam shrugged. "I don't get to the library very often, and like you said, I probably won't have time to read for pleasure, especially such a childish subject." He flashed his perfect teeth in a wide grin at Tracy. "Hi. Adam Mandel."

"Tracy Batton. How do you two know each other?"

"Damsel in distress on the side of the road with a flat on Friday. No big deal."

Dina flinched. Something was off. She barely knew

him, but the Adam talking to her friend was the guy she *thought* he was when she first met him—not the potential serial killer part, but the shallow guy she'd dismissed.

"Really? You didn't tell me about your knight in shining armor," Tracy said, turning to her.

Two could play this game. She flipped her hands, as if it were no big deal.

He blinked. Before he looked away, remorse flashed across his face, but it was gone before she could be sure. Tracy looked between the two of them and cleared her throat. "I guess I'll go inside, now. Nice to meet you, Adam. See you later, Dina."

Dina rose. "No, I'll go inside with you. Bye, Adam."

With barely a backward glance, she followed Tracy. Once the heavy wood door closed behind them, Tracy spun around. "What was the attitude about?"

Boy, was she wrong. Better to find out early though. Next time, she'd listen to her first thoughts. "No idea."

****

Adam adjusted the starched sleeve of his shirt beneath his wool suit jacket and pulled on his silk tie. Even he recognized he acted like an ass.

In what was starting to be a regular occurrence, his morning sucked. His father gave him busy work, the paralegals in the office whispered about him, and James, his main competition for a promotion, walked around like he'd won the lottery.

Apparently, someone spread the news and implied he threw Ashley under the bus for his own ineptitude.

He'd needed a break, so he'd taken a walk,

enjoying the early spring day. As his steps led him toward the library, he'd decided to see if Dina was there. Something about her piqued his interest. In fact, he thought about her at the oddest times—once while he was at the gym, Saturday night at a bar with the guys, and today while he drove to the office.

When he saw her sitting outside, he'd stopped and watched her for a few minutes, wondering what about her intrigued him. She wasn't his type physically— petite, curvier than women he normally dated, and her clothes and hair would never be featured in a magazine, unless it was a "Tame Your Frizz," article. But her smile when she talked to Tracy warmed him. He wished she'd direct that smile at him. He'd walked up to her.

And everything fell apart.

Because Dina had talked about his love of superheroes. No one knew about his secret nostalgia. It was something he and his mom shared. And then she had left. He wasn't stupid enough to think she'd left because of his love for Captain America, but she'd known him better than anyone. She'd supposedly loved him. Yet she'd left anyway. His dad was an ass. If he thought about it, he understood why she'd wanted to leave her husband, but her son? She must have seen something terrible in him. Obviously, he was nothing like a superhero. So he buried what was inside and worked hard to maintain his image—a fast-rising, über-successful lawyer. Nothing would get in the way of his making the right connections, climbing the ladder of success, and drawing the right people toward him. Those people would ensure his happiness. If his image caused people to draw false conclusions about him, it was an acceptable risk to take.

Dina acted like his love of superheroes wasn't weird. Maybe it wasn't, but it wouldn't help his image, any more than his love of science fiction or indie bands. The right image would make him successful and prevent people from walking away. Hearing her mention superheroes in front of Tracy threw him. He'd reacted without thinking.

He owed her an apology for his attitude.

Which was why right now, at the end of the day, he waited outside the library for her. With flowers.

The door opened for the hundredth time. It still wasn't her. He gave a vague smile, the kind that said, "I'm not waiting for you," and shifted from one foot to the other as his impatience grew. It was cold with the sun setting. Maybe she'd gotten off early. Maybe she'd left from a different entrance. Maybe she decided to stay after the building closed in order to avoid him.

As he was about to give up, she walked outside.

"Dina."

She stiffened. He'd swear she considered returning inside. A sudden vision from his childhood of his mother walking away snaked into his head. He blinked to clear it. Like at lunch, her dark frizzy hair was pulled into a ponytail, but it showed off her cheekbones and the shape of her face. Raising her chin, like she prepared for battle, she approached.

"Adam."

"These are for you." He held out the bouquet of flowers.

Her violet eyes softened to heather. She reached for the flowers and frowned. "Why?"

He stuffed his hands in his pockets. "I'm sorry about before."

She started to walk past him. "Don't be."

Heat flushed through his body. He hurried to catch up with her, matching his stride to hers. "I was rude."

"It doesn't matter."

"Yes, it does."

She spun around to face him. "The flowers are lovely, but there's no reason to apologize. Give them to your girlfriend." She held them out to him, but he didn't take them.

"I don't have one at the moment."

She raised an eyebrow as if she didn't believe him. Frankly, he couldn't believe it either. After two months of being single, it was his longest dry spell since he could remember. But he wasn't going to tell her.

"Give them to your mother."

He swallowed. "Don't have one of those either." He cursed himself for saying anything.

Dina stepped closer.

If she interrogated him about his mother, he would turn around and leave.

She held out a finger, ran it along the petal of one of the yellow roses. "They're pretty."

"Women like roses. I thought yellow suited you."

"Actually, my favorites are daisies."

He'd seen a bouquet of those, but he'd thought they looked cheap. Roses made a better impression. "Why?"

"Why what?"

"Why do you like daisies?" Why the hell did he care?

"They're cheerful and overlooked, usually, for more expensive, prettier smelling ones."

Her reaction tugged at his heart. "Seems like an

odd reason to like them."

She shrugged. "You asked."

"If I asked you out, would you say yes?" Whoa, where did this idea come from?

"You'd never ask me." She started walking again, this time around the side of the building toward the employee parking lot.

He followed. "I just did."

"No, you didn't. You tested the waters, like what a political candidate does before announcing his candidacy."

"I'm pretty sure you're insulting me," he said, beginning to enjoy himself.

She stopped in front of her beat up car. When she didn't speak, he filled the silence. "Go out with me."

"No."

He stepped back. "Why not?"

"Because you don't really want me to go out with you. I'm not your type."

"How do you know what my type is?" He stilled.

She looked him up and down, like a piece of meat. "Pretty, wealthy, popular and not too smart. Not dumb, but average."

His face burned as he recognized the truth in her statement.

She laughed. "Go home, Adam. Thank you for the flowers."

He watched her drive away. He wasn't sure what happened, but it wasn't what he'd intended.

****

The next day, he stood outside the front entrance of Dina's library when it opened.

"Don't you have a job?" she asked.

He shifted from one foot to the other, an endearing action, despite how he annoyed her. "For the moment."

"You'd probably have a better chance of keeping it if you were there, instead of here."

He chuckled. "Probably."

"Why are you here?"

"I wanted to talk to you."

She sighed. "Give me a minute."

When he started to follow her, she paused. "Wait here." She pointed to the lobby and waited until he'd settled himself onto an upholstered bench before entering the employee area and taking the elevator upstairs. She deposited her purse and sweater at her desk, waved to her boss and returned downstairs to the lobby. Adam was still there. Her stomach lurched. She shook her head. He was an annoyance, like indigestion, nothing more.

"Yes?" For some reason, she didn't know what to do with her hands. When they started fluttering at her sides, she folded them across her middle. Better to look the stern librarian than like a bird about to take flight.

He rose and shifted from one foot to the other. "I'm sorry about yesterday."

"You already apologized."

"I know, but I want to make it up to you."

"Why?"

"I have no idea."

"Is this normally how you woo women? If so, does it actually work?"

He blew out a breath, reminding her of a racehorse. "I'm usually a lot smoother than this."

Her inner smile was harder and harder to hide. He reminded her of Dorothy in *The Wizard of Oz*, when she discovers she's not in Kansas anymore. She kept it to herself, however—he didn't seem like the type of man who would appreciate the comparison with a girl, even if said girl was a character in a literary classic.

"Threatened by the smart girl?" She held her breath as the words escaped her mouth. She meant it as a joke, but some jokes weren't funny. Then again, he'd dismissed her yesterday.

"If I say yes, will you take pity and go out with me?" A teasing grin played about his mouth.

He was persistent, she had to give it to him. The last time a "pretty boy" pursued her this hard was when she was a freshman in high school, taking a senior-level chemistry class. One of the senior boys wanted to cheat off her lab report. She didn't let him cheat, because she was morally opposed to it. He'd continued to bother her about it for the rest of the year, as if the nagging would change her mind. It hadn't worked then, but it started to work now. And that would never do. Maybe the best way to get rid of Adam was to agree to go out with him.

"Fine."

She'd expected him to grin some plastic, car salesman-y grin. Instead, his eyes lightened to emerald, backlit with a warm glow. Her heart lurched.

"How's Friday night?"

Blinking, she tried to focus on his words. "Um, actually, I go to temple on Friday nights."

He nodded. "Okay, how about Thursday night? There's a bar in Newark with live bands Thursdays. They're usually pretty good."

A bar? He wanted to take her to a bar? In Newark? Visions of a quiet dinner or a show popped her bubble. She resigned herself to another night where she didn't fit in. High school all over again. It was too late to change her mind now. "Okay."

He confirmed her phone number and gave her his, promising to call later in the week to arrange specifics. He'd probably change his mind. But she wouldn't tell him. Finally, he left, and she returned to her desk.

"You have a date, how wonderful!" Rose, an older woman who worked with Dina, clapped her hands in glee.

"I wouldn't get too excited. He's totally not my type."

Rose winked. "Sometimes, those are the best kinds, sweetie. Shave your legs and bring protection."

"What?" Dina couldn't believe Rose said this. In a library of all places. "I would never sleep with him on the first date."

The salt-and-pepper-haired woman gave a knowing look. "You do know you don't need protection for sleeping, right?"

"You mean you weren't talking about ear plugs for noise?" Dina asked, eyebrow raised.

"He's handsome and likes you. Be prepared."

As Dina returned to her desk and thought seriously about bleaching her ears, she discounted Rose's assessment. Adam didn't "like" her. He felt guilty, sure. He was concerned about what she thought of him, okay. But like her? Please.

Chapter Three

On Monday, Adam walked straight to the paralegals. "Hey, Kim, I brought in my old study guides for the Bar." He'd spent all day Sunday putting them in order. A single mom whose husband walked out on her and her two children, she'd told him about her desire to become a lawyer, and he'd encouraged her, helping her out the last two years, entertaining her kids, and smoothing the way for her to leave early to study. She was in the home stretch, and he was proud of his friend.

She jumped, looked around, and gave him an awkward glance. "Thanks, Adam."

Others in the area watched the exchange. It was weird. He held out a binder and after swallowing, she reached for it.

"Everything okay?" he asked. "I know the exam can be stressful, but with all the real-world experience you're getting here, and how hard you're studying, you're going to do great."

Her cheeks colored. "Yeah."

She was usually a lot more talkative. "If you want, I can give up my lunch hour today and help you study. I still remember the tricks and techniques I used."

"No, it's okay. But thanks." She rose from her desk, skirted around him, and walked over to one of the other paralegals, who shot him a glance before whispering to Kim.

He stood there, feeling awkward, before he returned to his office.

On Tuesday, he passed Kim at the copy machine. "Did you take a look at the stuff I gave you yesterday? If you need anything—"

"Adam, really, I'm fine. Thanks. I've got this on my own now."

"Are you sure? I can take Oliver and Jared out for ice cream again, or a movie, like last time, if you need time alone to study."

"I'm sure. Look, when you accuse one paralegal, you accuse all of us. I don't think it's a good idea—" She looked around before she focused on him. "—for us to be together, at least not right now. I need to work with these people, at least until I become a lawyer…"

He stiffened, gave her a nod, and walked down the hall to his office. Sinking into his ergonomic chair, he buried his face in his hand. Kim and he were friends. Did she really believe Ashley over him? They spent hours together and never once had he ever blamed anyone else for his screw-ups. She knew him. Or she should.

By Wednesday, any doubts about whether or not Kim believed him disappeared. His history with her was irrelevant, because Ashley convinced all the paralegals he had it out for her, and if they weren't careful, he'd go after them too. He'd tried to talk to her, but she wouldn't budge. Most worrisome of all was he couldn't find the paper trail on his computer he'd left himself for such a thing as this happening. He'd searched everywhere for it and it was gone.

This was three marks against him. One of which lost them the case and unless something happened quickly, might result in the loss of the client. His father was pissed. Ashley was unshakeable. The other paralegals avoided him. Not only was it impossible for him to work if he had to do everything himself, he would never make junior partner if this continued.

He wracked his brain, trying to figure out why Ashley would do something like this. Other than one time where he'd given her an assignment and she'd messed it up, their interactions were fine. Professional. Sure, she didn't like staying late, but it came with the job. He was always friendly and respectful. He'd greet her in the morning, like he did everyone else. He asked her about her weekend, like he did everyone else. He couldn't think of anything out of the ordinary. Could he have possibly said something to anger her? And if so, why didn't she tell him, either at the time, or now? He would have apologized immediately.

In the meantime, the paralegals gave him wary looks, Kim no longer wanted his help, and his father gave him grunt work. Putting aside how his friends and father abandoned him, how the hell was he supposed to prove himself ready for the promotion to junior partner if he was relegated to handling things a first year could do with her eyes closed? He started to sweat. Why did everyone assume the worst of him?

He stared out the window to the street below. A woman with curly hair walked by, reminding him of Dina, and he smiled for the first time in days.

Dina was sweet. She was funny. Images of her smiling at him, leaning forward to ask questions, flitted through is mind. Her face was round, with clear, pale skin, long lashes, and full lips. Her eyes—he still couldn't believe they were violet—were beautiful.

Maybe she wore contacts? Her hair fascinated him. It was different from the smooth, straight tresses he saw everywhere. Hers was a deep brown, almost black, with thick, frizzy waves. He wondered what it would feel like against his cheek. Would it be soft or springy or something he hadn't considered?

There was something about having all those curves to himself—to explore, admire and discover—that made him think about her more than he'd like. She was curvier than the women he typically dated, but those women were model thin and complained about every calorie they put in their mouth. Half of his dinner conversations with them involved food, and not in any way he found fascinating. His conversations with Dina, on the other hand? They made him think.

He expelled a breath. It didn't matter. No matter how much he might have enjoyed dinner with her, he couldn't date a woman like her, a woman who could see through him as easily as Dina. A woman who would leave him if she discovered the real him—like his mother, and now, apparently, Kim.

He groaned. Dina was more religiously observant than he was if she went to temple every Friday night. Except last Friday night they ate dinner at the diner. Was temple an excuse to avoid him?

No, somehow, he thought Dina would be more direct. And now, despite his concerns, he was taking Dina out to a bar tomorrow night. He didn't do commitment, and his dating record showed it. Dina, on the other hand, probably wanted a long-term relationship, which should make him nervous. Except she didn't seem to want to go out with him in the first place.

So why the hell was he taking her out?

****

Adam was due in forty-five minutes. She'd already stood in front of her walk-in closet for close to fifteen. Who did that? She owned work clothes. She wore weekend clothes. She had temple clothes. She even owned clothes to go on a date. But this was Adam, "Mr. Flashypants."

Women probably flaunted their cleavage and leg on a regular basis. Her boobs were too big for her to be comfortable showing cleavage. She wasn't a mini-skirt kind of person. Which left...not too many options.

Ten minutes later, she settled on black boot-cut jeans. A drape-necked green cashmere sweater accentuated her eyes. Black boots, chunky silver earrings, her silver Jewish star necklace, minimal makeup and she was done. Why she tried to impress him, she had no idea.

When her apartment intercom buzzed, she grabbed her purse and jacket and met Adam on the porch of her converted Victorian.

Once again, he greeted her with his slow, small smile. A frisson of excitement went through her. He wore a black button-down, open at the neck, and gray slacks. The dark colors set off his lighter hair and made his green eyes pop. He leaned over and kissed her cheek, surprising her. His soft lips teased her skin. She inhaled his spicy clean scent.

"You look pretty. I like what you did to your hair."

All she'd done was pull it off her face in a low half-knot. He probably said this to all his dates. She fisted her hand at her side to keep from touching it. "Thanks."

She wouldn't think about her cheek he'd kissed.

He led her down the cement walkway and held open the car door. Up close, and in the daylight, she realized his car was a convertible. Of course it was. Luckily for her hair, the top was up.

"Nice car. Did you know Germany started making BMWs because after the Treaty of Versailles they were prohibited from making warplanes or warplane engines?" She gulped after the fact slipped out. She really needed to stop.

He looked at her, chuckled, and eased onto the street. Jazz played through the car's sound system. She stared out the window as they drove along the highway and eventually onto the streets of Newark. She didn't know what to say, but the silence didn't seem to bother him. Adam pulled into a parking garage.

He opened the door for her, pocketing the ticket. "Come on, the bar's this way."

The area near the restaurant was busy with young professionals unwinding after a long day at work and older people grabbing a quick bite before the show at the performing arts center down the street. As they walked along the city streets, Adam chatted about the types of bands he liked. She didn't recognize most of the names—her musical tastes ran more to classic rock. Once there, he gave his name and the host sat them downstairs in a cozy booth in sight of the stage, but not too close. The room was dark, with silver up-lighting and multi-colored wall sconces.

Everything about this place screamed, "What are you doing here?"

Sitting across the silvery speckled-granite topped table from each other, Dina studied his face while he opened the wine menu. He was more handsome than she'd remembered. Her stomach knotted.

"What's wrong?" Adam put the wine menu down.

"This is all foreign to me."

"What do you mean?"

"Nothing. Never mind."

He fixed his attention on her, as if waiting for her to continue, but she wasn't about to pour out her discomfort to someone she'd never see again. She nodded toward the menu. "Is there a particular wine you were thinking of?"

"What's your preference?"

"Anything but Manischewitz."

He laughed. "Hey, we have the same taste in wine."

Dina couldn't help but see the irony. Maybe he recognized how incongruous they were too. "Good to know. Because it might be a deal breaker."

"You really have no preference for red or white even?"

"I'm open to trying something new."

The slow smile spread. Motioning for the waitress, he gave their wine order. Returning his attention to her, he leaned forward. "So, do you get first dibs on the new books?"

She laughed again. "Not exactly. I mean, I get to see what's in stock, so I know what to add to my list, but we usually have a waiting list of people who want the books, and I don't get to jump ahead in line."

"The people you work with seem pretty nice. What's your friend like, the one from the other day?"

Wait. Why was he asking about Tracy? "What do you want to know about her?"

"How'd you two meet?"

The question was innocuous. The knot in her stomach loosened. "We work together. She started a few years before I did. She took me under her wing. I filled in for her when she took maternity leave."

"Are there a lot of people our age working there or just you and Tracy?"

It was a good question, and an easy one. "There's a pretty decent mix, actually."

They paused to study their menus and order and when the waiter left, Adam continued with his questions. "Do you two socialize outside of work much?"

Dina relaxed as she thought about her friend. "She's pretty busy with her family, but we go to lunch. Occasionally we'll go shopping or see a movie on a weekend."

"Oh, the Morristown movie theater is great—their seats are really comfortable."

"Yeah, although I wish they'd get more classic movies, but I guess those don't appeal to as many people."

"The black and white ones? There are a few great ones I've seen. Citizen Kane was one of my favorites. What's yours?"

"Orson Welles was terrific in it," she said.

"'I don't think there's one word that can describe a man's life.' I love the line."

"Why?"

Just then, the waiter brought their dinners, a steak for Adam and filet of sole for Dina. The meat sizzled. Its garlicky scent mixed with the smell of the fish and the fruity salsa, making her stomach growl. Once they'd each tasted their food, she prompted him. "The movie line?"

"Oh. I like how it's such a simple way to describe the complexity of a person. It's not dramatic, it doesn't exaggerate things, but it shows there can be more to someone or some situation than meets the eye."

Her heart thudded. Mr. Flashypants had a soul. A fairly deep one.

"Discovering those hidden facets can be the most rewarding part of getting to know someone."

A flicker of uncertainty passed over his face. He sat back in his chair, adjusting his napkin on his lap. "Unless there's nothing there."

"What do you mean?" The sole was melt-in-your-mouth delicious. She hadn't stopped eating since the waiter set the plate in front of her. Now, however, she put down her fork and wiped her mouth.

His gaze shifted from the food in front of him, to the wall behind her ear, to the center of the room, and he shrugged. "Some of us are exactly what we seem."

"I don't believe it. I think we all hide pieces of ourselves. No one walks around with a sign around her neck proclaiming this is the real me."

He sliced another piece of steak, finished chewing before he spoke again. "And you? Who are you?"

Like she would tell him. "I'm a vampire," she whispered, focusing on his blood-red meat.

"Ah, I guess seeing you out in the daylight and sharing this garlic bread with you really fooled me," he said with a wink. His posture loosened and, once again, he relaxed.

They finished their meal together as the band took the stage. Intrigued, Dina watched as they tuned their

36

instruments before beginning their set. The music was a mix of new age rock with a little jazz and funk thrown in. She was surprised at how much she enjoyed it and tapped her hands on the table to the beat. The other surprising thing? Adam knew the music, singing along at parts. She never would have pegged him as someone who liked this music style—it wasn't flashy or trendy enough. At least, she didn't think it was.

Her nostrils filled with his spicy clean aftershave. Something about his scent made her want to move closer to him, which was insane. She barely knew him, and they were in public with a table of food between them.

"How do you like the band?" he asked.

She nodded. "They're great. I've never heard of them before." Of course, she wasn't up on music, so it didn't mean anything.

"They're indie and fairly new. Originally they're from Chicago. Glad you're enjoying yourself." He shifted his chair closer and placed his hand on the table close to hers. Their fingers brushed against each other. The contact sent jolts of electricity up Dina's arm.

He twined his fingers through hers, and she stilled. Did he feel it too? Or was this how he acted with everyone? When the set ended and the lights came on, she expected him and his supple fingers to move to his side of the table. But he stayed where he was and took a dessert menu from the waiter. "We can share," he said. The waiter walked away. "See anything you like?"

An insane desire to say, "Yes, you," burbled in her throat. But he meant dessert. Her face heated as her mind wandered a path it really shouldn't go on a first-slash-second-date-that-didn't-mean-anything-and-would-never-go-anywhere. She shook her head to clear it and tried to distract herself.

Glancing over at him, she realized he still waited for an answer. Despite the fact the menu was right in front of her, she didn't notice the items. "I'll have some ice cream."

He nodded, ordered for the two of them, and fiddled with the silverware on the table.

"I never would have pegged you for someone who liked indie bands," she said.

He gave a wry grin. "Me neither. It appeared on my Pandora one day while I was jogging."

"You run?"

Nodding, he flipped the fork first one way then the other.

The motion of his hands mesmerized her—the play of the tendons as he spun the fork, the stretch of his fingers as he strove not to drop the utensil on the table, the light glinting off the silverware and the gold chain around his wrist.

"Five miles a day," he said.

She started. *Five miles…oh, yeah. Running.* "Great exercise."

"Do you run?"

"Only if someone chases me. Even then, I'd probably surrender. I prefer walking, preferably in the woods."

The server returned with their bowls of ice cream. The cold, creamy treat cooled Dina's mouth, if not the rest of her.

"Have you walked any of the county trails?"

She started to nod, but the lights dimmed. The band came back for their final set. This time, his nearness distracted her—the touch of his shoulder as he rocked in his seat in time to the beat, the thrum of his voice as he sang a private concert for her. She remembered the first set for the music, but this second set was all about Adam. Spotlights from the stage glinted off his hair, creating streaks of white gold and copper. His silhouette reminded her of Greek sculptures in the museum—proud nose, firm chin, prominent cheekbones, wide forehead. Muscles in his forearms flexed beneath his black sleeve as he played air guitar or imitated the drummer.

When it was over, her chest constricted, making it difficult to breathe. She took a hasty sip of water.

"Ready to go?" he asked.

When she nodded, he held out her chair and walked with her toward the door, his hand against the small of her back.

"Adam Mandel?"

He dropped his hand from her back. "Hey, Seth, how ya doin'?"

Like a flick of a switch, Mr. Flashypants was back.

"I didn't know you liked this band," Seth said.

The sound of Adam's laugh sent a chill along her spine. "You know me, always willing to try something new." But the tone of his voice indicated otherwise. "See you around, Seth."

Whereas before, Adam's hand on her back warmed her, this time, when he put it there again, it was as if he steered her away from public view. She stayed silent on their walk to the car, Adam's nonchalant whistle grating on her ears.

Once inside his car, she looked out the window at the city lights. There was nothing to see, but she didn't want to look at Adam.

"I'm glad we did this," he said, as he pulled onto the highway.

Her mother taught her manners. No matter how uncomfortable she was, she would live up to them. "The band was great. The food was delicious."

"Sorry about back there," he said. "I should have introduced you."

"It can be shocking to run into people in odd places." Except it didn't fully explain his change in demeanor.

She half listened to his small talk in the car as they drove the rest of the way home, trying to figure out why he demonstrated two such different sides of his personality.

He walked her to her door, paused outside it, looking around as if to see if anyone watched them. "I had a lot of fun with you tonight," he said. "Thanks for giving me another chance."

"You're welcome."

He reached a hand out and traced the side of her face. Prickles of goose bumps followed his finger. She shivered. Did she want him to kiss her? Before they ran into Seth, she would have said yes. Now she wasn't sure. Noise from another building intruded.

He dropped his hand to his side. "I'll call you tomorrow?"

Nodding, she fished her keys out of her purse. He waited for her to get inside before raising his hand in a wave and jogging to his car.

****

Adam let himself into his high-rise apartment after dropping off Dina at hers. She was a surprise he enjoyed discovering. When their hands touched over dinner, he'd felt...something. "Sparks" was stupid, but he didn't know what else to call it. From the way she'd jumped, he'd bet she'd felt something too, especially when she didn't pull her hand away as he wound his fingers around hers. Standing at her door, he hadn't wanted to let her go.

He'd wanted to taste her lips. Her soft skin left him dying to touch her again. If only Seth hadn't intruded, and those people hadn't interrupted them. Next time. He'd have to make sure there was a next time, even if he was supposed to cool off his social life for the time being.

The red light of his answering machine glowed. His body tensed. Only one person called him on his home phone—his father. Tossing his keys onto the black granite counter, he hit play.

"Adam, it's Dad. Where the hell are you? It's a Thursday night. Please tell me you're not out partying. You're supposed to improve your work ethic, not abandon it. Call me."

Jabbing the Erase button, he stalked out onto his balcony. He gripped the railing as he stared into the night, no longer picturing Dina's face. His apartment complex was next to the train station, but if he looked out instead of down, he could see silhouettes of the trees on the Green in the distance.

When did his life turn to shit? Out of all the conclusions his father jumped to, he immediately leapt to partying? Maybe a work engagement kept him out late. Or research at the library. Or an appointment with Kim to help her study for the Bar exam. He shook his head. With the types of assignments his father foisted on him, there was no need to work late. The library? Hadn't stopped there since law school—stopping outside to talk to Dina the other day, or waiting for her in the lobby, probably didn't count. Helping Kim? His father didn't know about her.

He shifted from one foot to the other. No wonder his father was suspicious. Although would it kill him to have a little faith in his son? He berated himself. His father's faith in anyone disappeared when his wife left twenty-two years ago. Adam pushed away from the railing.

Returning inside, he looked around at his modern luxury bachelor pad. He wasn't in the mood to go to bed. He didn't feel like being alone. But there weren't any friends he could call. His gaze fell onto his law school graduation photo perched on the white marble-topped coffee table. He stood next to his best law school friend, Jacob Black. They hadn't talked in a few months, but Jacob knew his father and Adam. Maybe he'd be able to give him career advice.

Pulling the name from his contacts, he dialed.

"Jacob. It's Adam."

"Hey, it's been a while."

The sound of his buddy's voice made him feel better. "Yeah, how are you?"

"Great. Busy with work, as I'm sure you are."

Adam swallowed. "Any chance you're free to catch up?"

"Absolutely. Tomorrow night?"

Dina might go to temple every Friday, but he didn't. "Sure."

Chapter Four

The next evening, Adam rode the commuter train to Hoboken and fidgeted with his phone. Should he call Dina? She'd probably know some obscure fact about trains. He started to grin. He didn't think she would ever understand his rules. Rule number one being no strings. Rule number two being if you get attached, reread rule number one. He'd had a nice time with her last night. Hell, more than a nice time. Despite her sense of humor, which was subtle like her, she possessed depth. She was different from everyone he knew, and her depth appealed to him. However, he couldn't afford depth and he didn't want to hurt her. Frustrated, he shoved his phone in his pocket and as the train stopped, disembarked with the other passengers onto the streets by the water. A short walk later, he entered the loud commuter bar where he'd arranged to meet Jacob.

His friend sat at a table halfway back and raised his arm to flag Adam down.

"Hey, good to see you," Jacob said, shaking his hand. "It's been too long."

"You too. Tell me what's happening with you." Adam listened as Jacob filled him in on married life to Aviva and his job with a boutique law firm in Jersey City. Adam's stomach clenched. The beer he swallowed soured. Another one with a perfect life.

"You're usually a lot more talkative, Adz. What's going on?"

Adam opened his mouth, about to brush him off with his usual flip answer. But this was Jake, the one person he opened up to, if only a little bit. He gripped the neck of his beer tighter and rubbed the condensation away. "My life's a mess." He gave him a quick rundown about the debacle at work.

Jacob winced. "Oh man, that's rough. Has your dad forgiven you yet?"

"Nope, and in the meantime, I'm doing scut work at the office. I'm also benched socially. Sort of."

"What's 'sort of' mean?"

"It means normally, I'd drown my sorrows with some gorgeous babe, but I can't, since hooking up only fuels my dad's fire. I need to keep my nose clean. Which, for the most part, I am."

"For the most part?"

"There's a woman but she's totally not my type."

Jacob raised his brows. Adam banged his head against the exposed brick wall. "She isn't. She's everything I don't look for in a woman. Seriously, my father needs to forgive me so I can get on with my social life and forget about this." And her.

"Isn't your social life what landed you in this mess to begin with? Maybe the woman is exactly what you need."

Adam took another swig of beer. "I was sure Ashley would take care of it." He blocked out images of Dina's creamy skin and stared off into the distance. "And Dina? I don't see it happening."

"Why not?"

He shrugged. "She's not a 'no-strings' kind of

woman."

"You're positive you're still a 'no-strings' kind of guy?"

Didn't matter what he wanted. She wouldn't want him when she found out about him. His mom, the one woman who was supposed to love him no matter what, hadn't given him a second thought when she'd left and cut off all contact. Even his father, who'd stuck around and supposedly knew him, wanted little to do with him. "Please. Not all of us are boring like you."

Jacob laughed. "Don't knock it 'til you try it. You know if you want, I can have my mother set you up."

Adam pulled away from the wooden table in horror, his chair legs scraping against the plank floor. "*Yenta* Karen? You'd sic her on me? Are you kidding?"

"Yep. Just wanted to see you sweat."

"I love your mother, but there's no way I'll let her meddle in my life."

"I think you're missing out on a great opportunity," Jacob said with a wink. "I think you should reconsider Dina. Something in the tone of your voice when you talk about her makes me think your feelings for her are different."

"There's no point."

****

Dina walked into temple Friday night and let her worries fade away. The peacefulness of the sanctuary, with its stained glass windows depicting biblical scenes from the Torah, the ornately carved mahogany doors of the Ark where the Torah scrolls rested, and the dim lighting calmed her. It was the place she needed to be after a week filled with such uncertainty about Adam and her feelings toward him.

She sat in the pew toward the front and waited for the Rabbi to begin her service. A rustling next to her brought her attention to Rebecca, her husband, Aaron, and their three children sliding into her row. Scooting over, she made room for them and handed prayer books to them as they settled.

After the service, she followed Rebecca and her family into the Social Hall for the *oneg*, where everyone socialized and ate dessert after reciting brief prayers over the wine and the *challah*.

"I love showing my children how many people come to services on Friday nights," Rebecca said to Dina as she watched them run over to the dessert table for cookies and juice.

"And I love coming here Friday nights," Dina said. "It helps me settle after a week of stress."

Rebecca nodded. "We missed you last week."

"I was out to dinner and it ran late."

Rebecca's face lit up. "With anyone special?"

Dina sighed. She loved Rebecca. About ten years older than she was, Dina enjoyed having a friend at temple to keep her company and to talk to, but Rebecca always tried to fix her up. "I got a flat tire and this guy stopped to help me. I was a little rude to him and to apologize, I took him to the diner."

"You invited a random stranger to the diner?" She covered her mouth with one hand and gripped Dina's shoulder with the other. "Are you crazy?" When Dina rolled her eyes, Rebecca shook her head. "What's he like?"

Dina pulled Rebecca off to the side, away from the other congregants. "Completely different from anyone I've ever dated."

"Different how? You're dating him?"

"No, he's flashy and seems concerned about his image and what other people think." *But he's got depth.* She'd heard it when they talked, usually when he wasn't aware of it. Rebecca's look of concern made Dina hold out her hand. "Don't worry, he's not my type at all."

Rebecca put her arm around her. "Well, I think I have someone perfect for you. Let me know and I can set you up with him."

Did she want to be set up again? Maybe. "Who are you thinking of?"

"He's a really sweet guy, a few years older than you. He's a researcher in Aaron's lab. Very smart. I think you two would be perfect together. He lives in Madison."

He didn't sound bad at all. "Okay, sure. Why not?"

"Great. I'll give him your phone number. His name is Zach Epstein."

When Dina left fifteen minutes later, she promised to let Rebecca know about her plans with Zach. If he called.

****

The large envelope embossed with her high school logo made Dina's palms sweat. As she pulled out the invitation to her tenth high school reunion, visions of the popular girls whispering as she walked in the hallways clicked through her brain. She was too smart in high school to fit in with anyone. The nerdy kids didn't want to hang out with her—they'd giggled when she'd wanted to discuss the themes in *The Scarlet Letter* and looked at her like she was a bug when she'd proved she could recite the Constitution from memory.

The only things to get her through those years were her teachers and books. Now she was supposed to reunite with them and talk about the good old days? No way.

Morbid curiosity made her read the invitation, rather than throwing it in the trash unopened like she did the five-year one. She frowned. It was a dinner dance on a Saturday night two months from now at a fancy hotel about an hour away in Princeton. The organizers went all out. She started to slide the invitation inside the envelope when her phone rang. Tossing the invitation on the distressed table by her front door, she answered her phone as she walked further inside her apartment.

"Hello, Dina? This is Zach Epstein. Rebecca and Aaron Kopf gave me your name."

"Hi, Zach. Rebecca told me you might call."

"Oh. Good. I wondered if you'd like to go out for a drink one night this week?"

She swallowed. No harm in seeing what happened. "Sure."

"Oh. Good. How's tomorrow? There's this neat place in Madison called The Game Set. It has board games. Do you like board games?"

Board games? "Sure, sounds fun."

After getting the address, she hung up. She'd never heard of the place, but it would be different. And he sounded much more her type than Adam, who never called despite telling her he would. Even if in her imagination, Adam was the one she pictured on the date.

Chapter Five

Dina stood in the doorway of The Game Set. The place was rustic, with a wooden floor and yellow walls. To the left was the bar. Game tables, shelves with board games stacked on them, and groupings of comfy-looking chairs and mismatched sofas occupied every other free space. Toward the back was a room with a doorway marked Billiards. The place was filled with people of all ages and she walked through, looking for a guy on his own.

Movement from the bar drew her attention and a man with wire-rimmed glasses and dark, wavy hair waved to her.

"Zach?"

"Hi, Dina. Nice to meet you. You look like Rebecca said you would." He shook her hand. His grasp was cool and firm and when he made eye contact with her, she noticed his warm, brown eyes. "Would you like a drink?"

He placed their orders and once their craft beers arrived, he directed her to a vacant table with two high stools. She climbed up, grateful she took his advice and wore jeans. He did too, with a button-down blue Oxford. He was tall and rangy with a mellow voice and a piercing stare.

"So tell me how you know Rebecca and Aaron," he said, when they'd settled, turning his stare on her.

Such intensity made her self-conscious and she could feel her cheeks heating. *Great, I probably match my pink sweater.* "We belong to the same temple. I've known her for years. And you work with Aaron?"

"Yes, I'm a research director in the lab next to his. How's your beer?" He jiggled his knee.

She took a sip of the dark brew. "A little bitter, but not bad, thanks. I've never heard of this place. Do you come here often?"

"Some of us in the lab come here for their game tournaments. It's a fun way to let off some steam." His face lit up. "Would you like to play one of the games?"

She would much prefer to talk and get to know him, but he didn't seem like much of a conversationalist. "Sure, why don't you pick one?"

He walked away for a few minutes and Dina checked her watch. Thirty minutes. She'd never checked her watch when she was with Adam.

When Zach returned, he brought Battleship. "I love this game," he said as he set up the board.

It wasn't one of her favorites. "It's a great one. Did you know it used to be known as Salvo?"

"I had no idea. How fascinating!"

As they played the game and talked, Dina tried hard not to compare him to Adam.

Zach wasn't flashy. He wore a smart watch, but it didn't cost more than her entire paycheck. His shirt was wrinkled in the back and his jeans were functional, not designer.

Zach wasn't smooth. His hair wasn't slicked off his forehead and he didn't seem to have a set of responses he took out and used.

Zach wasn't popular. Despite his claim he and his

friends came here often, there was no line of groupies waiting to talk to him while sizing her up.

Zach was…normal. He was smart, average-looking…and boring.

She sighed. "You sunk my battleship."

He nodded at the commercial reference as he added points to his side. He was acknowledging the reference, right?

"I remember those commercials," he said, and relief trickled through her.

He pulled out the pegs in his board. "Want to play another one?"

Goodness, no. "I really enjoyed this one, but it's late and I think I need to get going." Okay, it was nine o'clock, but some people might consider it late. If you were seventy.

"Ah, sure. Can I walk you to your car?"

Think of Rebecca. "Sure."

She followed Zach out the door and walked with him along the quiet main street of Madison. Lit store windows and bright street lamps offered a kaleidoscope of black, yellow and shades of gray for them to walk through, and at times it reminded Dina of an old movie. He pointed out restaurants he and his colleagues ate at, stores he'd stopped in, and interesting facts about the town, such as its nickname of The Rose City. "In the 1800s it had a flourishing rose-growing industry. In fact, the Morris and Essex rail line enabled the industry to flourish and for farmers to sell their produce in Manhattan."

"How interesting." And it was. As a lover of obscure facts, she could appreciate his knowledge. She looked at him. He looked proud of knowing the information. And he'd thought her information about Battleship fascinating. His intelligence sat well on him, truly becoming a part of who he was, unlike Adam, who hid his intelligence behind a veneer. Would Adam have known something like this? Would he have told her? And how would he have acted if he did?

"Oh wait, I see a colleague of mine ahead," he said. "Come on, I'll introduce you."

Taking her arm, he led her half a block to a group of people outside a restaurant. "Mark, Lena, how are you?"

"Zach, funny running into you here."

"Let me introduce you to Dina. She and I were at The Game Set." He made the introductions, and everyone chatted with one another. Dina made small talk for a few minutes until Zach made eye contact with her.

She pulled up short. Unlike Adam, Zach made a special effort to introduce her to his friends. He didn't act ashamed of her. Her intelligence didn't embarrass him.

As they left the group and he walked her to her car, she wondered what she should do. Was she too hasty in her judgment of him? She had no idea if she'd see Adam again anyway. Maybe she shouldn't write Zach off yet. He was kind and solicitous. His friends welcomed her. She could tell by the way he looked at her he liked her. He was exactly the kind of guy she could picture herself with.

"It was great meeting you, Dina," he said. He leaned over and kissed her cheek. "I hope you had as much fun as I did."

"I enjoyed getting to know you, too, Zach." She

smiled at him, and the relief on his face pushed her to make her decision. "I hope we can get together again."

Nodding, he opened her car door for her and held it while she got herself settled. "I'd like to," he said. "I'll call you."

As she pulled away, she hoped he would. Because she wouldn't wait around on the off chance Adam decided to call.

****

Monday morning, Adam looked at his phone, scrolled through his contacts, and dialed Dina's number. The sound of her voice rolled over him, enveloping him like a warm blanket, but when he realized it was her voice mail, he rolled his eyes. "Hey, Dina, it's Adam. Give me a call." He left his number and concentrated on editing his brief. When it was finished, he emailed it to the managing partner before stopping at the threshold of her spacious office.

"Hi, Florence, I emailed you the brief on the Hatchet case. Are we still set for court next week?"

"Oh, Adam, I was going to call you. James will come with me instead."

Adam frowned at the gray-suited woman. He walked into her office. With light-colored furniture and cheery paintings on the wall, it was the complete opposite of his father's. "What's going on? I've worked on the case with you. I thought everything was all set."

She moved behind her light pine desk and peered over her reading glasses. "It was, but your father suggested it might be better to have James work on the case. We really need it to succeed, and well, to be honest, I can't afford any careless mistakes. I hope you understand."

He masked his facial features and gave her a bland nod as his pulse pounded in his ears. "Sure, of course. I'll send all my files over to James."

"Thanks, I appreciate it. I'm sorry about all of this, Adam. You're one of the smartest lawyers I've worked with—and I'm not saying it because your father is my boss."

He left her office, hands in fists at his sides, lungs constricted. Yeah, right. Of course he was smart. But intelligence didn't prevent Ashley from accusing him of throwing her under the bus or lying—because he was convinced she lied—about giving her the motion to file. Intelligence didn't convince his father or anyone else in this office to believe in him. He couldn't even count on Kim. And his father? Fat chance. His head hurt. "Smart" wasn't getting him anywhere.

Trying to banish the thoughts, he returned to his office and put together the files for James. It took him twice as long as it should have, because his hands shook. By the time he was finished, the workday was over. He had a raging headache. He needed to get away, to forget about everything at work.

Dina.

Before he could think about why she was the first person to pop into his mind, he grabbed his phone. He checked his messages, but she hadn't called him back. He'd stop at the library and pick her up to go somewhere. Anywhere. She'd take his mind off of here. Maybe they'd go into the city to a club.

Ten minutes later, he was in his car, screeching into a spot in the library lot. The woman who was friends with Dina—what was her name—? walked toward her car. Tracy. That was it.

"Hey, Tracy, is Dina around?"

She shielded her eyes from the sun. "Adam? No, she's at home today. Everything okay?"

"Sure is," he said with a grin. Pulling out of the lot, he drove to Dina's apartment.

He pulled up to the old Victorian building. He found an empty spot on the street, locked his car, and tried the front door. It was locked. He buzzed #2.

"Hello?"

Dina's voice made him smile, his first genuine one all day. Some of the tension left his neck. "Hey, Dina, it's Adam."

"Adam. Um, come on up."

She buzzed him in. He took the stairs two at a time. The converted house was well kept, but old fashioned. The hallway smelled musty like ancient buildings, and an antique-looking railing protected the staircase. As pretty as the building was, with colorful shutters and a shaded front porch, it wasn't his style. He preferred his modern apartment complex with a gym and underground garage. She waited for him in the doorway of her apartment, her thick hair pulled in a ponytail, dressed in a long sleeved T-shirt and sweatpants. Most women he dated would be mortified to be seen so underdressed. Yet she looked perfect. His gaze focused on her pink lips. What would they taste like?

"Get changed, we're going out."

Her brow wrinkled. "Did we have plans I forgot about?"

"No, I thought it would be fun to go somewhere. We could go into the city to a club, drive along the waterfront, whatever you want." He jingled his keys against his leg. He peered over her shoulder, trying to get a view of the inside of her apartment. He glimpsed a kitchen counter, some overstuffed furniture, and a mix of colors.

"Adam, I can't just pick up and go off with you. I have plans. I was about to start getting ready."

"Cancel them. Come out with me."

She stared at him. He fought the urge to squirm.

"Come on in."

****

From her bedroom, she called Zach. "I'm sorry, I need to postpone tonight. Can we reschedule? I have a semi-emergency I need to take care of. I'm sorry. I don't usually do things like this." She never canceled plans, but something about Adam, the look in his eye, made her do it.

"Oh gosh, is there anything I can do?"

She thought about Adam currently sitting in her living room—jittery, upset, needing her. "No, it's something I have to take care of on my own. I'm sorry to do this last minute though."

"No problem. I'll call you later in the week and we can reschedule. I'm busy the next few days with an experiment I'm running. I can tell you all about it when I see you next."

"Terrific. Thanks for understanding."

She hung up, glanced in the mirror, and shuddered. Well, Adam would have to deal with her looking like a schlump—it's what happens when you show up unannounced. Returning to her living room, she watched him pace, filled with a frenetic energy she didn't understand.

His eyes reflected hurt and sadness. She wanted to fold him into a hug, but he wouldn't stop moving. He probably wouldn't want her hug anyway. "What's going on, Adam?"

"Nothing. I was in the mood for a good time and thought of you."

She cringed at the implication. He threw his hands up as if in surrender.

"No, wait, I didn't mean it."

"What did you mean?"

"Let's go somewhere, do something, drive fast."

He raked his hands through his short blond hair. A part of her wanted to feel its texture between her fingers while another part of her wanted to run and hide under her covers.

"Adam, I don't do spontaneity."

"Why the hell not?" He spun toward her and grasped her upper arms. Despite his quick movements, his hands were gentle. The hurt in his expression lessened. But it was still there. His hands were warm, his breath minty. She couldn't decide if she wanted to run away or melt into him. "Because I'm a planner."

"And you have plans?"

His gaze raked her from top to bottom, leaving a trail of heat in their wake. Only the heat wasn't desire, it was embarrassment, because she knew very well what she looked like. She folded her arms across her chest. "I did, which I cancelled when you showed up."

"You were going to the gym?" He raised one side of his mouth into a lopsided grin.

She would have laughed if she found his comment the least bit funny. "No, I was relaxing before getting ready to go out with someone who doesn't care what I look like." She inhaled as soon as the words left her mouth. "I…I didn't mean…"

He gave a bitter huff. He shuttered the last of the emotion she'd thought she'd seen. "Of course you did. I should have considered you might see someone else. My bad."

He edged toward the door. "Go 'uncancel' them. See you around."

Before she could say anything else, he strode down the stairs. The click of the door as it closed gently reverberated. He was gone.

Chapter Six

Hours later, Adam returned home from aimless driving, bleary eyed. Every muscle in his body ached from the tight control he maintained and wasn't able to release. Parking in the underground garage, he stumbled his way to his apartment. When the elevator doors opened into the gold-carpeted lobby, he stopped short.

Dina was curled in one of the red leather chairs. What the hell?

Bending down, he smelled coconuts in her hair. He inhaled, imagining her wrapped naked around him, lying on a beach with the waves lapping at their toes. But they weren't at the beach and she wasn't naked. She also wasn't supposed to be here.

Anger, embarrassment, and desire combined as he looked at her, trying to figure out what the hell he was supposed to do. He couldn't leave her here—it was one in the morning. He wasn't an ass, despite what others might think. It was rude. She'd be embarrassed. He wasn't that guy.

He knelt and gently shook her shoulder. She was warm beneath his hand. "Dina?"

She blinked, her eyes eggplant in the dim light of the lobby, and slightly unfocused. Extending her legs out from their curled-in-a-ball position, she let out the faintest of squeals as she stretched. His heart thumped.

She reminded him of a cat stretching in the sun. His imagination went into overdrive as he pictured her naked in his bed, waking after a night of making love. He fought the urge to pull her against his chest and nuzzle her hair. As if slammed by recognition, she started and sat straight.

"Adam! What are you doing here?"

He raised an eyebrow. "I live here. The question is what are you doing here?"

She looked around. The color of her creamy skin deepened like an overripe peach. "I must have fallen asleep."

Holding out a hand to her, he helped her up. "Come on upstairs."

"No, I need to go home."

"You haven't told me why you're here." He steered her toward the elevator.

"I came to apologize. But you weren't home, so I waited. Now you're back. I shouldn't have said what I did."

Adam pressed the button on the elevator and held the door while waving her inside. "I'm not sure exactly why you're sorry. If anyone should apologize, it's me."

She leaned against the wall and angled herself until she could make eye contact. "You were upset. I should have tried to help you."

He froze, key clenched in his fist. How the hell did this woman read him? And more importantly, how could he stop it? "It was no big deal."

"Yes, it was."

He folded his arms across his chest and turned to her, nostrils flaring as all of his previous fears rushed back. "How the hell would you know?"

"Anyone who knows you could tell."

What the hell was she talking about?

"I can tell you're still upset."

"No, I'm annoyed by a woman who camped out in my lobby." He should have left her there.

"Right." She didn't look convinced. After a few moments of silence, she sighed and stayed in the elevator. "It's late, I need to go. Goodnight."

It was one o'clock in the morning. She was barely awake. "Please," he said. He ushered her to his door. "Come inside."

"Your apartment?"

"Yeah."

"Now?"

He looked around. "Yeah."

"Why?"

He rubbed a hand across his face. "Because it's too late for you to go home alone and I'm in no shape to drive you." Not waiting for her to argue, he put an arm around her and steered her inside. She fit well in the crook of his arm, all soft and warm. He searched his brain for a reason to keep his arm there. But apparently his brain was more tired than usual because he couldn't come up with a single one. And he called himself a red-blooded male. "Sit down," he said and pointed to the black leather sofa in his living room.

She sat, back straight, perched on the edge, as if she were afraid of—he didn't know what. Not him, right? There was no reason for her to be afraid. But she looked uncomfortable.

He left her seated in his living room and went to the linen closet. Grabbing an extra blanket and pillow, he returned to her and pointed toward the hallway.

"My bedroom is there. You can sleep in my bed."

She frowned. His finger itched to trace the crease in between her eyebrows. Hell, his whole body itched to touch any part of her body. Instead, he squeezed the linens in his arms.

"With you?"

God, he wished he could say yes. "No, I'll sleep here."

"Why?"

"So you can get some sleep."

She jumped up. "You want me to sleep in your bed?"

Heat flooded his groin at the mental picture his mind painted. He gritted his teeth. "Yes."

"I can't do this. I have to go home."

He threw his head back and withheld a scream. "It's late. You're tired. Stay here."

"But I'll have to leave in the morning."

"It's usually what's required to get to work."

She bit her lip. "No, in the morning it will be light. People will see me."

Oh my God, the walk of shame. She thinks people will see her and assume—desire mixed with sympathy. He doubted anyone would think anything of it. But the thought of waking in the same apartment as her made him hard, and he didn't even plan on touching her.

"It will be fine," he said, when he could get the words past his strangled throat.

"Give me those and I'll sleep out here." Before he could protest, she grabbed the blanket and pillow.

He never meant for her to sleep on the couch or for her to use—his arm froze as he reached out for the blanket, but she pulled it onto her lap, sat cross-legged on the couch, and turned. "If you make me stay, then you have to talk to me."

He liked talking to her. As long as he didn't reveal too much. And as long as she didn't notice the pattern on the blanket. "Let me get changed." And maybe find something else for her to cover up in. When he returned to the living room in pajama pants and a T-shirt, he carried another blanket. But she was already wrapped in the first one, and he would draw too much attention if he made her change blankets. Instead, he held onto it and eased onto the recliner next to the sofa.

"What's wrong?" she asked.

He didn't know he was obvious. "Muscles are sore."

She nodded. "What's making them sore?"

He shrugged and then winced. "No idea." She didn't need to know why he was tense.

"What happened today to make you upset?"

This is what she wanted to talk about? He would much prefer to talk about other things. Like her. "So tell me about the guy you were seeing tonight."

"There's nothing to tell," she said. "You showed up and I cancelled my plans."

His hands clenched at the thought of her going out on a date. "Must not be a great guy if you were eager to cancel on him."

"He's nice."

"That's it? Nice?"

"And isn't embarrassed to be seen with me in public."

What the hell did she mean? Oh. Right. Dammit. "I—" What was he supposed to say to her? He was concerned about what others thought of him and he raced to establish his reputation, forgetting about whom he might already be with and how they would feel? "I'm sorry. My behavior was inexcusable, but you don't embarrass me."

She picked at the blanket. "Cute," she said.

Damn. She noticed. His stomach knotted. Kim's kids gave him that superhero blanket as a thank you for spending time with them. "Except when you make fun of my blanket."

She wrapped it tighter. His embarrassment disappeared, replaced once again with desire. Even tired, he couldn't stop staring. Her face was clear, open and warmth emanated from her. He wanted to soak some of it up.

"So why are your muscles sore?"

She was also stubborn. He shrugged.

"Okay, what freaked you out at my apartment earlier?"

He needed to change the subject, fast. He thought about his brief time in her apartment. He hadn't noticed much of it from the doorway, except it was homey and sweet, like her. There'd been a big fancy envelope on the distressed table near the front door.

"What was the fancy invitation for at your place?"

Her face blanched. For a moment he thought she would faint. Who fainted these days? Maybe the same women who worried about the walk of shame? She didn't seem like the fainting type. But her cheeks regained their color, and more. She looked at her lap. Mission accomplished, although his distraction came at her expense.

"It's nothing, just my high school reunion."

"Which one?"

"Tenth."

"Are you going?"

She folded her arms. "Absolutely not."

"Why?"

"Because I don't feel like either being ignored or talked about. High school was not a fun time for me."

High school reunions offered the chance to show up all the people who thought little of you. "Of course you're going. We'll go together."

"What?"

Yeah, what? Did he really offer to accompany her? "You and me. Your high school reunion." Apparently he did.

Her ponytail whipped back and forth like some overzealous spectator at a tennis match. "You're crazy."

"You need a little crazy in your life. It'll be fun."

"You have no idea what it will be like. Popular girls who thought I wasn't fit to wipe gum off their shoe. People who only talked to me to beg me to give them my homework to copy. People who hid their intelligence in order to have friends and ignored me. Trust me, there's no one I want to see."

Adam stretched his shoulders at her description of people who sounded a lot like him.

Dina stared him down, as if daring him to do his worst. Ha, she obviously didn't know him. His worst chased his mother away. His worst turned his father into a slave driver and an entire office against him. He couldn't allow himself to give her his worst. So he'd give her his best.

"I'm sure they've changed. Or at least grown older and fatter. You shouldn't miss it, especially if it scares

65

you."

She yawned. "You're crazy, but I'm too tired to argue right now."

She snuggled into the blanket. A desire to join her overpowered him. He reached his hand out to hover over her leg. When she moved it as she got settled, his hand skimmed the blanket. A jolt of electricity zinged up his arm. He frowned. How was he attracted to her? She wasn't the sexiest woman he'd seen. She wasn't the prettiest even. But she possessed a quality about her that made all his other dates seem shallow. Somehow, he couldn't get enough. It scared the hell out of him.

****

Dina woke a couple hours later, the room still dark, her mind whirling, her body completely still. She didn't want to take the chance he'd come out and find her wide awake. She didn't want him to come out here at all, wearing whatever he wore to sleep—did he wear clothes when he slept? Possibilities danced through her mind, but unlike sheep, counting them would not help her sleep.

She turned carefully onto her side, brought her knee toward her chest. She rested her hand on her ankle, the same ankle Adam touched earlier. Even now, warm streaks zinged along her calf from his touch. She wondered what it would feel like for him to touch her in other places. She buried her face in her pillow.

No, this couldn't happen. He wasn't attracted to her—she didn't fit his profile. She wasn't tall enough, skinny enough, or sexy enough to claim him. She definitely wasn't experienced enough. Oh, how he'd make fun of her if he knew how a simple touch on her ankle through a blanket affected her. The men she was used to, the fewer she'd slept with, never woke her out of a deep sleep—achy and twitchy, wanting more of…something. She was completely out of her depth with Adam.

She needed to fall asleep in order to handle tomorrow. Because tomorrow, she had to leave here with her dignity intact.

****

The aroma of ground coffee and the whistle of steam brought her to the surface of consciousness. She blinked at the darkness. As her sight adjusted to the lack of light, outlines of masculine, geometric furniture in the room appeared. She glanced toward the large window on the opposite wall. Streetlights glowed from outside. How early was it?

Wrapping the superhero blanket around herself, she walked into the galley kitchen. The clock set in the stainless steel oven said five thirty. She should leave, now, before too many people woke and saw her. But oh, coffee. Dina inhaled. The toe-curling smell filled her nostrils and woke her without the benefits of the caffeine.

"Smells good, doesn't it?"

She shrieked, glared at Adam as he let out a low, throaty laugh from the doorway behind her. He wore the same white T-shirt and pajama pants from last night. She swallowed. "You scared me on purpose."

"No, I didn't. But I will not deny finding it amusing."

She drew the blanket closer around her body. "I should go."

"And miss my coffee? If I say so myself, you'd deprive yourself of something amazing."

For a moment, she wasn't positive he referred to coffee. "Okay, I'll try it," she said, making sure to be crystal clear in her answer, regardless of what he referenced, "but then I really need to leave."

Adam walked toward her. He reached around her and opened the cherry cabinet next to her head. This close to him, his nearness overwhelmed her. Warmth radiated from him, his cotton T-shirt brushed her cheek as he stretched his arm beyond her. His particular scent—spice and soap and, for the moment, sleep—battled with the smell of the brewing coffee, making her dizzy.

He grabbed two mugs and handed her one. Their fingers touched. She swallowed. "You're less likely to run into people if you wait until later, after most people have left for work."

"Work! Oy, I forgot. I have an eight o'clock meeting." She took a sip of the coffee, moaned as she savored the nutty flavor. He was right. It tasted amazing.

"Good, isn't it?"

Her cheeks warmed. His smile indicated he'd heard her moan. She wondered when he'd call her out.

"Why don't you skip work and we can have an adventure," he said.

She raised an eyebrow over the rim of her mug. "Your dad would be okay with you playing hooky?"

Adam's face lost all expression. "He probably wouldn't care," he said.

He leaned against the black granite counter drinking his coffee, but Dina wasn't fooled. His shoulders were set, and his fingers gripped the mug hard enough his knuckles glowed white. This was the

Adam she remembered from her apartment before he'd distracted her with other things.

Taking a last sip of her drink, she set the mug on the counter, walked over to him, and removed his mug from his hand. His look of surprise quickly shuttered.

"What are you doing?" he asked.

"What's going on with you and work?"

"Nothing."

"You and your dad?"

"You're very nosy for someone so short."

"Don't think you're going to distract me by turning this conversation toward me. Talk to me, Adam. There's no one else around."

Standing this close to him, she could see a vein pulse in his throat. His eyelid twitched. He avoided her gaze. It wasn't hard. She only came to his shoulder. But he'd never avoided her before.

"Adam."

He sighed.

She watched his chest swell. Clenching her hands at her sides, she resisted the urge to run her hands over the muscles beneath his shirt. She needed him to talk to her, but she also needed to get to work. She didn't think touching him would speed the process.

"My dad is giving me a hard time about something and limiting the amount and type of work for me. He's making it harder for me to make junior partner."

Despite his words, his tortured expression told her it was a big deal. There was more to it.

"It must be really hard working for your father. Don't give up though. Talk to him about it. Let him know how you feel."

He looked at her as if she'd said he could fly. She

waited for him to say something, but he remained silent. Then, clasping her upper arms, he pushed her gently away, grabbed his coffee cup, and walked out of the kitchen. As he left, he called over his shoulder, "Don't forget to text me the information about your high school reunion."

Crap.

Chapter Seven

Dina returned to her apartment in the evening, yawning. She kicked a yellow petal on the front sidewalk before she dragged herself up the stairs and into the front hall of her Victorian building. More petals intermingled with leaves lay scattered on the carpeted hallway. She frowned as she opened her mailbox. Some flower delivery service made a mess.

After a mostly sleepless night at Adam's and a full day of work, all she wanted to do was draw a bath in her claw-foot tub and go to bed. Immediately. She followed the trail of petals and leaves upstairs to her front door. Taped to it was a kelly-green envelope. She yanked it off and opened it.

Tracy said it was okay.

Her mind was too sluggish to process the meaning of the note. She unlocked her door and gasped. Yellow flowers of every variety covered all the visible surfaces in her apartment. Centered on the occasional table in her front hallway was a vase of yellow sunflowers. Tossing her keys next to them, she moved into her living room, where vases of blanket flowers and daffodils littered her coffee table. Walking over to the windowsill, she sneezed at the goldenrod.

Kicking off her shoes, she walked barefoot into the kitchen. Roses sat on the counters, ligularia rested in the sink and Blackeyed Susans perched on the stove.

Stunned, she peeked into her bedroom. Snapdragons sat on her dresser, tickseeds rested on her night table and coneflowers lay tied in bunches on her bed. It was as if the pages of The Encyclopedia of Plants and Flowers came to life. Another kelly-green note lay on her pillow and she sank to the floor to read it.

Please go to your high school reunion with me.
Adam

It was only when she saw each word alternating between green and gold she realized Adam chose the flowers to coordinate with her school colors. She leaned against the side of her bed. Mr. Flashypants struck again, and he was a romantic. Apparently with Tracy's help.

Taking her time, she stopped to examine all of the flowers, except for the goldenrod, which she carried at arm's length out to her balcony—allergies. Her lips twitched. He was the one who left the petals and leaves trailing from her front porch to her apartment door. It was…sweet and romantic and over the top. Pulling her phone out of her purse, she dialed Adam's number. He answered right away.

"So will you go with me?"

Happiness washed over her. He'd waited for her call. "Thank you for the flowers." She tried to keep her voice modulated and steady, though her heart beat fast.

"Did you like them?"

"Everything except the goldenrod. They make me sneeze."

"I'm sorry."

"It's okay. I put them out on the balcony where I can see them anyway."

"I'll remember it for next time."

Next time? "Mm hm."

"So, will you go with me?"

"It's *my* reunion. Shouldn't it be, 'can I go with you?' "

"Details."

She chuckled. "Yes."

****

The smile on Adam's face lasted the rest of the night as he watched TV and lay in bed. Dina invaded his dreams, which featured a silhouette he'd swear was hers. He woke beaming the next morning and it didn't dim as he walked from Starbucks into his office. Only his father's voice through the intercom, ordering him into his office at his "earliest convenience" made it disappear.

The man sure knew how to ruin the mood.

Plastering a neutral expression on his face, Adam sat in a blue wing backed chair across from his father's massive mahogany desk.

"What's up?"

His father frowned. "Is this how you speak to me?"

Neutrality was difficult to maintain. Kudos to Switzerland. "I apologize."

With a nod, his father leaned forward, tented his hands, and rested his elbows on his desk. "Bradley & Company is threatening to take their business elsewhere, thanks to your carelessness."

His stomach plummeted to his toes.

His father's look of distaste matched Adam's feelings at having his father think poorly of him.

"It's all bullshit!" Adam hurled himself out of the chair and paced his father's office. The plush carpet deadened his footsteps, taking away some of the satisfaction from stalking back and forth.

"Sit down."

Shooting pain ringed his scalp as a tension headache formed, but he sat.

"And the paralegals are unhappy working with you," his father said

"Even if you think I was careless with the account, which I wasn't, you know my concerns about Ashley are legitimate."

"Are you sure?"

Adam cradled his head in his hands before raising his gaze. The man was in his fifties with an ageless white-male privileged look about him—a full head of white hair, skin tanned and leathery from endless tennis matches at the club and a powerful stance to make him look as formidable in court as his winning record implied.

"Yes."

His father focused his famous prosecutorial stare at him. Adam felt as if he were turned the wrong way in a wind tunnel.

"You need to fix your relationship with the paralegals. As for your carelessness, I can't afford any more of your screw-ups. You're taking time off."

Was there really no one in the paralegal department who would vouch for him? He might be the boss' son, but he always thought he had genuine relationships. Maybe he could talk to Kim again in private.

The logical side of his brain said his father had no choice but to take away his caseload. Bradley & Company was an important client with far-reaching influence. If they left, it would be significant loss to the law firm. But the rest of him thought making him hide away was the equivalent of announcing his guilt to the world. He'd never make junior partner this way. He wouldn't be able to move anywhere else without a good reference or a winning track record on current cases. He was screwed.

"You won't back me on this? I'm your son."

His father stared past Adam's left ear. "The firm can't suffer, Adam. You know I'm right."

He'd heard the phrase all his life, but never directed at him.

****

Dina stepped off the elevator into the impressive waiting area of Mandel & Ryan, Attorneys at Law, and looked around wide-eyed. First, Adam wanted to be more than friends and now, she was surprising him at his office. Her stomach flopped. She thought she had no more nerves left.

She was wrong.

The smell of money—amounts of which she could never hope to have—practically assaulted her nostrils as she looked around the space. Everything she'd ever read about corporate law offices was true. The carpet beneath her feet was so soft, she wanted to roll around on it. The furniture was expensive wood and she thought the door into the inner sanctum might actually be zebrawood. A woman in a suit straight out of a fashion magazine looked at her over platinum-rimmed glasses. Her hair was perfect. Dina ran a hand over hers in discomfort.

"May I help you?"

Unlike some accents that identified the speaker's geography, hers identified her amount of money—lots. *Wow, even the office receptionist makes more money than I do.*

She shifted from one foot to the other. "Um, I'm here to see Adam Mandel."

"Is he expecting you?"

"N…not really." The idea of taking Adam out to lunch to thank him for the flowers was a spur-of-the moment one. It sounded great in the security of the library stacks. Here, not so much.

The receptionist frowned. At least, Dina thought she frowned. Her face didn't move, but somehow managed to look more disapproving than before. "I'll see if he's available."

Dina perched on the supple brown leather sofa and studied the magazines on the marble table in front of her—Islands, Yachts International, Saveur, Unique Homes, Upscale Living, Architectural Digest, and the Robb Report. As if she didn't already know the second she walked in here, she was way out of her league.

"I'm sorry, but—"

The zebrawood door opened and interrupted whatever Little Miss Botox was about to say.

Adam looked awful. Tension lines bisected his brow and a thin white line outlined his lips. He stopped dead when she caught his attention, and she thought maybe she'd made the biggest mistake of her life. A wash of red passed across his face and he looked around.

"Uh, Dina. What are you doing here?"

It was not the "Hey, I'm glad to see you, Dina!" reaction she hoped for.

"I thought I'd take you to lunch."

A variety of emotions played across his face, but the zebrawood door opened a second time and halted his speech. A thirty-year-older version of Adam stepped through and Dina didn't know whether to be impressed or frightened. Like Adam, he was tall with broad shoulders. His white hair was slicked back. His piercing blue eyes were sharp, and he stood as if a bubble of impenetrability surrounded him. He scanned the room, looking down his aquiline nose.

"Adam, your key."

Adam stiffened, and Dina reached a hand out and placed it on his upper arm. His muscle was rock hard—too hard for anything other than tension to cause it. His jaw bulged, and he ground his teeth together.

Why would he have to turn in his key?

Adam's father turned his stare to her. "May I help you?" It took all her resolve not to cringe. Instead she stepped forward.

"I'm Dina Jacobs." She held out her hand. "It's a pleasure to meet you." The words almost got stuck in her throat.

Little Miss Botox practically fell over the reception desk eavesdropping, and Mr. Mandel must have noticed, because he stepped forward and took Dina's outstretched hand. His handshake was firm. Hers was too and surprise flashed across his face before he banked it down.

"Noah Mandel. How do you know my son?"

"Dad!"

She put a calming hand on Adam's chest. "We've been seeing each other for about a week now."

She didn't know whose face was more comical, Mr. Mandel's or Little Miss Botox's. Both mirrored each other—open fish mouth, raised eyebrows, flared nostrils—which was quite a feat for the receptionist, and a little reassuring somehow for Dina.

Adam's father, on the other hand, alarmed her. Adam didn't mention her at all?

He cleared his throat, looked at Adam, and cleared it again. "Is this true?"

Finally finding his voice, Adam spoke, "Yes, Dad, it is."

"Do you think it's wise?"

"Yes, I do."

Suddenly, Adam put his arm around her shoulder and pulled her against him. He'd never shown her affection publicly. Pleasure, similar to when she saw the flowers, flowed through her. Remembering how similar to a gasping fish the other two looked, she did her best not to let her jaw drop.

But she couldn't do anything about the warmth permeating throughout her body, or the lightheadedness she got from standing this close to him, or the zings of pleasure traveling through her body and pooling below her stomach.

She might not fit in with his lifestyle, but she could make someone comfortable and her parents taught her manners. Looking at Adam, she said, "Thank you again for the flowers." Turning her focus to his father, she added, "He gave me the most beautiful flowers I've ever seen. You taught him well."

A hint of a frown crossed Noah's features before he inclined his head. Without another word, he turned toward the office. When the door closed, silence stretched. Dina stayed in Adam's embrace, afraid to break the spell. Finally, when even Little Ms. Botox returned to work, Dina glanced at Adam.

A wide grin stretched his cheeks, showing off his

dimple.

He pulled her out of the reception area, into the building's hallway outside his firm's office. After the office's opulence, the hallway was utilitarian at best. "You're a genius."

She was, but it wasn't something she mentioned during the first week of a relationship, so she doubted he referred to her IQ. "What are you talking about?"

"My dad is on my case about being more responsible, improving my image, etc. When he saw you with me, he backed down. This is the solution to all our problems."

This time she stiffened. He couldn't be…

"You need me to take you to the reunion. I need you to help my dad see I'm mature enough, attentive enough, for the promotion."

…he was. Did she misread his intentions after he sent her those flowers?

"We were already going to the reunion together," she said. "And shouldn't your performance at work determine whether or not you get a promotion?"

"I need a hidden weapon outside of work. And you, my dear," he planted a kiss on her forehead, "are it."

No, no, no. "You don't need a weapon. You need to have a conversation with your dad to fix things."

"My dad doesn't work your way."

The sinking feeling in her stomach increased. Because while she had started to feel something for Adam, he'd turned her into a career asset for his own ambition.

"You'll help me convince my father, right?"

His green-eyed gaze sent shards of heat into her soul, and she did all she could to extinguish them. He might not care for her in a romantic way, but she could see he cared for her as a friend. And she didn't have a lot of those. Certainly not male ones willing to take her to a reunion and save her the embarrassment of dealing with her old high school enemies alone.

She could help him with this ruse until after the reunion. By then, she'd have gotten through seeing her old classmates, and his father would see how deserving he finally was. It was less than two months.

"Yes," she said.

It was the only thing she could do.

Chapter Eight

This was the dumbest idea on the planet. No, in the galaxy. Maybe the entire universe. *Yay, aliens, I've let you all off the hook!* And now, not only did she talk to herself, she talked to imaginary aliens. Obviously, she should call Adam and tell him she was sick, too sick to go to his father's house for dinner, too sick to participate in this charade.

Instead, she stood in her blue-tiled bathroom and tried to force her frizzy, gravity-defying hair into something chic and sophisticated to go along with her black slacks and pale pink V-neck top. No matter what she did, her hair resembled a Brillo pad. Figures—today was the one day it mattered.

Observing the futility of her endeavor, she pulled her hair away from her face with two combs, added pale pink lipstick and hoped it would be enough. She walked to her lace-curtained window and stared at the street below. In the distance, a motor raced and a moment later, Adam's fancy-schmancy sports car pulled up. When her buzzer rang, she grabbed her purse, whispered *beh-hahts-lah-khah*, Hebrew for good luck, and jogged down the steps.

Adam exited the driver's side and opened the passenger door. As she started to slide in, he pulled her toward him and brushed her lips. He tasted minty and before she could analyze how his kiss made her feel, he pulled away.

"You look great."

She slid into the butter leather seat as he sauntered around and started the car.

"Thanks."

He gripped the steering wheel and Dina watched him, wishing for easy camaraderie, but at a loss for how to get it. The tendons in his hands were taut and the muscles in his jaw bulged. When they stopped at the next traffic light, Dina rested her hand on his. Adam let out a breath and flexed his fingers beneath her hand. His jaw unclenched and he turned. "It's not you. I'm not looking forward to this dinner."

"Because of me?"

"No. You're the only good thing about it. Because of my father." He pulled her hand toward his mouth and kissed her fingers. "I like your hair."

She snorted. "Seriously? I mean, I guess I should say, 'thank you,' but my hair does not deserve a compliment."

Reaching across the center console, he grabbed a hank of her hair and squeezed and released it. It bounced, like the spring in a pogo stick. "I like it. I will not stop complimenting something I like. And I like you. So get used to it."

"Yes, sir."

His cheek twitched, and the hint of a smile crossed his face before he stifled it. But the mood in the car lightened, at least until they turned into a drive between two carved stone posts. Massive lions topped them. As he steered the car around the curve, a huge brick Federal-style mansion with white stone pillars came into view.

Dina swallowed and peered out the window, half expecting a line of servants to stand outside in greeting. This is where his father lived, and all she worried about was her hair?

Parking in front of the broad stone steps leading to an elaborately carved double door, Adam hopped out of the car and came around to Dina's side.

"Ready?" he asked as he led her up the stairs.

"Sure." *Fake it 'til you make it, baby.*

He rang the bell and as the musical chimes echoed inside, Dina turned to him in puzzlement.

"Wouldn't it be easier to walk in?"

Before Adam could answer, an older woman in black dress slacks and a white cotton blouse answered the door.

"Mr. Mandel. Your father is in the living room."

Dina walked with Adam behind the woman, her feet sinking into the Aubusson carpet, and resisted the urge to reach for his hand. She could do this.

Outside the doorway of the living room, he reached for hers. His warm skin against hers and the press of his fingers reassured her. Whether he needed the support, or whether he did it for show, didn't matter. They were together for the moment.

His father rose as they entered, Adam gave her hand a last squeeze, and walked to his father. They nodded to each other, and his father turned his attention to her.

She held out her hand and he grasped it. While Adam might be Mr. Flashypants, his father was The General, complete with military posture.

"It's a pleasure to see you again, Mr. Mandel. You have an impressive home."

He released her grasp and nodded. "You're quite different from Adam's usual dates."

Oof. Adam inhaled, and from the glint in his father's eye, Dina wondered if he looked for a reaction. Her first impression of him hadn't been great, and he sure wasn't helping his cause now. But she was here for Adam, and she'd live up to her side of the bargain.

"I'm sure I am," she said, a wide grin on her face. Looping her arm through Adam's, she looked at him, hoping his father could read her expression of adoration.

"May I offer you a drink?" The General asked.

When she nodded and Adam's father reached for the whiskey decanter, Dina blurted, "Did you know if you laid the 99 million cases of Scotch exported each year end-to-end, they would run the distance between Edinburgh and New York six times?"

Dina froze as the words left her mouth, for the expressions on the men's faces were…odd. The General's hand froze in midair above her tumbler, his mouth slightly open, his white brows furrowed. Adam looked between her and his father, nostrils trembling.

"No, I did not know. How…interesting," The General said. "Adam, would you like one?"

He nodded, eyes sparkling.

They sat in front of the white marble fireplace, glasses in hand and Dina listened to The General and Adam make small talk. Or attempt to. They were really bad at it. The General mentioned the weather and Adam answered with a word or two. Dina launched into a description of cloud formations. Adam mentioned baseball and The General nodded. As the awkward exchange became unbearable and Dina was about to break in with baseball stats, the woman who'd opened the front door for them entered the room after a soft knock.

"Dinner is served."

The General nodded, reminding Dina of an emperor surveying his subjects. He led them out of the living room, across the expansive foyer and into the dining room. If Adam didn't hold her hand, she would stop dead in the entryway.

The dining room—to call it a room was probably an insult—was awe-inspiring. From at least a twelve-foot ceiling dangled a crystal chandelier with enough lights to power a small country. Mirrors on either end of the room gave it the illusion of extending far further than its thirty feet. Decorated in taupe, mauve and cream, it exuded elegance. Dina wasn't sure she was dressed well enough for the room.

However, no one stopped her and no one offered her a change of clothing. She sat in the Louis XVI chair Adam held out for her and stared at the bone china and silver laid out on the cherry table and pretended she fit in.

"This room is lovely," she said to The General, who inclined his head. "Did you know Louis XVI hated cats?"

It was as if her mouth possessed a mind of its own, which would be great if it involved kissing Adam, but in this instance, she didn't think obscure facts about furniture, or the kings after whom the furniture was named, endeared her to Adam's father.

But this time, he chuckled. "Cats? Really?"

Spreading her cream linen napkin on her lap, she nodded.

"Well, I'll be damned. I guess the dandy might have had some good qualities."

A raised eyebrow from Adam prevented her from listing others. Instead, she cleared her throat, tasted the creamy butternut squash soup, and listened as the two men talked about law. The subject didn't particularly interest her, but their interaction did. Adam asked questions, as if to draw his father out. The General initially gave one- or two-word answers, but Adam persisted. Dina's heart broke listening to him try to get his father to talk. She slid her foot forward beneath the table until it bumped into his. His gaze shot toward her and he paused midsentence.

His father noticed. "See, this is what I mean. You lack focus. Careless mistakes are inevitable if you don't pay attention."

Dina's gasp was lost in the quiet clatter of her meal being served. "I'm sorry," she said, "but it was my fault. My foot hit Adam's and distracted him."

The General raised an eyebrow, reminding her of his son. "My son could do with fewer distractions."

Adam's hands clasped into fists and he was poised to rise from the table. She was supposed to help him. Now was not the time for him to get into a fight with his father.

Instead, she blinked. "Well, if we eliminated all distractions, neither of us would be here tonight," she said, and The General's jaw dropped.

Dina switched her attention to the meal in front of her—according to the person who'd served her, it was grilled filet mignon with a brandy peppercorn sauce, roasted fingerling potatoes, and fresh spinach. It was delicious, and she was glad of the break to focus on her food.

"Would you like more wine?" Adam held the bottle and she shook her head.

"No, thank you. I'm good."

"Temperance," The General said. "Another good quality. Adam, you could learn a lot from her."

Adam's jaw clenched and Dina had enough. "Actually, I've learned a lot from Adam as well."

Adam lowered the wine bottle to the table, but kept his hand clenched around it. She wanted to reach out, cover his hand and soothe him, but the table was too wide and climbing across it? Well, she wasn't that type of woman. Hoping he'd take her running her foot up his calf as a sign of comfort and not foreplay, she continued her conversation with The General.

"His knowledge of science fiction and mythology is extensive. In fact," she turned toward Adam, "I put aside some new reference materials and magazines you might be interested in."

His hand relaxed and rested on the table. "Thanks. I'll stop by to look at them."

"Since when are you interested in mythology?" The General didn't bother looking up from his plate.

"I was always interested in it. Don't you remember the class I took in college?"

"At Emory? No, I don't."

Dina came from a family who paid attention to every detail of her life. A particular class in college? Her parents could recall the day and time of the class, as well as the professor and her final grade.

She wiped her mouth and put down her fork. "What class was it?"

"Mythology and superheroes."

"I'll bet it was fascinating."

"Almost made me want to get a PhD."

His father snorted.

Dina turned to The General. "Have you always loved the law, or was there something else to pique your interest?"

A look passed over his face with a dreamy quality she would never have believed.

"I took a theater class once."

Adam paused mid bite. "Really? What kind?"

"Musical. My advisor told me it was helpful for public speaking." He smiled as if lost in a memory. "It was a lot of fun."

"I didn't know you could sing," Adam said.

"I'm more of the shower variety." He hummed a few bars and after a couple of seconds, The General turned.

"I like this woman. I don't know how you found her or what she sees in you, but if you're as smart as someone with my DNA is supposed to be, you'll keep her."

Chapter Nine

"Adam, before you go, can I speak with you a moment?"

They were about to leave this mausoleum filled to the brim with memories of his mother, and Adam stepped away from Dina with a sigh. She smelled good. Turning his back on his father, he brought her into the living room and made sure she was comfortably ensconced in a chair near the window. He placed a hand on her shoulder. Beneath the pale pink cashmere sweater, he could feel her delicate bones. The contrast between soft and sharp made him groan. He wanted to let her textures overwhelm him, not his father's commands or whispers of his mother's unhappiness. "I won't be long," he promised before he returned to the foyer and his father. "Sure, Dad." He followed his father down the marble hall.

Clicking the heavy door shut behind him, he stood in his father's home office, the man's inner sanctum. He waited for the other shoe to drop. Because there was always another shoe.

"I've convinced Bradley to stay with us, but you're not allowed to work with them."

"Ever? They're on retainer."

"Doesn't matter. And while you can come back to the firm, you'll have to work without a paralegal for now."

"How about I contact the president of Bradley and apologize."

He squared off the papers on his desk. Adam stared. His father liked orderliness more than anything else. He didn't want to think where it left him. He'd never been orderly.

"I can't have you anywhere near them right now. The agreement I made with him is tenuous at best. I have only our best people working with the company. And if you say or do anything to hit them the wrong way, they're gone. I won't risk it."

"I swear it wasn't me, Dad."

"I wish I could believe you, but you've screwed up twice before this. If you were anyone else, I would have fired you."

Adam ran a hand through his hair and tried to ignore the sudden nausea that made the food they ate threaten to come right back up. There was nothing left to say. He rose from the chair, his body leaden. As he turned to leave, his father stopped him.

"The promotion you want? I need to see a complete change in how you conduct your professional life, Adam. Because there's no way I can justify your promotion without significant changes in your behavior. You need to put your work first and your personal life second. Too many people know what happened, and it causes doubt and distrust. You have my last name, and with the name comes responsibility. You, more than anyone, have to be above reproach. Your reputation applies to your personal life as well. No more stories around the office of how you rush out early to hit a club or stagger in late in the same clothes you wore the day before because you were with some random woman. This Dina of yours seems like a good start. Let's see if you can keep her."

Keep her, like a coveted toy? Or maybe a grade point average? Or possibly a wild animal needing to be tamed? What the hell did his father think of him? The irony of his father pushing him to commit to one woman, when he couldn't keep Adam's mother from leaving, wasn't lost. The issue begged for a much longer discussion than he had the time for right now. Dina waited for him in the living room. Instead of rising to the bait, he nodded.

"Thanks for dinner."

His father followed him out of the office and to the living room, where Dina waited.

"It was a pleasure to meet you, Dina."

She smiled, looked between Adam and his father. "It was an enlightening evening. Your house is beautiful and dinner was lovely. Thank you."

Between memories of his mother leaving and admonitions from his father, Adam couldn't get away from the house fast enough. He ushered Dina out the door. Swinging his car around, he drove down the long driveway. When he could no longer see the house in the rearview mirror, but had not yet reached the street, he put the car into park.

"What are you doing?" Dina asked. "Is everything all right?"

He gripped the wheel with both hands at ten and two, as his driving teacher instructed him years ago. His thumbs rapped out a beat on the wheel only he could hear. He needed a moment to regroup—

"Adam?"

He breathed in through his nose and out through

his mouth, inhaling her coconut scent that perfumed his car. Unlike other women, her fragrance didn't make his eyes water. It reminded him of the beach. Turning toward her, he reached out and cupped her cheek. She stared at him, a quizzical look on her face. He ran his thumb over her cheekbones before he buried his hand in her hair. His life had turned to shit, and all he could think of was her.

"I...You..." He groaned and pulled her toward him, brushing his lips against hers. They were soft, giving, like everything about her. After the intractability of his father, he welcomed the change.

He needed the change. But he needed Dina more.

She gripped his elbows, and he kissed her. She tasted like wine and chocolate. His hands memorized the outline of her body beneath her sweater. In a corner of his mind he wondered if his hands distracted her as much as hers distracted him. Because hers currently played with the hair on the back of his neck and sent chills along his spine.

The thought came to him in a rush of panic. Like everyone else he'd ever cared for, she would leave him.

He leaned forward, determined to make her stay. The gearshift dug into his rib, but he ignored the jab, needing to get closer. Pulling her against him, he traced kisses along her jaw. He nuzzled the skin behind her ear, smiling as she gasped. His hands roved her body, slipping under her sweater, sliding up her sides and stroking her breasts. Heat shot through him straight to his groin. He groaned. When her mouth opened, he plunged his tongue inside. She stilled before her tongue met his.

He moved too fast. He shouldn't rush her. She was

the only woman who made him feel good about himself. He needed her to like him, to care about him, to not leave. How was he supposed to achieve his goal?

She raised her hands to his face and pulled away so their noses touched. He wanted her mouth on his. He reached, but she stilled him with her hands.

"Shh," she said. "What's the rush?"

He rested his forehead against hers as his breathing slowed. He was afraid if he didn't rush, she'd find a reason to leave. But she was right, he moved too fast. He pulled away. She really would leave him.

Turning his focus to the wheel, he swallowed. "Sorry. I'm sorry. It won't happen ag…"

Now it was she who leaned over and pulled his face toward her. She kissed him long and deep before pulling away. Again.

"I didn't say stop. I said slow down." She placed her hand over his on the steering wheel.

Flipping his hand, he grasped hers and kissed it.

"Sorry, I got carried away."

"And you were avoiding something?"

How the hell could she know? "My father said some things…" He stopped.

"…and they upset you." She finished his sentence and squeezed his arm.

"Was it obvious?"

She nodded. "Do you want to talk about it?"

Never. "Maybe some other time."

She ran her hand through his hair. The touch of her fingers against his scalp sent shards of electricity skittering to his toes.

With a sigh, he put the car into drive. Outside of her apartment, he turned to her.

"Thanks for coming with me tonight."

"If you want to talk, just call."

He leaned over and gave her a chaste kiss on the mouth. He wanted more than "talk," much more, but he'd already moved too fast. With Dina, he needed to move slowly.

****

Three days later and Dina could still feel the imprint of Adam's kiss on her lips. She shivered at the little jolts of electricity running through her body at the memory of his touch. When she closed her eyes, she could smell his scent.

This was ridiculous.

Adam didn't date women like her. His father said as much. She suspected he dated tall, thin, and gorgeous. No matter how kind and considerate he was to her, the only reason he dated her was to help him with his father. Even if his kisses made her toes curl.

As she sat at her computer, she tried to stop thinking about the way the sound of his voice made her stomach vibrate and focus on the "little-boy-lost" look whatever his father said to him caused.

"Are you ready?"

She jumped as Tracy's voice sounded behind her and she swung her chair around. "Ready for what?"

Tracy rolled her eyes. "OMG, you can't possibly have forgotten we're going shopping for your reunion dress now, can you?"

Crap. "No, of course not. I was preoccupied."

Tracy grabbed her arm and practically dragged her out of the office and into the sunshine, where Dina simultaneously squinted and rubbed her arm.

A dull throbbing started behind her eyes. "You

know, I have perfectly fine dresses at home."

Tracy kept walking. "How old are they?"

With a shrug, Dina trotted after Tracy, who personified a heat-seeking missile as she race-walked down the crowded midday sidewalk. She watched, mortified, as three random businessmen and two mothers with strollers rushed out of the way and glared at Tracy's back as she plowed through them.

Mouthing "I'm sorry," Dina caught up with her friend outside a small dress boutique. After seeing the scantily clad window mannequins, she opened her mouth to suggest they try a different store, but Tracy already disappeared inside.

The bell over the door jingled, drowning out the saleswoman's words.

Tracy gave a broad smile and turned toward Dina. "You can help her find a dress for her reunion."

The rail-thin Goth girl nodded. "High school or college?"

"High school," Dina replied, wondering why it mattered.

Goth Girl gave her a once-over and turned toward a clothing rack against the far wall. As Dina followed her, panic bubbled in her chest. Most of the clothes were in shades of mustard, olive, and rust. When Goth Girl pulled out a cream sheath with subtle ruffles along the hem, Dina's jaw dropped.

"The dress is perfect," Tracy said, grabbing it from Goth Girl.

She had to admit, it was lovely. But cream? Not exactly slimming. And the back had a huge cutout, which meant she couldn't wear a bra.

"I need a bra, Tracy," she whispered.

"No you don't. Sticky Boobs!"

Goth Girl walked to the accessory area and returned with a package for Dina, who took it as her face went up in flames. They pointed her toward the dressing room and she obeyed without a sound, if only to get out of the awkward situation.

Sticky Boobs.

She stared in dismay at her reflection in the mirror. You'd think these things would be made for large-chested women, as they couldn't afford to go without a bra. Except the models on the boxes were always waifs who looked as if they hadn't reached puberty yet. And, uh, how sticky was "sticky"? Sticky enough to defy gravity? God, she hoped so.

Once she read the directions and figured out how to apply the sticky boobs, she picked up the dress. The material was soft and slid through her fingers. The ruffles cut against the bias were sophisticated and the plunging back neckline added elegance. But on her? She put on the dress, letting it float into place.

Oy gevalt!

Who the heck was this woman in the mirror?

"Dina? Come on out!"

She blinked, but her reflection didn't change. Pushing open the curtain, she exited the dressing room.

Tracy and Goth Girl gasped.

"Oh my God, you look beautiful," Tracy said. "Turn around!"

Dina obeyed, feeling like the ballerina in a music box.

"You have to get this," Tracy said.

Dina bit her lip. "I don't know. I mean, the dress is lovely, but is it me? I have plenty of 'me' dresses at home I could wear…"

Tracy marched over and gripped her shoulders. "You are not wearing one of your old dresses to your high school reunion. You're wearing this one."

Goth Girl nodded her agreement. "It's über stunning."

Dina angled herself to show off her back. "But, it's so…"

"Perfect," said Tracy.

"I don't know."

"Trust me. You want to wow the mean girls from high school and this is the dress to do it. Besides, Adam won't be able to keep his hands off you."

****

"Kim, can I talk to you a minute?" Adam stood outside in the parking lot Friday evening.

She looked around and nodded. "What do you need, Adam?"

He ran a hand through his hair. "Look, I didn't mean to put you in an awkward position the other day, but I'm really confused and hoped you could help me. Why am I suddenly the bad guy with the paralegals?"

She opened her door and stuffed her briefcase and purse in the backseat of her minivan. "We're a tight knit group. Some of the lawyers don't always treat us well and we stick together. What you did to Ashley really got to us."

"I swear to you, I didn't blame her without cause. I gave her the motion to be filed. I actually handed it to her before I left, and I clearly stated the deadline."

"So you're calling her a liar?"

Adam shrugged. "I wish I wasn't. But I never would have expected her not to own up to her mistake.

97

And certainly not to have all the paralegals rally around her."

"Really? If a paralegal screws up and forces you all to lose a case, you really think she's going to admit it? We have to have each other's backs."

"Are you saying you'd lie?"

Kim closed her eyes. "No, but it's awkward to be working with the boss' son and expect fair treatment, especially individually."

"Wait a minute, hold on. I'll admit I was careless in the past. I'll admit to rushing out occasionally. But when I mess up, I admit it. You know I do, Kim. I've admitted mistakes. And I've never blamed any of you for something I've done. Why are you willing to believe her over me?"

"Actually, Adam," she said as she got into her car, "I'm trying to stay out of it completely. We do have each other's backs. I've had good experiences working with you and I appreciate all the help you've given me. But in this case, I'm keeping my nose out of everything. If you have an issue with Ashley, or any of the other paralegals, talk to them. Please leave me out of it."

Kim started her car and drove away, leaving Adam alone under the lamplight. Muttering a curse, he climbed into his own car and left. Ten minutes later, he pulled into a bar he and the other lawyers frequented.

"Adam!"

This late on a Friday afternoon, the bar was crowded with happy hour revelers, but despite the noise, Adam easily heard Ryan, one of the lawyers he worked with. Although going to a bar probably wasn't the wisest choice, Adam wanted to find out about Ashley's work from Ryan. Maybe if other lawyers had the same problem, he could use their experience as proof he told the truth. It was weak, but it was the best he could do. Following the voice and looking out for the raised hand holding a beer, Adam pushed his way through the crowd at the door. He made his way toward the other end of the bar.

"You want the usual?" Ryan asked. Turning to the bartender, he ordered Adam a beer before addressing him again. "Haven't seen you around the office much."

Adam took the beer from the bartender and swallowed deeply. He'd need about twelve of these to release all his tension, but one was a start. "About the office. How has Ashley worked out for you?"

"What do you mean?

"When you give her deadlines, motions to file, etc. Does she meet them?"

Ryan wrinkled his face. "I think so. I can't remember a time she hasn't. Why?"

"Because I gave her a motion to be filed—handed it to her specifically—and it never made it. She claims I never gave it to her. There was also a problem with a motion I gave her on the Hyde case a month or so ago. Now she's telling the paralegals I've thrown her under the bus to cover my own mistake."

Ryan took a gulp of his beer. "Sorry, I haven't noticed any problems with her."

Adam stifled a groan. Another one who couldn't point to any problems and therefore, couldn't help him.

"I do know she doesn't like working late, but, none of them do. Wish I could be more help." He eyed him over his beer. "You need to get laid, my friend," Ryan said. "You'll feel a lot better.

Sex was Ryan's answer to everything. In law

school, Adam might have agreed with him. Hell, before his father rode his ass, he'd probably have agreed with him. But now? Now he didn't know what the hell to do.

"Oh, do you see the one over there?" Ryan pointed to a hot blonde in the corner, and Adam winced. The blonde didn't appeal to him. He took another swig of beer and shook his head.

"What's wrong with her?"

"Hair's too smooth."

He felt as surprised as Ryan looked. Where the hell did the comment come from?

"Since when are you picky?" Ryan asked.

Since my father decided everything I do points to my being a waste of space. "I have no idea."

"Well, if you're not interested, I'm going to check her out." Grabbing his beer, Ryan sauntered over to the blonde.

Adam watched them as Ryan leaned in and said something. The blonde nodded, and Ryan held up his hand for the bartender. When did he become such a stick in the mud? There was nothing wrong with what Ryan and the blonde were doing. He'd done it countless times.

"How the heck do I get him to pay attention to me?"

A female voice near his ear made Adam jump. He turned toward a brunette with an up do and heavy bangles on her wrists.

"Pardon me?" he asked. What kind of pick-up line was this?

"Ugh, this bartender is impossible to flag down."

Oh. "Here, let me try. What do you want?"

Her lips curved in a smile, but it didn't carry to her

eyes. "Martini."

"Shaken or stirred?"

She frowned. Dina would have gotten the reference. He turned to the bartender and raised his voice. "Hey!"

The bartender turned. Adam gave the order. *Not the most elegant way, but effective.*

"You're much better at this than I am." She held out her hand. "Yvonne."

"Adam." She had a firm handshake and well-manicured nails. The bangles on her arm clinked and reminded him of change jingling. The noise could get annoying.

"Are you here with anyone?" She craned her neck to look past him and refocused on his face.

Her voice rasped. He wanted to suggest she clear it. "Yeah." He pointed toward Ryan. "You?"

"No, I usually stop by here after work."

So she was a regular.

"So what do you do?"

"I'm a lawyer," he said. "You?"

"I'm a personal trainer. Do you work out?"

God he was tired of mindless conversation. Adam swallowed the last of his beer. Ryan was right, he was picky. Glancing toward Ryan and seeing him still occupied with his blonde, Adam tossed some bills on the counter.

"Well, it was nice to meet you, Yvonne."

"Leaving so soon?"

She placed a hand on his arm. He blinked, trying not to mistake her nails for talons.

"Long week."

As he escaped the confines of the bar, he took a

deep breath and tried to force himself to relax. Drinks with Ryan didn't help.

Dina's face flitted through his mind and pulled him up short. His hands curled into fists as he pictured her springy hair. His lips curved as he remembered her obscure trivia and her love of knowledge.

Dina.

He wanted her.

Chapter Ten

Dina's phone rang early the next morning, and she cracked an eye open as she looked at the clock on her night table. Seven eighteen. Who called this early on a Saturday morning?

"Hey, Dina, it's Adam."

She cleared her throat, hoped she didn't have too much of a morning voice, knew it was a futile hope, and prayed he wouldn't hear it. "Hi, Adam."

"Oh gosh, I woke you! I'm sorry. I…I wanted to talk to you and didn't think about the time."

So much for hopes and prayers. "It's okay."

"I'm really sorry. Go to bed, I'll talk to you later."

"Wait," she screeched before he could hang up. "It's fine. I need to get up anyway." It was a lie, but she'd never fall asleep now. She might as well talk. Besides, she'd missed his voice.

"Are you sure?"

"Adam!"

He laughed. "Okay, well, since you're awake, want to go for an early-morning walk?"

A walk? "A walk? Where?"

"I thought on one of the trails. It's cold, but sunny and I thought it might be nice. Although…"

Dina yawned. "Although what?" She thought he sighed, but then, nothing. "Adam?"

"Never mind. This sounded like a much better idea

103

last night when I got ready for bed."

"It sounds lovely, really. Did you have a particular trail in mind?" She'd never before seen this unsure side of Adam.

"How about the Loantaka Brook Reservation Trail? It's at the end of South Street."

"I know where you're talking about. Should I meet you there?"

"No, I'll pick you up. Can you be ready in an hour?"

Dina looked at the clock again. Seven thirty. "Sure."

"We'll stop for coffee first."

"Thank goodness!"

He huffed with amusement, and the echo of it lingered in her mind long after she'd hung up the phone. Which was ridiculous, because they were nothing more than two people fulfilling a bargain. Thinking of him in any other light would lead to heartache.

By the time she was dressed and ready to go, Dina had just about convinced herself to beg off from the walk. They'd grab coffee together and she'd go home. There was laundry to do and bathroom cleaning and grocery shopping.

When he pulled up to her door and flashed his high-wattage grin at her, her pulse thrummed and thoughts of laundry, bathroom cleaning and grocery shopping dissolved in a poof of cleanser bubbles. He wanted to walk, she'd walk.

"I missed you," he said, as she climbed into his car. He missed her? Heck, if he wanted her to run, she'd run, without needing anyone to chase her, even.

"It's good to see you too."

They pulled away from the curb into the empty early Saturday morning streets, and chatted about their week, Adam paying close attention and asking questions. By the time they'd stopped for coffee and arrived at the trailhead, she was ready to follow him anywhere.

He took her hand as he helped her out of the car and if she hadn't been staring at their joined hands, she'd swear flames raced up and down her arm. She met Adam's gaze. A frown line appeared between his eyebrows for a brief moment, disappearing before she could think about why it might be there.

Once she was upright, he dropped her hand and took a step closer to her, until mere inches separated them. He brushed his hand across her shoulder, lingering for a second or two before he moved away.

"Your hair was caught on your jacket collar," he said, a strange huskiness making his voice scrape across the space between them. Stuffing his hands in his pockets, he turned toward the trailhead, and Dina followed.

His stride wasn't overly long, but it was brisk, and she raced to keep up with him.

"Adam, wait," she said, when he didn't seem to notice.

He turned a sheepish glance toward her and waited. "Sorry, I was distracted."

A part of her wanted to ask what distracted him. Another part of her was afraid she knew the answer. She kept silent and the two of them walked the paved trail. The air was cold, the sky a clear blue, and the rising sun sparkled in the stream running next to the path.

"Hold on," Dina said, as she pulled her camera out of her pocket. She knelt and took a picture. "It's beautiful out here."

They continued walking, Dina stopping every few minutes as she noticed a pretty leaf or weed or view. Adam waited without a word each time. After photographing a brown leaf floating on the stream, she turned her camera on Adam. He stared off into the distance, hands thrust in the pockets of his navy down jacket, a pensive look on his face. Against the stark brown leafless trees, he made a striking figure, and she focused her camera, intent on capturing the shot. The click of the camera made him turn, and he frowned.

"Did you take my picture?"

"I did. Do you mind?"

"I wasn't looking at you."

"It's okay," she said. "It was a striking setup. Do you want to see?"

When he nodded, she showed him the photo. His frown deepened. "I wasn't smiling."

"I know, it was candid. You look good."

He raised an eyebrow. "Next time, tell me you want a picture and I'll smile."

She raised her camera. "Okay, smile."

The one he gave her reminded her of why she called him "Mr. Flashypants." It was broad with white teeth and reminded her of a car salesman. His muscles stretched, but it didn't reach his eyes. She snapped it anyway, since she told him she would, but inside, she preferred the other one. When she showed the smiling one to him, he nodded.

"This one is more like me."

She disagreed.

They walked along the stream until the path veered into the woods. Within the shade of the trees, the air was several degrees cooler, and Dina burrowed deeper into her pea coat.

"Cold?" Adam turned and stopped in front of her.

She nodded, and he adjusted her scarf, the backs of his fingers caressing her cheeks and jaw. His warm breath tickled her nose and up close, she could see flecks of silver and brown in his eyes. A small scar marked the top of his cheekbone, beneath his eye, and without thinking, she touched it.

He froze, a sharp intake of breath making Dina realize she'd actually made contact. As if the texture of his skin beneath the tip of her finger wasn't enough evidence.

"I'm sorry," she said, drawing her hand away.

"No, it's okay." He took her hand and held it against his cheek. She could see his pupils dilate, feel the rasp of stubble beneath her palm.

"How did you get it?" she asked.

"A fight in the third grade. Tommy D teased me for talking to the girl everyone used to make fun of in class. So I decked him. He got me back and we both got detention."

Dina couldn't help smiling. "Aw, you were her knight in shining armor."

He reddened. "You're the only one who thinks I was."

"Not true. She probably thinks so as well. Since I know who my competition is, I'll have to give you my ribbon to carry or something."

At his look of confusion, she continued. "In

medieval times, a lady gave her knight a favor, such as a ribbon, and he'd joust for her."

Taking her hand from his cheek, he raised it to his lips and kissed the backs of her fingers. "So you want me to fight for you?"

This was a direction she didn't want to traverse. "We're too old for fighting. But it's sweet you defended her."

A look crossed Adam's face, and she couldn't be sure if it was embarrassment or relief. He squeezed her hand. "Your fingers are icy cold." He rubbed them between his, trying to warm them up, which was weird, since the rest of her was on fire at his proximity. He pulled her onto the trail and continued their walk. His hand was warm and larger than hers and somehow, it fit.

Their feet crunched on the gravel path. Deeper in the vegetation and hidden among the trees, deer popped up their heads and watched them pass, the younger ones bounding away before they got close.

"Did you get in many fights as a kid?" she asked as the silence stretched between them.

"It was my only one. My father was angry—I don't think I was able to sit for a week. How about you?"

"Did I get into any fights?" Dina looked at him askance.

"What were you like as a kid?"

"You wouldn't have noticed me," she said. "I always had my head in a book. The teacher would have to call my name repeatedly for me to hear her."

His face took on a dreamy quality, as if he pictured her lost in her book.

"And now?"

"I still keep my nose in books. The worlds they create are wonderful. I can live anything I want, be anyone I want, without consequence."

Adam huffed. "It has a certain appeal." His fingers tightened around her hand, not enough to hurt, but enough to tell her he'd tensed, and she struggled for a way to change the subject. Not knowing what upset him, she didn't want to ruin their walk.

"I bought a dress for the reunion," she said.

"What's it look like?"

She grappled with a way to describe it—fashion wasn't her strong suit. "It's cream, with a ruffle and…" No way would she mention the Sticky Boobs.

"And?"

Her face heated as she tried to figure out how to fill in the "and." "Tracy helped me, and she says it's perfect, but I'm not sure."

He slanted his gaze toward her and squeezed her hand again. This time, the squeeze wasn't filled with tension. "I can't wait to see it."

His confidence in her appearance should have made her happy. Instead, it only gave her anxiety. She suspected he was used to fashion model-types, not girls with frizzy hair and hips. And if she passed inspection when he first noticed her, once he saw the rest of her classmates, she was sure he'd find her lacking.

Well, she could spend the next few weeks worrying about it, or she could suck it up and accept herself for the way she was.

She hoped Adam could do the same.

****

"Adam, your father wants to see you," Diane, his father's secretary, announced as he walked into the office Monday morning.

Adam continued walking to his desk, his stomach clenched.

"I think he'd like to see you right away," she said.

She would have reminded him of a puppy, with the way she followed his father around doing his bidding, if she wasn't sharp and ferocious. Maybe a rat terrier? With her hair pulled in a tight bun, small pointy glasses, and bright red nail polish, he could see the resemblance. He nodded to her and changed his direction.

Adam knocked on his father's door, not bothering to wait for him to answer. There must be some perk to being the boss' son. These days he was hard pressed to come up with any others.

"When are you bringing Dina to the office?" His father spoke without looking up from his desk, his attention still on whatever was on his computer screen.

Two could play this game. Adam sat, crossed his leg over his knee. He waited for his father to look at him.

After a moment, his father met his gaze.

"Why would I bring her here?"

An expression appeared on his father's face Adam could only describe as patronizing, the kind you give a small child who doesn't understand the simplest of commands. "I thought we went over this, Adam. You need to change your image. Completely. Bringing Dina here, introducing her as your steady girlfriend, would help you. It would make you seem more stable and thoughtful."

Bile rose in Adam's throat at his father's blatant use of Dina. And his. Because wasn't it why he started dating her in the first place?

"Seems to me it would only prove I slack off, since I wouldn't be working when she was here."

"I don't recall your working on anything important enough you couldn't have a small break to show your girlfriend around."

Man, he'd have to look into getting a Kevlar suit made if his dad continued to sling insults his way, no matter how veiled they might be. He rose from the chair.

"She works at the library—she might not be able to get time off."

"She stopped by once. I'm sure she'd love to visit her boyfriend's law office again and meet his high-powered co-workers."

Adam returned to his desk, nauseated. His manipulative father was using Dina. He was too. Because really, wasn't he going out with her to get his father off his back? A part of his conscience agreed, but there was a small piece of him that rebelled. Her skin yesterday on the trail, when he'd adjusted her scarf, was softer than anything he'd touched in a long time. He'd lingered, adjusting the scarf in miniscule movements to try to prolong contact. If they weren't in public and in the cold, he would have removed the scarf, and everything else she wore, to feel if the rest of her was as soft. When she'd touched his scar? Heat radiated from her fingertip on his cheekbone to the edges of his scalp. He'd wanted her to touch more of him.

But those things spoke of physical attraction, which surprised him, given how different she looked from those he was normally attracted to. Yet, he'd kissed her in the car on the way home from dinner with his father. If she hadn't stopped him, he'd have gone much further.

But he loved talking with her, hearing how her mind worked, listening to her obscure trivia. When they weren't together, he missed her. Even if she scared the crap out of him. Because she got him. She knew him better than friends he'd known for years. He liked it. In fact, he was crazy about it.

Increasingly, he was at ease around her. It comforted him to know he didn't have to play a part, even if he couldn't help playing it anyway. Because there were times when he'd let his inner self shine through—like when they talked about his love of superheroes—and it was a relief.

So inviting her to his office would be difficult. Because he was using her, but he also cared. Balancing those two pieces would be tricky.

Back at his desk, he picked up the phone and dialed her number.

"Hello?"

Her voice filled him with warmth. He couldn't stop the smile from teasing his lips.

"Hey, Dina. Are you free for lunch?"

"Today? Yeah."

The pleasure in her voice made his request bittersweet. "Good, why don't you come to my office at twelve. We can go to a restaurant in my building."

"I'll see you then."

The busywork he still handled did little to make the rest of the morning pass, but somehow, the hands of the clock moved along until noon, when his phone rang. Without bothering to answer it, Adam sprinted to the reception desk and stuck his head around the door into the waiting area.

"Hey, Dina, come on in."

He wanted to kiss her hello, run his hands beneath her pea coat, play with her springy hair, but there were people around. Instead, he grimaced. "I'll give you a tour."

His stomach clenched a little as they walked through the office, waving to his friends behind glass walls. He'd do what his father wanted, but fast, and he'd have the rest of lunch to enjoy spending time with her.

"Have you known him long?" Dina asked as he pointed out his friend John behind a glass wall.

"Yeah, he's one of my close friends here." Close being relative, of course. He and John hadn't spoken much since Ashley made her accusations.

"What about him?" she asked, pointing to Paul, another one of his friends who also avoided him.

"Yeah, we often have lunch together."

He steered her around the paralegal department, rattling off a list of names and kept moving until they approached his office.

"Marie, this is my friend, Dina," he said to his secretary.

She waved. "Nice to meet you."

"You too," Dina said.

"And this," he said, opening his door, "is my office."

She took a cursory look around, glanced out his window, and nodded. "Nice."

Her reaction shouldn't have surprised him. An actual office, even one with a window, wouldn't impress someone like her.

She fidgeted. When he opened his mouth to speak,

she turned to his bookshelves. Of course. Bending down, she examined the law books on his shelves as if they fascinated her. He examined the shape of her rear, which he found much more intriguing.

"Are you ready for lunch?"

"Sure," she said.

With his hand on the small of her back, he ushered her out of the office and downstairs to the restaurant off the lobby. She was silent during the entire elevator ride. He didn't know what to make of it. Once they sat and looked at menus, he put his aside.

"So, what did you think of the office?"

"Um, it was very nice." She squirmed.

He frowned. What was going on?

She sighed. "Adam, why did you invite me to your office?"

Well, this question was a little trickier. "I thought you'd like to see it."

"The building or the people?"

"What do you mean?"

She blew a strand of hair out of her face. "I mean, did you want me to meet the people you work with or see the place you spend hours of your day?"

He shrugged, confused. "Dina, I don't know what you're talking about."

"Do I embarrass you?"

He gaped. "Why would you think you embarrass me?"

"Because every time I'm with you and we meet someone you know, you act like you don't know me. Because rather than introduce me to the people who are your supposed best friends at work, you rushed me past their offices before I had time to wave."

Oh God. "Dina, you've got it wrong."

"Do I?" She rose and dropped her napkin on the table. "I don't think so. If you'll excuse me, I'm going to go clear my head. I'll talk to you later."

"Dina, wait!"

He rose to go after her, but a body in his way stopped him short.

"Hey, Adam, how are you?"

Stephen, a guy in another law firm in the building, approached him.

"I can't talk now, Stephen, I'm sorry."

"You know, you really need to manage your time better."

Adam stopped short and swore to himself. He couldn't get away from his reputation if he wanted to. The desire to straighten out Stephen's assumption made him start to turn back, but he paused. Now wasn't the time. He needed to find Dina and fix her assumptions first.

But when he looked for her, she was gone.

Chapter Eleven

The buzzing intercom pulled Dina out of a daydream that evening. The daydream in which she and Adam had a relationship instead of the bargain they'd struck. With a sigh, she rose from the table where her dinner sat untouched and looked at the video screen on her security intercom. Adam's image greeted her, and she jerked back.

If I wait, he'll get bored and go away. It would be best for both of them. She needed time to get herself fully on board with their value to each other—a means to an end. He wasn't interested in her, not beyond body chemistry.

Leaning against the cool steel door, she repeated, "We have an agreement," over and over in her mind.

He buzzed again.

He didn't get the hint.

He leaned on the buzzer without stopping.

Oy gevalt. Lovely.

He made patterns with his buzzing.

He possessed more of an attention span than she'd expected. Her neighbors, however, had little patience for noise. Unless she wanted them to let him in, she had to answer. Repeating "We have an agreement" to herself one more time, she pressed the button, opened her door, and listened as he climbed the creaking stairs.

"You're very persistent," she said, hands clenched

together behind her back. His hair was mussed, and she wanted to run her fingers through it to smooth it.

"You didn't answer."

She blinked. Standing this close to him, she could smell his spicy clove aftershave, and it was all she could do not to throw herself at him. But they had an agreement and throwing herself into his arms wasn't part of it.

"Can I come in? We need to talk, and I don't think we should do it in front of your neighbors."

"I don't know. Mrs. MacAvoy loves gossip. It would be a shame to deprive her."

He raised an eyebrow and she suppressed a smile. What she would give to see his eyebrow raise all the time. She moved deeper into the apartment and let him follow her inside. What would he think of where she lived? It was completely different from his: all colorful fabrics, gravity-defying stacks of books, and mismatched furniture with Judaica scattered around. It probably screamed "single girl" to him, but at least she didn't have a cat. Yet.

She perched on her favorite wing chair, a purple one with daisies she'd bought at a garage sale and pointed to her gold overstuffed sofa for him to sit. She'd curl up on it later and inhale his lingering scent, dreaming of an impossible future. For now, she needed space.

"I'm sorry about what happened in the office, Dina. Truly."

She shook her head. "Don't be. I overstepped."

"No, you didn't, but you did misunderstand."

Their relationship? Of course she did. Was he about to reiterate their deal? She opened her mouth to stop him, but he held out a hand.

"Let me finish."

She shut her mouth to avoid looking like a fish, or a mouth-breather. Neither was attractive.

He ran a hand through his hair and stared at his feet for a moment before he continued. "I'm sorry I didn't introduce you to my friends at the office. It wasn't because of you, it was because of me."

Was he really going to use the "it wasn't you, it was me" argument?

"I'm having a problem at the office. I've become sort of a pariah. I was afraid if I brought you into their offices or stopped to talk to them for long, they'd say something about it to you."

"Why are you a pariah and why would I take their side?"

"Everyone else has."

"I'm not everyone else," she said.

It was like she'd stuck a pin in him and let out all the excess air. "You're right. And I'm sorry."

Dina nodded. Why was he a pariah?

He mumbled something. It sounded like the word "father," but she couldn't be sure. "Pardon? Why are you a pariah?"

He fidgeted. "Work politics. But I should have called you my girlfriend when I introduced you to Marie. I don't know why I didn't. Maybe I was being careful…"

"No, you were right."

"I was right?"

She swallowed and plunged ahead. "I'm not your girlfriend, not really. We have an arrangement." Getting involved in his work politics was pointless.

"An arrangement."

"I'm helping you get in your father's good graces and you're escorting me to my reunion. We might enjoy each other's company, we might have gone out on a date, but we shouldn't make this into anything more."

"Dina—" He looked stricken.

"No, Adam. I'm not your type, and frankly, you're not mine, either." God forgive her for lying. "I overreacted."

"You overreacted?"

She nodded, glad he finally understood. "I'm sorry your friends are behaving the way they are. You're probably right, though. Introducing me to them would only have hurt your reputation with them." She didn't need to delve any further into his difficulties at work.

He frowned and looked at his hands.

"I'm glad we got this straightened out," she said as she rose and led him toward the door. Saying the words, reminding them both of their agreement, was useful. It made things clearer, like drawing a map or an org chart.

He followed her. "Everything will be fine, Adam. I don't usually overreact, and I won't do it again."

He wore his "little boy lost" look and it was all she could do not to react to it. She needed him to leave before she wrapped him in her arms. Opening her front door, she waited for him to step over the threshold. It took him a while, but when he did, she leaned against the doorframe.

"We should grab lunch again sometime," she added.

"Lunch?"

Friends ate lunch together, right? "I promise I won't walk out on you," she said. Smile, she told herself.

"Walk out on me?"

She raised the corners of her mouth, and it lasted while he turned and walked down the hallway, after she closed the door, and until she sat on the sofa he'd recently vacated.

Her stomach fluttered at his scent in the fabric of her sofa and a shiver of desire ran up her spine. Tears coursed down her cheeks.

She'd done it. She'd restored their equilibrium. They were friends.

****

Adam climbed into his car and shut the door before opening it and slamming it again, hard enough the car shook. He pounded his hands on the steering wheel. The force sent shock waves up his arms and jarred his teeth. He flared his nostrils as he blew air in and out in an attempt control his raucous breathing.

What the hell happened?

She wanted to be friends.

The only kind of "friend" he wanted to be with her had "boy" attached to it. No, it wasn't true. He did enjoy her friendship. It added depth to their relationship and prevented it from being a purely physical attraction. Because he loved talking to her, hearing her opinions, sharing himself with her.

But the physical part was also important. He was attracted to her. They'd only kissed, but the one kiss, the unbelievable kiss, haunted him. His lips still burned where they'd touched hers, his insides still turned to jelly when he thought about it. In fact, he'd hoped there would be more kissing in her apartment once he apologized for his gaffe.

But she'd focused on their arrangement and her overreaction, and here he was pulling away from the curb into rush hour traffic.

She thought he dated her only to impress his father. If he were one hundred percent honest with himself, he'd acknowledge the partial truth in the statement. But the more time he spent time with her, when he wasn't royally screwing things up, the more he wanted to move beyond their arrangement.

His head was another matter. It still focused on not making a fool of himself, on maintaining the right reputation, on spinning the right message.

But listening to his head was probably what got him into this mess in the first place. As unbelievable as it might sound, it was time to follow his heart.

****

Dina's phone rang late that night.

"Dina, it's Adam."

She blew her nose, which was stuffy from crying. "Hi."

"Are you okay? You don't sound like yourself."

"It's allergies." People had winter ones, right? Dust, mold, nonexistent cats…

"Are you sure?" His voice was deep with concern.

Dina's eyes watered. "What's up, Adam?"

"Nothing, I wanted to check in with you. See how you are."

He'd seen her earlier in the evening. What was left to check in on? "I'm reading."

"What book?"

She picked up the closest one. It was a book she'd read more times than she could count. "*Little House on the Prairie.*"

"Really? I remember my teacher reading it to us in third grade."

"Did you like it?"

"I was more interested in running around the playground than sitting and listening to a story."

She smiled.

"Anyway," he continued, "I wanted to thank you for forgiving me earlier."

"It's okay."

"So, I need a book to read and thought of you, my favorite librarian."

Her insides warmed. "Really?"

"Really. I thought maybe you could recommend something, so…"

They talked for an hour, moving from books to TV to movies. The next night he called as she ate dinner.

"Hey, how was your day?"

"Sad. There was a homeless woman hanging out in one of the reading rooms. I've seen her before and I leave her alone, other than to wave, because it's a place for her to stay warm and she's harmless, but there was this other woman who objected to her presence so my boss made her leave. I felt really bad for her."

"I don't understand how people can ignore someone suffering," he said. "There's an old man near my dad's office and I give him spare change when I see him. I've talked to him a few times. He's a war veteran. He could be anyone. Even you or me."

Dina swallowed at his unexpected side. Her chest expanded at his compassion. She'd moved onto the sofa, settling deep into the cushions as they spent the rest of the evening talking about volunteer opportunities and politics. This evening he'd called to tell her a funny story about a friend of his, but she was getting ready for Temple.

"I'm sorry, Adam, but I'm in a rush. Can we talk later?"

Apparently, telling him they were friends made him more inclined to, well, act like a friend and talk to her. It was nice, but it was also hard. Because the more they spoke, the more attached she grew—both to him as a person and to him as a man. He was much deeper than he made himself out to be. This was the Adam she admired.

At least their conversations took place over the phone, where all she needed to do was ignore her attraction to his husky voice, reminding her of flannel and leather and the sound an engine makes when it's warmed up. She'd never tell him—he'd probably object to being compared to flannel, even if it was warm and cozy. As long as it wasn't in person, at least until she could get her mind and her heart and her body on the same page, she'd be fine.

She finished dressing in gray flared suit pants and an orange button-back V-neck sweater. Her Jewish star necklace, hoop earrings, and she was set. Shrugging into her black pea coat and swinging her purse over her shoulder, she went to temple, determined to put Adam out of her mind for now.

The chilly wind blew her hair across her face. She entered the foyer of the synagogue with relief. Shivering, she hung her coat in the coat closet and walked into the vestibule outside the sanctuary.

She stopped dead.

Adam.

So much for Shabbat peace. She pasted a smile on

her face and walked over to him.

"Shabbat Shalom," she said. "I didn't expect to see you here."

His face glowed, and her heart stuttered in her chest. He leaned over and placed a kiss on her cheek. It shouldn't have affected her—everyone did it—but her knees wobbled.

"I thought it would be a nice place to be tonight."

Her lips trembled and she eyed him askance. "Really?"

He shrugged. "Well, you come every week. There must be something you like about it. I thought I'd try it."

He tried to hide his uncertainty, but it peeked out, like a child who sneaked out of bed to spy on the grownups, and her heart melted. "I'm glad you're here. Let's go sit down."

He took her elbow as they entered the blue and gold carpeted sanctuary, greeted the ushers, and found a seat halfway down the center aisle. They sat together, Adam's arm across the back of her chair.

"Hi, Dina," Rebecca said. "Can we join you?"

Rebecca, Aaron, and their kids scooted into the row while Dina made introductions. "Adam, this is my friend Rebecca and her family." He leaned forward and shook everyone's hand. "Rebecca, this is my friend, Adam."

Dina busied herself in picking up the correct prayer book, but not before Rebecca gave him an appraising glance. The Rabbi walked to the *bima* and nodded to the Cantor, who hummed a *niggun*. Its wordless melody washed over her, saving Dina from having to say anything further to Rebecca.

Throughout the service, Dina kept watch over Adam out of the corner of her eye. He was familiar enough with the prayer book and most of the prayers and joined in singing many of the songs. His singing voice was beautiful—deep and husky—and made her feel as if he whispered words of love only to her. He'd moved his arm, but it now rested next to her. Every fiber of her being told her to move her arm to touch his, even if it was only through cloth. But they were in temple and they were friends. She dragged her gaze forward and focused on the service.

When it was over, they joined the entire congregation in the social hall for the *oneg*. Usually, talking to people over refreshments was one of Dina's favorite parts of the service, but this time, Adam stood too close and she couldn't concentrate.

"Would you like something to drink," he asked after they'd said the prayers over the wine and the *challah*.

"Water would be great," she said, as much to put some distance between them as to soothe her parched throat. Adam left to find her a drink and Rebecca moved closer.

"So, 'friends,' huh?" Rebecca asked, laughter adding golden sparkles to her brown eyes.

"Yes."

"Are you sure? Because he doesn't look at you like a friend, and you don't respond to him like one."

"None of it matters. We can't be anything more."

"So does this mean you're interested in Zach?"

Dina sighed. "I should be. He was great."

"But?"

She shrugged. "But...I don't know."

"I think you do," Rebecca said as Adam returned with a glass of water.

Chapter Twelve

"Come to dinner with me tonight?" Adam asked Dina during what she thought of as her daily phone call.

It being Saturday, he'd called in the morning. Eleven to be precise. After spending time together last night at temple. What was left to talk about? Apparently eating.

"I'm not sure I can."

"Someone else taking you out?"

His tone was light, but she could hear an underlying edge to it, betraying nerves he covered with a laugh. It could be interpreted as mean. Adam was many things, including Mr. Flashypants, but "mean" wasn't one of them.

"No. I told Tracy I'd watch the baby for part of the afternoon so she and Joe could get some errands done. I'm not sure how late they'll be." She also wasn't sure she could handle seeing him two days in a row.

"I think you need some adult company."

Adult company sounded slightly obscene when Adam talked about it. "Um, you want to hang out with a baby? Don't you have other things you'd rather do?"

"I'm not doing it for the baby, I'm doing it to see you."

She pressed her hand against her stomach and tried to stop the smile. Somehow, she didn't think saying no was going to be easy. And come to think of it, she'd never watched a baby before and she'd been trying to calm her nerves all morning. "Have you spent time with any babies before?"

"I'm a baby expert."

Once again, he came to her rescue. "Great, because I've never done this before. Why don't you come to Tracy's at two?"

"I'll pick you up instead and we can drive over together."

She gobbled a tuna and tomato sandwich and thought and rethought her babysitting outfit—having Adam see her meant her "relax with a baby" outfit needed serious rethinking—several times before Adam buzzed her apartment intercom.

When she climbed into his car, she did a double take. "You do know we're watching a baby, right?"

"I didn't forget," he said as he pulled away from the curb. "Hello, by the way."

"You obviously weren't paying attention, since you're wearing a white shirt." She pulled her brown turtleneck toward him. "Brown hides stains best. And hi."

He shook his head. "Bleach, my friend. There won't be any problem bleach can't handle." His gaze pierced hers. "You look pretty," he said.

"No I don't. I look like an overgrown chocolate bar."

"There is never anything wrong with chocolate," he said.

She hated when he was right. Dina bit her lip and looked out the window. He apparently was good at laundry. If she were interested in him as a potential boyfriend, it would be a huge plus.

"Dina!" Tracy said as she opened the door, looking like a prisoner about to be sprung from jail. "You brought reinforcements."

Reinforcements? How much trouble could one miniature person be? "I hope you don't mind."

"Not at all," she said, pulling her inside and kissing Adam's cheek. "Thank you both for this. Here's where we'll be." She handed Dina a piece of paper with the name and address of three stores and a restaurant. "And here's her schedule."

This list was longer. So long, in fact, Dina's eyes widened as she turned the eight-and-a-half-by-eleven-paper over.

"Mackenzie is sleeping, but I'll show you where everything is."

Silently, they got a tour of the apartment and after another ten minutes, Tracy and Joe left. Dina looked at Adam, who smiled.

Flustered, she looked at the list. "It says feed her at one-thirty." She turned toward the baby's room.

"Wait." Adam grabbed her arm. "She's sleeping."

"But the instructions say to feed her now."

"Haven't you ever heard the advice not to wake a sleeping baby?"

"Yes, but I know Tracy. And she wouldn't give us instructions if she didn't want us to follow them."

Adam leaned against the kitchen counter and folded his arms across his chest. "Do you always follow the rules?"

Having shucked his jacket, all that stood between her and his skin—aside from a few feet of air, of course—was a white cotton long-sleeved polo. His stance emphasized his chest and arm muscles and her throat went dry. She shook her head to clear her mind.

"You don't?" he asked. "Somehow I didn't picture you as a rule breaker."

He spoke. What had he said? Because all she'd focused on were his muscles. "Wait, what?"

"Earth to Dina. I asked if you always follow the rules."

"Oh, um, yeah, usually."

"Why did you shake your head no?"

Crap. "I don't know."

He took a step toward her, put his arm around her shoulder, and ushered her into the living room. "Okay, it's obvious the baby's overwhelming you a little. Let's sit and wait. We can always wake her if we need to, but it's damn hard to unwake her."

She let him pull her toward the sofa and she sank into it, running her hand absently over the cloth upholstery. "Maybe I should call Tracy and ask," Dina said.

"And make her think we have no idea what we're doing?"

Something in his face made her think he might not be joking. "Don't you know what you're doing?"

"Not a clue," he said. "But how hard can this be?"

"Wait a minute," she said, rising, and putting her hands on her hips. "I thought you said you were a baby expert!"

"I might have exaggerated a little."

The baby's cries prevented her response, which was probably good for Adam.

He'd lied to her.

She rushed into the lavender-painted nursery and reached for Mackenzie, whose face was scrunched like a withered apple.

"Shh, it's okay," she crooned as she pulled her against her chest.

"What can I do?" Adam asked, standing in the doorway.

He could stop making things up, for one.

She nodded toward the supplies. "Can you get out a fresh diaper and wipes?"

Adam rushed to get what she'd asked for and hovered near the table, holding the items in the air like they'd fly away if he let go—or bite him.

"Wait," he said. "Are you sure we should change her? It doesn't say to do it on the list."

She tried not to laugh at the sudden role reversal. "Well, I'm pretty sure if they were able to predict exactly when she'd need a diaper change, she'd be potty trained already, so for this one thing, I'm not worried about the list."

He looked properly chastised, and she changed her mind about his intentions. Maybe he didn't lie *per se*. Maybe he'd exaggerated. A lot. The question was why, which she'd examine after she changed Mackenzie's diaper.

Dina figured out the snaps on the onesie, cleaned her up, and put on a fresh diaper. And still she cried.

"Here, can you hold her? The list said to give her a bottle."

Adam's mouth opened and shut. "How about I make the bottle and you hold her?"

"It's frozen breast milk."

"Come here, Mackenzie. Let Uncle Adam hold you."

With a grin, Dina went in search of the milk. Three

minutes later, she approached the nursery and stopped in the doorway. There was singing and cooing and nose-to-nose touching and all of it came from Adam. She double and triple checked to make sure there wasn't some TV or radio playing she didn't notice before.

There wasn't.

His lips moved and sound emerged. And while Mackenzie was still fussy, she wasn't screaming her head off.

Adam calmed her.

Maybe he *was* an expert. Or if not an expert, a natural.

You know what he also was? Bone-meltingly sexy. Whoever said men with babies were sexy knew of what they spoke.

"You going to give me the bottle?" Adam asked in a singsong voice.

She jolted out of her reverie and handed him the bottle, watching as Mackenzie lunged for it and gulped it down. Adam couldn't have looked more pleased if he was able to nurse her himself.

When the bottle was empty, Dina reached for her. "Here, I'll burp her."

"No, let me." He tilted the baby onto his shoulder.

"Wait!"

Too late. Mackenzie spit up all over his shirt. Dina bit the insides of her cheeks.

"Maybe you should take her after all," he said.

She grabbed the diaper cloth she'd tried to hand Adam before the spit-up incident, flung it over her shoulder and took Mackenzie. "Do you want help cleaning up?"

"No, I got it. And hey, at least I wore a white shirt." He winked at her and her stomach fluttered.

Maybe she was hungry.

She patted and rubbed Mackenzie's back until she burped, then looked at the instructions Tracy left. There was a half an hour before she was supposed to check her diaper. Now what?

"Hey, I found this, think she'll use it?" Adam walked in carrying a bouncy thing.

Well, it probably had a name, but Dina had no idea what it was called. There was a seat for the baby and things to play with. And it bounced. Yeah, it would do.

"We can try."

She placed Mackenzie in the seat and Adam spun some of the toys. Mackenzie giggled and bounced as she kicked her legs. Excellent. Problem solved.

They sat on the floor watching her. Adam made funny faces, which entertained Mackenzie.

"You're quiet," he said to Dina as he played with Mackenzie's toy.

"Did you know a baby can't taste salt until they're about four months old? It's thought the delay is related to—"

He grabbed her hand and rubbed his thumb across her palm, and she forgot the rest of her sentence.

"What's wrong, Dina?"

She swallowed. "Wrong?"

"You're nervous."

"Why do you say I'm nervous?"

"Because you're quoting random facts. You only do it when you're nervous."

He was not supposed to know. "I don't do it when I'm nervous."

Adam arched one eyebrow, making Mackenzie giggle again. "Even she agrees with me."

"No, she's just laughing at your face."

"My…you…!" He tried to frown but couldn't pull it off, and Dina elbowed him gently in the ribs. Joking around, she could handle. Adam with a baby was more difficult to deal with.

"Seriously, why are you nervous?" he asked. He focused on her, sending emerald-colored lasers direct to her heart, which thumped.

"I'm not sure what to do with her," she said. Or you.

"She's easy."

Did she imagine a stressor on "she?" "She's a baby who doesn't talk," she said.

"With a mother who provides instructions which rival IKEA's."

True.

He pulled the instruction list toward him while rattling one of the toys on the bouncy thing. It really needed a name.

"We change her diaper in twenty minutes. Afterward, we have time until she needs to eat again. Want to go for a walk?"

"Does it say we should?"

He smiled. "It doesn't say we shouldn't. And Tracy left us the stroller all set up near the door. In fact, we could probably change her now and leave early."

"No! She said a half hour after eating. We should wait."

"Boy, you really are a rule follower."

"Well, neither of us seems to know anything about babies," said Dina. "We probably shouldn't deviate from the schedule too much."

He squeezed her hand, and she tried to join in playing with Mackenzie. When her phone alarm buzzed, she took the baby and went to change her diaper.

"Want help?" Adam asked.

"No, I think I've got this."

She laid her on the changing table. "We can do this, right?" she whispered.

Opening the diaper, she cringed. Mackenzie was filthy, and it was everywhere. She thought about calling Adam for reinforcements, but doubted he'd be much help. Screwing up her face, which caused the baby to giggle again, and breathing through her mouth, she cleaned her as best she could before diapering and redressing her.

"Oh, it was nasty," she said as she returned to Adam. "You should be very glad you didn't do this one."

She handed Mackenzie over to Adam who took her and pointed at Dina's shirt. "Um…"

"What?"

Looking down, she frowned, pulled her shirt to her nose, and sniffed. "Oh no!" she said as her face heated.

Adam raised an eyebrow. "Guess it's a good thing you wore brown."

"I have to go clean this."

Dina ran into the bathroom, thankful there was a door she could shut. It was a good thing she and Adam were only friends, because she'd be mortified if this happened otherwise. And the flush on her cheeks? Must be from the heat. It was going to be scorching hot summer—even if it was only March.

"All fixed?" Adam asked as she emerged from the bathroom.

Nodding, she focused on Mackenzie seated in the stroller. "Don't you think she needs a jacket?" Her cheeks might still burn, but she didn't think it was contagious.

Adam dropped his chin to his chest. "Oh, yeah."

Together, they unstrapped her, zipped her into her fuchsia jacket, and strapped her into the stroller.

"Hat?" Adam asked.

"Probably." She looked around and found one on the half wall next to the front door. "Okay, I think we're set."

"Yeah, except for *our* jackets."

Right.

As Mackenzie started to fuss, they hurried into their jackets and finally maneuvered the stroller outside, locked the door and walked along the sidewalk. They settled into a rhythm, the fussing stopped, and Dina breathed a sigh of relief.

"Made it," she said.

"Did you doubt it?"

She glanced at Adam askance. "Honestly? Yes."

"Ye of little faith." He elbowed her gently in the ribs, and she huffed.

Dina pushed the stroller, and Adam rested his hand on the bar next to hers. Their silence was companionable and for the first time in at least an hour, Dina took in a deep breath.

"Feel better?" he asked.

"I don't know what you're talking about."

He elbowed her again without removing his hand from the stroller. They approached an older woman walking toward them who glanced from the baby to them.

"Your daughter is adorable," the woman said as she approached.

She should protest. Adam was her friend. They weren't a couple, much less the parents of a baby. She really should say something. But instead, she nodded to the woman and continued walking.

****

He would have bet money Dina would have corrected the woman. Dina was the one hung up on their being friends.

Friends.

The more he thought of the word, the more ludicrous it became.

A friend didn't look at a woman with lust in his eyes. A friend didn't ache to touch the other's skin. A friend didn't hunger for the sound of the other's voice.

He had no idea how she felt, because she'd stuck him squarely in the "friend zone," a foreign land with its own language, manners, and rules. He should object to it—he'd heard enough scorn about it from other guys. But there was something refreshing about getting to know a woman, really know her, without having to deal with the sexual side of things. Still, he did his best to break out of it. Inch by infuriatingly sexy inch. Because the more he got to know her, the more connected he felt.

The old woman drew attention to their un-friend-like status. He'd expected Dina to recoil in horror before babbling on about some obscure fact about friends, babies, or friends with babies.

Instead, she'd smiled.

His heart melted.

He wanted to go kiss the old woman, except it probably wouldn't win him any points with Dina. It might draw attention to the idea they looked like a family, rather than friends. She didn't need any help there. He forced his feet to continue on the cold, hard pavement.

And walked right into a fire hydrant.

"Ow!" He hopped on one foot, gripping his knee with the other, muttering curses under his breath.

"Are you all right?" Dina placed a hand on his arm. Though he couldn't actually feel her skin through his coat, he imagined he could. He started to speak, cleared his throat, and tried again.

"Yeah, I'm fine." He limped along next to her.

"Maybe we should go back."

"No, let's keep going."

She looked at him like she didn't believe him. "They're probably going to be home soon."

Without waiting for his response, she swung the stroller around and walked in the opposite direction. At home, by the time they'd taken off their coats, unwrapped Mackenzie from the layers of clothes they'd bundled her in, and stored the stroller, Tracy and Joe walked in.

"Did you guys survive?" Tracy asked as she unwound her scarf and put her bags down.

Dina walked toward her, carrying Mackenzie, while Adam limped behind. Tracy's gaze flickered from one to the other. Her mouth twitched. She turned to her husband. As one, they laughed.

"Oh my, you two look like you've been through the ringer."

Catching up, Adam put his arm around Dina. She stiffened. He stroked her shoulder with his thumb. "Nah, we're good. A little spit up, a little poop, a little bruise. No big deal."

She didn't relax into his embrace, as he hoped, but she didn't move away either. "He's right. It was fun."

Later, after they'd left, Adam turned to her in the car. "Want to go out tonight?"

She looked at her shirt. "I'm pretty sure I smell."

Her brown shirt was stained. Her hair was wild. Her lip was caught between her teeth. She'd never looked more beautiful.

He sniffed the air. "I don't smell anything." He turned and sniffed his shoulder. "Well, maybe some spit up."

Her smile made her eyes sparkle. Had he never noticed it?

"If you don't mind, I think I'll pass tonight. I'm exhausted. Another time?" She grabbed her coat and opened the door as he pulled in front of her apartment. "But thanks for the offer. And for today. You were a huge help."

He nodded, wondering what she'd do if he kissed her. Before he could test it out, she climbed out of the car. As he watched her go into her building, he wondered how much longer it would take to persuade her to the idea of a relationship with him.

Because he wasn't sure he could wait.

Chapter Thirteen

Waiting was hard. Dina picked up her phone and put it on the table next to her bed three times, before grabbing a book and marching into the living room to read. But her mind wouldn't focus on the words. It focused on sharp green eyes, tawny hair, and warm skin with a trace of cloves.

She couldn't stop thinking of Adam, which annoyed her, since she shouldn't be thinking of him at all. They were only friends, at her insistence. And if she did think of him—and friends thought about each other—she most certainly wasn't supposed to think about puddles of goo. Because it was how he made her insides feel, in a delicious, warm, tingly kind of way.

And it couldn't happen.

So she left her phone—her lifeline enabling her to hear his voice once more—where it lay in her bedroom and once again tried to focus on the cozy mystery she read. She couldn't remember the plot. She could barely remember the mystery. She did know there was a cat, because the description of it in the book reminded her of Adam's soft cashmere sweater, the one he'd worn the last time they'd eaten together.

Ugh!

It was only a day since they'd last spoken. She'd come to depend on his daily phone conversation. Usually, he called around seven thirty. Seven forty-five if he was busy. But it was eight thirty and he hadn't called her yet.

Would he?

Maybe she should ring him. Friends called each other. She and Tracy were friends and they did so all the time.

Except Adam was a guy. Would he look at her phone call as an admission of her attraction to him? Because she was hard put to deny her attraction to him any longer, even if she didn't want to announce it.

They had an arrangement and acting on her attraction would complicate things and make her seem pathetic.

She flung her book across the room, and then raced to get it. Picking it off the floor, she brushed it off and examined it to make sure it wasn't damaged. Librarians didn't throw books. It was against their code of conduct. The only thing worse than throwing a book would be to dog-ear the pages. She was pretty sure they'd revoke her masters in library science.

Placing the cozy mystery on the end table, she walked into her bedroom and picked up her phone. This was crazy. She'd call him. She could always plead a wrong number.

She dialed his number and held her breath while she waited for him to pick up.

"Heyyyy, it's Adam! Leave a message!"

Dina exhaled and hung up before the beep sounded, which would have required her to leave a message. Only she didn't have one. Because anything she said would make her sound desperate and clingy.

Later that night, as she was about to go to sleep, her phone rang.

"Hey, Dinaaaa…"

Adam's voice slurred. He was drunk.

"Adam?"

"I called you before," he said. "No, wait, you called me. Right?"

"Right. But it wasn't important. We can talk tomorrow." A conversation with him when he was drunk wasn't fun.

"No, should…should talk now."

There was silence and Dina waited for him to continue. When he didn't, she sighed. "Adam, let's talk tomorrow."

"You have a pretty voice, d'you know?"

She sighed. "Thank you." Why was he drunk? "Are you having a party?"

"Hah! No, I'm not having a party. A party would be fun. I'm not supposed to have any fun."

This was new. "Why not?"

"Nev…mind."

Dina paused. If you got past the fact he was drunk and you ignored the slurred, sloppy speech, there was something off in his tone of voice. He tried to be a happy drunk and failed. Why did he call her when he was drunk? Maybe something was wrong.

"Can I come over?" she asked.

"Why do you wanna come here?"

The Adam she knew wouldn't have asked why. There was definitely something wrong. "I want to see you."

"You want to party? The lib…libar…book lady wants to party?"

She'd laugh if he were sober. "Can I come over now?"

"Shhhurrrre."

Throwing on jeans and a long-sleeved pink T-shirt, she grabbed her keys, black leather purse, and pea coat and ran out the door. The streets of Morristown were quiet at this time of night—it was after eleven—and she made it to the lobby of Adam's high-rise apartment in less than ten minutes. The guy behind the security desk in the marble and mirrored lobby called up to his apartment and nodded to her.

She rode up the elevator, jiggled her car keys in her hand, and tapped her sneaker-clad toe on the gold carpet as the elevator crept to Adam's floor. She glanced around briefly at the familiar hallway as she got her bearings—black carpet with silver flecks plush enough to deaden her footsteps; gray walls with white trim; and geometrical-shaped mirrors interspersed along the hallway—as she wondered whether or not this was a good idea.

She knocked on the door and it swung open as if he'd waited for her.

"Dinaaaaa!" He reached for her and stumbled, and she half hugged, half caught him, pushed him into his apartment and shut the door behind her.

He smelled like a distillery and his hair was spiked as if he'd run his hands through it numerous times—the way she'd fantasized doing herself.

"Adam, what's going on?"

"We're having a party!"

She frowned. "No, we're not."

"Don't bring it down, Dina. You said you wanted to party." He grabbed her hand and stumble-danced down the hall. He gripped her against him and she could feel his heartbeat against her chest. They banged into the wall and she winced.

"Oh, shit, Dina. Are you okay?" His gaze grew surprisingly clear and his eyes reflected his worry for her for a moment before glazing over again.

"Yeah, I'm okay. Maybe we should sit down, though."

He took her hand and led her into the living room. Once again, the heat from his hand warmed her entire body. She tried not to focus on it.

He sprawled onto a black leather sofa and pulled her beside him. Now the sides of their bodies touched, from their shoulders to their hips and thighs. It was worse.

"Better?" he asked. He didn't let go of her hand, and he played with it, running his fingers along her palm and wrist driving her crazy. Mr. Flashypants was also the King of Distraction.

"Tough day?" she asked.

"Don't wanna talk about it." He frowned, his gaze focused on her hand. "Your skin is so soft."

His body was close enough to her, she could almost hear his heartbeat. Or was it her own pulse racing in her ears? "Thank you."

"Why do you put up with me?"

"What do you mean?"

"I'm going to chase you away."

"I doubt it. Did you have dinner with friends tonight?" She needed to focus and figure out a way to get to what bothered him. The direct approach wasn't working.

"Tried to."

"What do you mean?"

"My dad showed up at the restaurant and made a

scene." She raised her eyebrows.

He lifted his whiskey glass to his lips, but it was empty, and he started to rise. She pulled at his waistband and he fell onto the couch. "Oh, is this what you want?" He leaned toward her, his breath a mixture of whiskey and him. She pushed against his chest until he once again sat next to her.

"First, tell me why your dad made a scene."

He glared at her but didn't move.

His eyebrows were caramel-colored, a shade deeper than his hair, and she pressed her hands together to keep from running her finger along his brow.

"He said I needed to learn my lesson."

"What lesson?"

He lurched off the sofa and over to the sideboard, where he sloshed whiskey into his glass. "Want one?"

Someone needed to stay sober.

Apparently, he'd overruled her, because he brought the glass over and handed it to her. "Drink up."

She took a sip and the amber liquid burned her throat. Coughing, she held the glass out to Adam, who banged it on the marble coffee table, relieving her of having to drink any more of it.

"What lesson, Adam?"

He focused his troubled green eyes on her, and she wanted to wrap her arms around him and promise everything would be all right. He rose, banged his leg on the edge of the table, and paced the room. The only way he'd feel better is if he got out whatever tormented him. Instead, his jaw clenched, his body was rigid, and he wouldn't look at her. Each time their gazes met, his took off in a different direction.

But he continued to return to her and it was only a

matter of time before he had no choice but to stop and talk. She waited.

After a few more circuits around the beige area rug, he sank onto the couch next to her, his forearm covering his eyes.

"What lesson?" she asked again.

"Honoring the family name." His voice was low and a little fuzzy, but understandable.

"Why would he think you weren't?" What kind of father would say it in public?

"Screwed up three cases. No one wants ta work wi me. Giving firm a bad name. Time for me ta get out on my own."

"Did you talk to him? Find out what you can do to fix things?"

"Does'n matter. Can't change his mind."

"You did say you wanted to get a job in Manhattan."

"Ha!" It sounded more like a bark, really, and he jumped up, again. "Like I'll get any sort of accep...acceptable ref'rence now."

"I'm sorry. What can I do?"

He squinted. Looming over her as he was, she felt at a distinct disadvantage, so she rose. Still, she needed to tilt her head back to meet his gaze—although staring at the column of his throat wasn't such a bad thing, especially where it disappeared into the collar of his shirt.

She swallowed. This was ridiculous. She was here, in Adam's apartment, to make him feel better, not to come up with more reasons to fantasize about him. Dina met his gaze.

His pupils widened. This close to him she could

see the striations of brown and green in his irises and the individual lashes surrounding them. His eye muscle jumped around his cheekbone as he clenched and unclenched his jaw. She swallowed again.

"Who are you?" he whispered.

"You know who I am." She wanted to cup his face and stroke his cheek.

As if he read her mind, he lifted his hand, but instead of stroking her cheek, he ran his fingers through her hair, squeezed the curls and released them. His hands weren't gentle, but each tug of her hair sent ripples through her body. He slid his fingers over her scalp and around the nape of her neck, and she stifled a moan. Shivers ran along her spine and she inhaled, leaning toward him. Her breasts brushed against his chest. She jerked as they tingled on contact.

"Yurre the only one who's ever believed in me, the only one who hasn't left," he whispered. "Why?"

"Because I care," she whispered.

He lowered his head. His lips approached hers, their breath mingled, and it would take barely any movement at all for them to meet.

He was going to kiss her. Or maybe she was going to kiss him. She couldn't tell at this point. Despite her best efforts to prevent it, despite all her reasons it shouldn't, it was happening.

He was drunk, but she didn't care.

When their lips finally met, she melted, like butter left outside on a ninety-five degree day. His mouth was firm and decisive. It brushed hers, back and forth and she opened for him. When she did, he swiped his tongue along her lips and delved deeper into her mouth. She did the same, tasting the whiskey. They explored each other's mouths together, each of them thrusting and receding in equal measure. She remembered learning in biology the tongue was the only muscle in the human body to work without the support of the skeleton, but she was loathe to mention the fact now—if she did, Adam might stop and it was too delicious to stop. He brushed his hands across her back and she imagined what it would feel like to have his hands on her bare skin.

She rested her hands on his shoulders. His sleek muscles flexed beneath her palms, before she let them drift along his neck to cup his jaw, like she'd wanted to before. Her fingers played with his earlobes and threaded through his hair, and he groaned against her mouth.

"Dina."

He grabbed her elbows, stood, and backed her against the wall without breaking contact with her mouth, and she was grateful for the support. Her knees turned to jelly and without the wall and his hands, she would have dissolved onto the floor.

If he never got another lawyer job, he could hire out as a professional kisser. Or maybe not, since he'd have to kiss other women and she wanted him all to herself. She pressed her body against him, her softness melting into his hardness as he grabbed her hips.

She shifted, and his breath caught. He pulled away from her mouth and trailed kisses along her jaw and neck, sucked her skin, no doubt leaving marks. Letting her head fall back, she gave him access and he continued kissing his way south to her collarbone. She whimpered and ran her hands up and down his ribcage, feeling the play of his muscles beneath his shirt. She hooked her fingers in his belt loops, locked him to her, and rotated her hips against him.

He hissed and pulled the hem of her shirt, loosening it enough to slide his palms beneath it. Finally, he touched her bare skin, leaving a trail of heat in their wake. She growled and took his lips between her teeth, nipping them and making him chuckle.

"You're as wild as your hair," he said, plunging his tongue once again into her mouth.

Taking a cue from him, she slid her hands beneath his shirt. His skin was warm, and she ran her fingers over the ridges of his abs. When she reached his chest, she played with the hair there, and from the reaction of his tongue, he liked it.

"I want you." His whispered words formed against her mouth.

Her whole body stilled. He was drunk. Would continuing this take advantage of their friendship?

Adam pulled away from her with great care, one body part at a time, as if he couldn't bear any part of him to be separated from her. Desire and need matched her own.

With a nod, she pulled off her shirt.

He took a step back, swayed and reached for her. His hands landed on her breasts and his thumbs caressed her nipples through her bra. She arched as her nipples tightened, and he offered a wolf-like grin.

"You like this."

Sensations overwhelmed her, and she couldn't speak. She nodded and reached for his shirt. Her fingers fumbled with the buttons until he ripped it open, popping the rest of them. Out of the corner of her eye, they landed on the fluffy carpet, but she couldn't avert her gaze from his muscular chest.

Now she could see what her fingers touched, and she wanted more. Leaning forward, she licked his chest and he gasped.

"Woman, you're killing me." He groaned, and his hands shook on her shoulders.

With a low chuckle, she continued, trailing her tongue and lips across his chest, tasting salt and sweat and man.

Without warning, he pulled away from her, bent and with one arm around her back and the other beneath her knees, lifted her as though she weighed nothing.

Dina knew it not to be true.

"What are you doing?" Despite her state of undress, his body warmed her.

"Having my way with you," he said, stalking to the sofa and lowering her onto it. He followed. She leaned against the sofa and he braced his knees on either side of her hips and stared. His gaze took in every inch of her, and she realized he was the hero in her very own romance.

"You're beautiful," he said and reached out to undo her bra clasp. When her breasts came free he filled his hands with them. If his thumbs aroused her through her bra before, they almost sent her over the edge now.

She bucked, and he tightened his thighs around her, following her body's movements as if he rode her. Her hands rose restlessly, and she reached for him. She shifted beneath him, and he hardened. Something fluttered low in her stomach.

"I need you now." His voice was hoarse, and he leaned away from her, undoing his belt and yanking at his pants.

Oh my God, she was going to see him naked.

Her heart thudded in her chest. She thought about stopping him, but the fluttering inside her increased and all thoughts of stopping or slowing down disappeared. She wanted him, needed him, too. He climbed off her and watched as she wriggled her hips to remove her pants. His nostrils flared at her movements and within moments, they were naked.

Together.

He pulled open a condom packet from the pocket of his jeans and laid her beneath him. She stared into eyes so green they reminded her of emeralds. Skin against skin, all kinds of tingling sensations pulsed through her, zeroing in low in her belly as he rolled the condom on. He kissed her, open-mouthed and his tongue gave her a preview of what they would do. She rotated her hips and he trailed his hand from her cheek, along her neck, around her breasts to where her body pulsed. His fingers teased her folds, and her breath came in short gasps. He rose and hovered over her, the cool air between them frustrating her. She needed him in her. Now.

As if hearing her silent demand, he lowered himself and entered her, pausing barely a moment for her to adjust before rhythmically moving inside of her. She stretched, trying to accommodate him, wanting to feel the pressure build once again. When he brushed his fingers against her, she gasped.

She ran her hands along his back, reveling in the feel of him as their hips rocked together. His breathing grew heavier and her need built. He withdrew partially before he plunged inside of her once again, and the pressure built within her, exploded into shards of light behind her eyelids. His climax followed close behind hers, his shout echoed off the walls, before he collapsed against her.

Their hearts beat together as slowly their breathing calmed and their sweat cooled. He made lazy circles on her arms as his head rested on her chest. She was blissfully spent with no desire to move.

If she did, they'd have to talk about what they'd done and why. They'd have to discuss where to go from here.

Chapter Fourteen

The first thing he noticed was the pounding behind his eyes. The second thing he noticed was the smell—a mix of alcohol and sex.

Dina.

Images of their time together flooded his brain, but fuzzy and out of focus, more like impressions really. The springiness of her hair, the scent of her skin, some stumbling around.

The utter bliss of making love.

He unstuck his cheek from the leather sofa. Sex was never about love before. But with Dina? It was a possibility. He squinted in the harsh sunlight bathing his living room. He was alone. Forcing down the panic this knowledge always caused him, he sat up, careful not to disturb the rocks in his head.

"Dina?" There was no answer.

His mind skittered to yesterday and the debacle with his father. He shut his eyes tight, as if it would block the memory from returning. He'd much prefer to think about Dina. But unfortunately, those earlier memories were clear and prolific.

His father, his own father, fired him.

Even though Ashley lied.

And he'd done it in public.

Pain sliced through him once again. He looked for a distraction. Where was Dina?

Looking around his apartment, he didn't find a note or any sign she'd been there. Well, maybe there was. The empty bottles stood lined up on the counter—he didn't think he had the presence of mind to line them up—and his clothes were folded on the recliner.

His clothes.

He looked down. Yup, he was naked. He was definitely hung over if he didn't notice he was naked.

Shit. He'd had drunk sex with Dina. The one person he cared about and who cared about him. What did he do? What did he say? Did he tell her about being fired? Did he make sure she enjoyed herself? Come to think of it, how did she get here? And now where was she?

He started to pat his leg to feel for his phone and would have laughed at the stupidity, but too many stupid things in his life weren't funny. Riffling through his stacked clothes, his fingers bumped the hard rectangle of his phone, and he pulled it out of his pocket. Maybe she'd texted him. He turned it on.

She didn't.

They'd had drunk sex. She deserved more than a text. He dialed her number. When her voicemail connected, his stomach dropped.

"Hey, Dina, it's Adam. Give me a call."

He probably should have said more. But what was he supposed to say when he didn't know exactly what he'd said or done? This conversation shouldn't happen on a voicemail, any more than via text.

****

Sitting in the coffee shop, muted noises of other patrons swirling around her, Dina watched Adam's name appear on her phone screen and let it go to voice mail. This was one awkward phone conversation she was not ready to have. As her voice mail dinged, indicating he'd left a message, Tracy walked to her table cradling her coffee cup like it was a pot of gold.

"Meeting for coffee this morning was a fabulous idea." She leaned over and kissed Dina's cheek. "Mackenzie didn't sleep all night, and I needed to get away from the house."

"Oh, I'm sorry." Dina stirred her tea, the delicate herbal scent drifting toward her nose. She could only imagine how difficult it was to be up all night with a baby and take care of the same baby all day. Lucky for Tracy, her husband was a huge help. Someday, Dina hoped to be as lucky. A vision of Adam rising over her flashed in her brain, and she squeezed her hands into fists.

"Comes with the territory. Now, tell me what's going on. You have a glow."

Dina reared back. "A glow? What kind of glow?"

Tracy leaned forward. "You slept with him, didn't you?"

"Wha…what are you talking about?" Sweat broke out on Dina's upper lip. Could she blame it on the hot tea?

The jig was up, and Dina let her head fall into her hands. "I'm in trouble," she said.

"Why? I'm surprised you waited this long."

"Tracy! We've only known each other a few weeks, and he keeps me at arm's length. Besides which, I don't sleep around."

"I hope there was more than sleeping going on," her friend said with a laugh.

Dina glared at her.

"Was it good?"

Dina bit her lip. "Yes and no."

"Details."

Bossy lady. "It was Adam, he doesn't do anything halfway." She smiled. "But he was drunk. It wasn't as romantic as…"

"You'd fantasized it would be?"

She expected flames to burst forth from her cheeks. In fact, she was surprised the coffee shop's sprinkler system didn't kick on to be safe. "It doesn't matter anyway, because it shouldn't happen again."

"Why not? And wait a minute, you can't skip over the good stuff. I want details."

"Seriously?"

"Absolutely. I'm an old married lady with a baby. The last time I had sex just for the hell of it, was I don't know when. I need to live vicariously through my exciting single friends."

"You should go make some," Dina said.

Tracy threw her napkin at her. "Don't make me beg."

With a sigh, Dina told her about the phone call, going over to Adam's apartment, trying to get him to talk, and how they ended up having sex.

"And you left?"

"No, I fell asleep, as did he. Then I woke up. And then I left."

"Why?"

"Because it will be awkward."

"I don't get it," Tracy said. "Lots of people have drunk sex. Why is this such a big deal?"

Dina swirled her tea in her cup. "Because we are supposed to be friends who made an arrangement. I help him seem more respectable for his father, and he accompanies me to the reunion."

"Okay. And you had sex. Why does sex change anything?"

"Because friends don't have sex!"

"Uh, Dina? Yes, they do."

"I know, but we weren't supposed to."

"Why not?"

"Because I didn't want to seem pathetic. I really like him, but I'm not his type, and he's not mine. There are still things he hides from me, I can tell. And he's only taking me to the reunion because I'm helping him with his dad. Except his dad is mad at him, and it's not really working. Which means he doesn't need me anymore."

"Anyone looking at the two of you knows he's not staying with you because of some arrangement you think you have."

"An arrangement I *know* we have."

Tracy gave her a look, and Dina squirmed.

"And leave without talking to him? You have no idea what he thinks or feels. You're never going to get those answers you want if you avoid him. Not to mention," Tracy leaned forward, "you missed out on all the good post-coital talk!"

"He left me a voicemail."

Tracy rolled her eyes. "What did it say?"

"I don't know. I didn't listen to it."

"Give me your phone."

"What? No!"

She held her hand out, and Dina gripped her phone in her lap. There was no way she would let her listen to the voicemail.

"Listen to it yourself."

Tracy grew up with three brothers. She was married to a guy who worshipped her. She was a kickass mom. Dina had no doubt she'd steal her phone and listen to the voicemail on her own. Flaring her nostrils, Dina pressed play and held the phone to her ear. A moment later, she put the phone in her purse.

"What did he say?"

"Just to call him."

"So do it."

"I will."

"Now. You're not going to feel better, or get the answers you need, if you push this off. And I think you're reading this all wrong anyway."

"Oh really?" Dina squeezed her hands together. Was Tracy a mind reader now? She did have the cutest baby ever. Perhaps whatever allowed her to produce gorgeous babies enabled her to read minds too. Pretty nifty trick, even if deep down she didn't believe it.

Picking up the phone, she redialed Adam. If she were lucky, he wouldn't answer.

She wasn't.

"Dina! Where'd you…never mind. Hi."

"Hi."

Tracy mouthed "speaker," but Dina shook her head.

"Where are you right now?"

"With Tracy."

"Can you come over when you're finished?"

"Um, I have errands and…"

"Please? You can do your errands after. I need to talk to you."

"Can't you talk to me now?"

"No, this needs to be said face to face."

There it was. He would tell her he didn't need her anymore. Her stomach dropped. It shouldn't hurt, but it did. And he expected her to come over to hear it?

She swallowed the lump in her throat. Tracy squeezed her hand. She'd forgotten she was there. Hanging up the phone, she wiped her eyes. "I don't want to go over. He can't force me, right?"

"Honey, I think you're jumping to conclusions here. How did he sound?"

"Like Adam. Normal."

"Go over and talk to him."

****

Adam paced his apartment, his sneakers squeaking on the wood floors before being muffled on the carpet. He wiped sweaty palms on his jeans. Something in her voice convinced him Dina didn't want to come over.

What was it about him to make women leave? His inner voice tried to remind him he was the one who usually insisted on casual relationships, and his mom left because of his dad, not because of him. But there was a part of him unable to believe his inner voice completely. Because even his dad was emotionally distant.

Why did Dina leave? Sex with him wasn't bad, was it? He'd never heard any complaints before… And though he didn't remember much, he was pretty sure he didn't tell her he lost his job. He stopped himself. Dina wasn't like the others. First they'd talk. Then he'd find out what the problem was. Afterwards, he'd fix it.

The buzzer made him jump. He barked "send her up" into the intercom. Three minutes later, the elevator chimed, and he opened his door.

This was it.

His heart sped up as heat rushed through him.

Dina. She possessed an inner glow. It made her cheeks rosy and her intelligent eyes soft. She looked at him like he mattered. She was beautiful, despite the misery giving her eyes a silvery amethyst tint. Her curly hair framed her face, her pale skin was almost translucent, but her shoulders hunched.

He wanted to take her in his arms and never let her go. He wanted to get on his knees and ask for forgiveness. He wanted to beg her never to leave. He wanted to tell her he might love her.

His body went cold. Love her? He rolled the word in his brain, and his body temperature returned to normal. The word didn't scare him as much as he expected it to.

But she looked at him with dread in her eyes, like she was afraid of him.

"Did I hurt you?" His voice sounded like a bullfrog. He cleared it. "Dina?" He motioned her inside.

Confusion crossed her features as she walked in. "Hurt me? When?"

"Last night." His body froze in place. If he'd hurt her, he'd never forgive himself.

"No, you didn't."

Gripping the doorjamb to prevent himself from falling to the ground as his knees buckled, he inhaled. *Thank God.*

She didn't want to be here. She would leave. He'd never get to tell her.

Backing up, he walked into the kitchen. He wanted to lock the front door, but it would be creepy. "Can I get you anything to drink?"

She blinked. "Water would be good."

Someone who wanted water wasn't walking away. Yet. Still, he kept watch over her as he grabbed a glass from the cherry cabinet and the filtered water from the Sub-Zero refrigerator. Handing it to her, their fingers touched. A charge ran up his arm, straight to his heart. He wanted to be the one to get her water, food, whatever she needed, always. He watched her take a sip. He wished he were the glass, because her hands wrapped around it as if she would never let it go. Pointing to the living room, he followed her. He watched her pause at the sofa before she sat in the recliner.

He swallowed. "About last night…"

"It's fine. I know everything is different now and it's okay."

"Excuse me?"

"Our arrangement. It's irrelevant now."

He must have drunk way more than he thought.

Running a hand over his hair, he rose and paced the room. "Okay, let's back up. Last night, I was drunk, you came over, we had sex. With me so far?"

She nodded without making eye contact.

"What arrangement are you talking about?"

"The one where I help you with your reputation and you go with me to my reunion."

"Yeah, it's the one I thought you meant. Only I have no idea what you're actually saying. What does one thing have to do with another?"

"Because I'm doing a terrible job improving your reputation, and your clodpate of a father isn't changing his mind." She covered her mouth. "Sorry, I shouldn't have said anything about him."

"Do I want to know what a 'clodpate' is?"

Her face heated. "It's an old-fashioned term for idiot. I don't know why it popped out."

Adam couldn't help the grin spreading across his face. Leave it to Dina to pick such a word. He loved this quirk of hers. Hell, if he was right, he loved everything about her. "It's quite all right. What I don't understand is why you think it has anything to do with our having sex."

"Because you don't need me to help your reputation. We have no reason to keep seeing each other."

Her face was the most expressive one he'd ever seen. Every emotion showed in her lovely violet eyes. What shade would they turn if he told her he loved her?

"Why do you think we had sex last night?" he asked.

"Because you were drunk. Which surprised me, because I didn't think alcohol enabled a person to have sex. But you…" She blushed. "You did quite well."

The woman who had "clodpate" on the tip of her tongue said he performed "quite well." He wasn't sure how to take it.

He reached for her hand across the space between the sofa and the recliner. Her skin was soft to the touch, her fingers thin and delicate. He held tight to make sure she didn't pull away. "We had sex because I can't get you out of my mind." *Because I love you.*

Her mouth opened.

"From the moment I met you, I haven't been able to think of another woman. Every time I'm with you, all I want to do is touch you, feel your skin against mine, taste your lips, play with your hair. Yes, I was drunk and it lowered my resolve, but we did not have sex *because* I was drunk."

She remained silent.

"Why did *you* have sex with *me*?" He swallowed, not sure if he wanted to hear the answer. For some reason, when he was with her, unexpected words tumbled from his mouth. Not vocabulary words like "clodpate," but words from his heart he kept hidden away from everyone else.

"Because you are irresistible."

Good Lord, if he didn't think he'd scare her with the fervor of his desire, he'd leap off the sofa, and take her again right there in the recliner. But the last time they'd had sex was on the sofa, and she now sat on the recliner. He needed to make sure she could sit somewhere in his apartment if he could somehow convince her to stay. Or return.

He wanted their next time to be different than their first—slower, more intentional, sober.

"We're supposed to be friends." Her voice wavered between accusation and dismay.

"We still are friends, but I've wanted us to be more than friends for a while now."

"What do we do about our arrangement?"

He rose and approached her with caution. Leaning over, he rested each hand on an armrest, effectively boxing her in with his body. He lowered his head until it was a hairsbreadth away from her face. Her lips glistened, and a blush rose from her neck across her cheek.

"Screw the arrangement."

Chapter Fifteen

The last time Adam's face was this close to hers, they had sex. From the looks of him, most notably his flared nostrils and his dilated pupils, he wanted to have sex again.

She must have smiled, because his lips widened slightly before parting. She could feel her pulse pound, hear his rapid breath and a part of her wanted to succumb to desire and let their bodies take over.

But first she needed answers. And this wasn't exactly a position conducive to discussion.

Pressing on his chest, she said, "No."

He reared away, and the electric charge in the air fizzled.

"No?"

She shook her head. "You can't kiss me again until you answer my questions."

His shoulders drooped for a moment. But when he met her gaze, it was with relief.

"I thought..." He clenched his jaw. "Well, never mind what I thought. I'll answer your questions. But first I owe you an apology."

She curled in the chair, since she had room, and waited for him to sit on the sofa. Instead, he paced.

"Why do you owe me an apology?"

"Because you deserve way better than drunk sex, and while it was amazing, it's not how I planned our first time to be." He ran his fingers through his hair, making it spiky and sexy.

"You planned our first time?" It wasn't just her.

Adam raised his head. "Planned, imagined, fantasized. And none of those fantasies included my being drunk. I haven't always acted in ways that might convince you, but Dina, you're the one I want to be with, and for more than sex, although I definitely want sex with you as well. I want to go out with you on a real date. I want to go the movies and the diner with you. Hell, I want to go to the grocery store with you, so we can buy ingredients for a romantic dinner to lead... well." He smiled. "And it didn't happen, especially last night. I'm sorry."

Her body filled with warmth. She didn't have to relegate him to "friends only." She could be herself. "Well, it's not as if you planned on your father screaming at you in public. He did scream at you, right?"

He gave her a humorless grin. "Yeah. So, what questions did you want me to answer?"

Dina fidgeted. He agreed to answer her questions. It was time to trust him and actually get answers. "So, about your dad..."

All the tension returned to his shoulders. "What else is left to say about him? He's a clodpate, as you put it, and I'm done."

"Why do I feel like there's something you're not telling me?"

Adam flexed and unflexed his fingers. "Someone lied about whether or not I gave my paralegal something to file. It didn't get filed and I lost the case. The situation took on a life of its own and hurt the firm's reputation. And it's not the first time a case I've worked on got screwed up. But no matter how much I beg him to believe I've changed and it wasn't me who screwed up," Adam swallowed in distaste, "good old 'clodpate' doesn't believe me."

"But he seemed okay at dinner." Not anyone she'd want as a father, but not someone who'd disbelieve his own son.

"He's great at putting on a show."

"Why is he set on not believing you?"

Adam sighed. "Honestly, I'm cocky, and I probably created part of the problem. I was careless in the past. But I've changed, only he doesn't see it—refuses to see it—especially now. The firm's reputation is too important to him to let someone like me screw it up. Do we have to continue talking about him?"

She wasn't finished. "What will you do about your promotion?"

Adam narrowed his gaze. "I'll figure it out. I don't really know. What I do know is I want to kiss you."

He leaned over and pressed his lips against hers, moving his mouth against hers as if to draw the kiss out of her in slow, deep pulls. This time she didn't stop him. This time, his mouth didn't taste of whiskey. This time, his lips were gentle. He ran his hands through her hair, massaging the back of her scalp. When she opened her mouth to moan at the delicious chills running through her body, he licked his way into her mouth, exploring her and getting to know her by taste.

It was glorious, and she wanted him.

He pulled away, panting.

"That was more like it," he whispered, running his thumb along her lower lip.

She wrapped her arms around his neck and reached to kiss him again, but as soon as her lips touched his, he pulled back.

"I can't believe I'm saying this, but no," he said, adding space between them. "We're doing this the right way this time. Nice and slow."

"I can kiss you slowly," she said, shocking herself at her own audacity. She must have shocked Adam too, because he flinched and let out a low chuff.

"Yes, you definitely can." He leaned forward and nipped her upper lip before once again pulling away. "But if we keep kissing, it will lead to more. Right here, right away. I don't want to rush anything. I want to discover everything about you I missed last night."

Heat pooled low in her belly. "So what does this mean?" she asked, her voice trembling with desire. She rose and rested her forehead against his shoulder.

"As crazy as it sounds, it means no more sex until we know each other in other ways. Much. Much. Better."

****

Adam closed the door of his apartment behind Dina after promising he'd call her tonight and took the first of what he suspected was many long, cold showers. Never before did he deny himself sex as he did with Dina. But Dina was special, and he wanted to do the right thing with her.

He dialed Jacob's number.

"Hey, want to meet me at the driving range?"

"Sure, when?" Jacob asked.

"One o'clock?"

"See you then."

He pulled into the parking spot, grabbed his golf

clubs, and walked into the driving range office. Jacob was already there. They walked to their cage, each carrying a bucket of balls. To their right a teenage girl practiced with her coach; to their left stood several boys, each in their own cage. Adam waved Jacob to go first. He adjusted his stance, shifted his hips, and swung his club. The ball soared through the air, coming close to the two hundred yard mark. After ten swings, Jacob stepped aside.

"So, what's going on?" Jacob adjusted his golf glove.

Adam bent to line up the ball on the tee. "My dad fired me." Uttering the words brought a bitter taste to his mouth. He swung his club, watched the ball skip over the ground and travel nowhere. Just like his career.

"What the hell did the bastard fire you for?"

It satisfied him listening to another person complain about his dad, though Dina had a better vocabulary.

"It's my word against the paralegal's, and well, my word doesn't carry much weight. Unfortunately, having me in the office made others think I received special treatment. Especially because all the paralegals think I threw mine under the bus and rely too much on my name."

He hit another ball. This time it sailed backward, hit the roof, before it rolled and landed two feet in front of him.

"Asshole," Jacob said, watching the golf ball.

"Exactly."

He swung his club again. Finally, it sailed straight and true, no more than one hundred yards, but at least it went in the right direction.

"Nice swing."

Adam nodded. He hit another seven balls before switching places with Jacob.

He took a deep breath. "So, I wondered if you might have any contacts I could speak to," he said as Jacob pulled out some balls with his club.

"New Jersey or New York?"

The Caribbean. "New York preferably, but I suspect I can't be too choosey." He should have known his friend wouldn't make an issue out of helping him.

"Don't panic yet. Your dad's known as a ballbuster," Jacob said. "If you get a job in New York, will you commute?"

He shrugged. "I don't know. I've always wanted to live in the city, but lately…"

"What about Dina?"

He was finally in a relationship that might last. Suddenly, the city held less appeal. "We can still see each other if I'm in the city, can't we?"

"So, you're seeing each other now?"

Adam filled him in as Jacob continued his flawless swing. He left out "love." No one would hear before Dina.

"What's she think about your getting fired?"

"She doesn't know about all of it."

Jacob sliced his ball far to the right. He swung around. "What part doesn't she know about?"

"The being fired part."

"Why not? She knows you well enough not to care."

Adam clenched his fist.

"Adz, you can't do this. You have to tell her."

A jolt of fear ran through him and his mouth dried.

He did have to tell her and based on what she knew already about him and his father, she'd be on his side, not his father's. But what if he couldn't find another job? Whatever respect she had for him would be lost. An unemployed guy wasn't boyfriend material. The thought of her leaving made his palms damp. He needed to tell her he loved her first. Maybe she'd stay. "It's a misunderstanding. I'll straighten it out with her when the time is right. First I need a new job."

"It's a helluva secret to keep from someone you care about."

It was exactly why he couldn't tell her. Not until he told her he loved her, and she loved him back. And then—"I've got it under control."

They finished each of their buckets. Before they left, Jacob clapped Adam on the shoulder. "I'll email you some contacts, don't worry. But you need to tell her."

****

Adam wrapped his hand around Dina's as they walked to the movie theater. The scent of buttery popcorn assaulted his senses. It was their first "official" date since his escape from the "friend zone." He was determined to do it right. After showing up with flowers—daisies, which she loved—and complimenting her on her outfit—jeans and a bright pink sweater made her lips look extra kissable—they'd walked to the movie theater down the street.

He didn't once let go of her hand, because he hated the thought of being apart from her, even by a few inches. Man, he was a goner.

Inside, he paid for the tickets, awkwardly doing everything with his one free hand, and taking twice as long as if he'd used two.

Jacob's advice still rang in his ears. He held on, determined to make himself the best boyfriend she'd known. When she eventually learned his secret—and he would have to tell her at some point—she'd stay. And maybe love him as much as he had begun to love her.

"Would you like popcorn?" he asked after they bought their tickets.

"I hate getting kernels in my teeth. But go ahead if you want it."

"Candy? Pretzels? Nachos?"

"I'm good."

"Are you sure?" She was his girlfriend. He needed her to know he'd give her anything she wanted. *Dude, you're toast.*

She turned to him, putting her free hand against his cheek and his heart stuttered in his chest. He turned his face into it, so he could kiss her palm.

"Relax," she said. "I don't eat at movie theaters. It has nothing to do with you. My parents were always obsessive about our eating habits, and it's stuck with me, at least as far as junk food in a movie theater goes."

He kissed her palm again. "You know I think you're perfect, right?"

The blush rising on her cheeks was adorable, and he vowed to make sure he caused it to appear more often. She looked away. No way. He took her chin in his hand and made her meet his gaze.

"Did your parents give you a hard time about your looks?" His blood boiled at the thought of it.

"I don't think they meant to, but when you're already insecure about your looks, it's difficult to brush off well-meant advice."

He drew her against him and gave her a hug. For as long as she was with him, he'd make sure she knew how perfect she was. She'd never feel insecure around him again. When it was his turn in the concession line, he ordered himself a bag of popcorn and a soda and walked with her into the movie theater. The leather reclining seats made the experience more like watching a movie in one's own living room than in a public theater.

As they waited for the movie to start, Adam wished they could share a seat.

She lifted the armrest separating their seats and scooted as close to him as possible. Could she read his mind? With a sigh, he put his arm around her and pulled her closer.

"This is better," she said.

He nodded and made small circles on the inside of her wrist with his thumb.

"You're going to distract me from the movie."

He looked at the ads on the screen. "It hasn't started yet."

"Did you know the first movies were under a minute long when they were invented in the 1890s?"

He huffed. "No, I didn't."

The previews started, and she faced forward. "This is my favorite part," she whispered.

Lights and colors flashed on the screen, but Adam was too busy watching Dina to notice it, other than through his peripheral vision. Her lips parted as she focused on the movie screen. For each preview, he could read her expression as summaries of each movie played—humor, surprise, confusion.

He liked her confusion best. She had this adorable

way of wrinkling her nose, making fine lines between her eyebrows, challenging him not to touch them. Later, he'd have to figure out a way to make her get those wrinkles back, so his fingers could be the ones to wipe them away.

When the main feature started—a romantic comedy he'd thought she'd like—she leaned over and whispered in his ear.

"She looks like she could use a plate of pasta more than a boyfriend."

He took a moment to examine the actress. She was right. The A-list actress was super skinny and although traditionally attractive, didn't appeal to him. He frowned. Before today, he'd always thought she was hot. In fact, a lot of the women he'd dated before Dina resembled her. Her neck looked stringy, the veins in her arms ropey. When he held Dina against him, her curves made him feel she melted into him, like the two of them became one person, even without sex.

When the actress and actor literally bumped into each other on the street corner, he leaned toward Dina. Her hair tickled his face, and he pushed it out of the way, more to give himself an excuse to touch it than because it bothered him.

"He's probably got bruises from her ribs."

Dina buried her face in his shoulder and trembled with laughter. He squeezed her hand, his cheek twitching from trying not to disturb anyone. The smell of coconuts wafted from her hair, and he focused on tropical islands, sandy beaches, anything but her silent laughter. Because if he thought about it he'd join her, and they'd get kicked out of the movie theater. Finally, she took a deep breath and pulled away, and while he was grateful for her control, his body missed her closeness.

They continued to make quiet comments throughout the movie—she pointed out "too stupid to live" moments, he pointed out how the male lead was equally treated as eye candy—until inevitably, the credits rolled and the lights came on.

Somehow, during the length of the movie, their hands became intertwined and their legs, extended in the red leather recliners, rested against each other. He didn't want to move. Ever.

"It was a pretty ridiculous movie," he said as they finally rose and filed out of the movie theater.

"Oh, but I loved it," Dina said. "It was ridiculous enough to be entertaining. What I love about those movies is you know exactly what you're going to get. There are no surprises, because there isn't much depth to the story or the characters, but it's exactly what you need at the time you're watching."

"I'll keep your thoughts in mind for next time." He gave her a sideways glance. This amazing, intelligent woman who could find meaning and joy in everything intrigued him.

"Good. Although we might need to discuss the genre next time. There are only so many skinny bimbos I can handle at one time."

He took her hand in his. "True. And that's the guys."

She laughed, and it was the sweetest sound. On their way home, they stopped for frozen yogurt, getting cups to go, and ate while walking.

Dina looked over at Adam's cup of yogurt, which was pineapple and coconut. "Um, we may have a problem."

Adam stopped dead. "What's wrong?"

Dina's lips twitched, and the pressure in his chest eased. "You don't eat chocolate. I think we might have a deal breaker."

Adam pulled her toward him and handed her his yogurt.

"My not eating chocolate is a deal breaker?" He drew himself up as large as possible and looked at her, focusing on her lips. There was a spot of chocolate in the corner, and he took his finger, dragging it across her mouth to wipe the chocolate away.

She nodded.

With the back of his hand, he caressed her cheek. Her skin was soft. "I would have thought it would be a good thing."

"Wh…" She cleared her throat. "Why?"

He licked his finger, slowly, and watched her mouth drop. "Because you don't need to share."

He bent toward her and kissed her cold lips. They tasted of chocolate. In the background he heard a "plunk," but to investigate would mean pulling away from her and he wouldn't. The coconut scent of her hair mixed with the coconut flavor of his yogurt, and he couldn't get enough of her. After what could have been hours or seconds, she pushed against his chest, and he took a step back, his breath in short gasps.

"I dropped the yogurt."

Chapter Sixteen

Adam called her every day over the next two weeks. They went out on dates during the week and spent at least one day a weekend together.

And they didn't have sex.

Prior to Adam, Dina would never have characterized herself as sex-starved. She never would have characterized herself as "sex" anything if she were completely honest.

She'd had boyfriends—mostly several years older, since she used to relate better to older men who appreciated a woman with a brain. She kept a box of condoms under her bed. The box was open, and several condoms were missing. But sex was never something she thought about very often.

After Adam?

She thought about sex constantly.

His desire to take things slow, to woo her, or whatever crackpot idea in his mind, while lovely, drove her mad.

The rom-com movie they'd gone to? She barely focused. The scent of his aftershave, mingled with the buttery popcorn smell, almost made her hyperventilate.

The night they'd gone to a karaoke bar? It was a damn good thing the words of the songs played in front of her, because his arm wrapped around her sent tingles up and down her spine and if not for the teleprompter, she wouldn't remember a single word.

She couldn't recollect the taste of any of the food they'd eaten, since the only taste she could recall was his mouth and his skin.

And today they were going ice-skating. She'd be lucky if the heat of her desire for him didn't melt the ice beneath her feet and send her plunging into the frigid waters.

At least she'd finally be able to cool off.

Her apartment buzzer sounded, and she grabbed her skates and skipped down the stairs to meet Adam. She would jump him after skating and convince him they needed to have sex. Today.

Still thinking about all the ways she would convince Adam to have sex with her, she didn't see him on her wide front porch until she was on top of him. He grabbed her by the elbows, ostensibly to keep them both from toppling.

It was the perfect opportunity to press herself against him and kiss his lips.

"Whoa, there," he said against her mouth. "In a hurry?"

To have sex with you. "I didn't want to keep you waiting." *I wonder what sex on the porch would be like?*

He nipped her lower lip, and she melted against him, dropping her skates and wrapping her arms around his neck. He groaned and pulled away.

"Come on, the ice awaits."

Definitely going to melt through it.

With a sigh, she picked up her skates and followed him into the car. "I thought Mennen Arena would be a better option," he said as he pulled out into traffic. "I never fully trust the lake is frozen, no matter how many people skate on it."

Well, at least she wouldn't drown when she melted the ice.

Once they parked and paid for ice time, they sat on the bench and laced their skates. Adam took her hand in his and they both stepped onto the ice. Pushing off with her left foot, she dropped his hand as she adjusted to the ice. Adam was a strong skater, and graceful, too. Dina hadn't skated since she was a teenager and was invited to some little cousin's birthday party. She'd spent most of the time supporting the younger kids so they wouldn't fall down, and her current skills were rusty. But with Adam's help, after a couple of laps, she perfected the rhythm and balance.

This time, she seized his hand and squeezed.

His mouth broadened in a grin. She tripped, and he grabbed her waist.

"You okay?"

They still moved, and Adam pressed her against his side, seeming reluctant to let her go though she'd regained her balance after a stroke or two.

"I'm fine." This time, she didn't look at his face. It was hard enough to concentrate pressed against him, feeling his muscles move, his warm breath tickling her neck.

He glided with ease, his strokes sure. They skated around the rink in silence, until he spun them around. She caught her breath and gasped as the lights in the rink twinkled and his warm body enveloped her. Closing her eyes at the dizzying sensation, she let him spin them across the ice, until finally he stopped in the center.

She opened her eyes to see him staring. "Like it?" he asked.

She nodded and took his hand as he moved. "Where'd you learn to skate?"

His stride faltered, but he righted himself. If she wasn't close to him, she probably wouldn't have noticed his misstep. He stared across the rink. "My mother taught me."

"It must have been nice."

He shrugged.

"Did you two skate together often?"

He waited so long to answer, she thought he would remain silent. But he finally answered.

"She took me skating every Saturday. Afterward, we'd go out for fresh donuts at this local bakery. It's no longer there."

The "neither is she" remained unspoken, but Dina heard it loud and clear. "How old were you when she left?"

He glided with her and from the corner of her eye, she could see him swallow. "Seven."

She squeezed his hand, wanting to say something comforting. But what did you say to someone whose mother left him?

"For a long time, I blamed myself," he said. "Now I mostly blame my father."

His "mostly" comment told her more than anything else he'd said, because no matter how much blame he'd shifted to his father, Dina would bet a part of him blamed himself. Especially when the father he blamed was distant as well. Suddenly, his questions about why Dina stayed with him made sense. Everyone who was supposed to love him had left, either physically or emotionally. Her throat hurt from the urge to cry. Instead, she squeezed his hand again and rested her cheek on his shoulder for a brief moment before concentrating on remaining upright.

"My dad used to take me to the library every Friday afternoon," she said. "He'd come home early for Shabbat, and we'd go borrow enough books to last me through the weekend."

"So that's where you get your love of reading."

She nodded. "To this day, my arms ache from carrying too many books every time I go into the children's section."

"Do your parents still live around here?"

She shook her head. "No, they moved to St. Louis when I was in college. My dad's a professor at a university there."

"And are they all as smart as you?"

She glanced sideways at him, but he didn't tease her. "My dad is a physics professor, my mom is a linguist, and my two brothers are doctors."

He turned so he skated backward, facing her. "Yeah, but are they as smart as you?"

It was the first time someone heard her family's professions and didn't make some comment about her only being a librarian. It was also the first time a man her own age valued her intelligence. She swallowed. Her heart rate sped up and the tears she'd swallowed before prickled behind her eyelids. She blinked quickly before she answered. "We're all pretty smart."

With a nod, he resumed skating. "It's hard living up to family expectations, real or imaginary," he said.

She never thought anyone would understand what it was like to live in the shadow of her brilliant family, but Adam understood immediately. A knot somewhere inside, one she'd always picked at, loosened. This man, this amazing, complicated man—

"I'm thirsty," Adam said. "Want to stop for a drink?"

It took her a few seconds to process what he said and by the time she did, they reached the exit. They hobbled over to the refreshment stand, where Adam ordered two hot chocolates and two bottled waters. Finding an empty table in the back, they sat and people-watched.

Or rather, Adam people-watched.

Dina Adam-watched.

His innate understanding of her, and his demonstration of vulnerability made him more attractive. He gulped most of the water in the water bottle. His throat worked, and the light shone on his skin. His hand wrapped around the bottle, the same hand that cupped her jaw when he kissed her, or her neck when he drew her close. His lips pursed around the mouth of the bottle, water moistening them, and she licked her own lips with desire. He returned the bottle to the table and the clap of it against the Formica made her jump.

She drank her own water, slaking her physical thirst, but leaving her sexual desire unfulfilled. Steam rose from her hot chocolate in wisps. She didn't need anything to make her hotter.

"Not a fan?" Adam asked. He nodded toward her cup.

"Oh, it's hot. I'm letting it cool a little." *And me.*

"What do you think their story is?" He indicated a couple two tables over. They both focused on their phones, looking to everyone else as if they paid no attention to each other.

"Brother and sister," Dina said.

Adam stared at them a moment longer. "I think they're sending each other dirty texts."

Dina choked on the hot chocolate she'd sipped and her eyes watered. Adam leaned over to help her and she waved him away. Her throat stung from the heat of the liquid, but she got herself under control and wiped her mouth with a napkin before she spoke.

"You're unfair."

"Why?" he asked.

"Because you can't tell a person something like that while they're drinking."

"Should I have texted it instead," he asked with a wink.

She rolled her eyes. "You're impossible." But her neck heated at the thought of the content of those texts and she tried to distract herself. "Do you have any?"

"Dirty texts?" He pulled out his phone and Dina squeaked.

"No!" People around them turned and she ducked, hearing Adam chuckle softly. "Siblings. Brothers or sisters."

His relaxed exterior changed once again, tightening, and growing wary. His jaw vibrated, as if he clenched and unclenched his teeth. "No, just me."

"I'll bet it has its advantages."

He stared into his hot chocolate. "I never thought about it really. What's it like having siblings?"

"Complicated. It's like being in an unending competition, where the stakes are constantly raised."

"At least they provide a distraction."

She waited for him to explain further, but he remained silent, and she could almost see him erect his walls. Only this time, they weren't quite as high. She'd knocked a few bricks down, and she was determined to tackle the rest. If he'd let her.

****

Adam forcibly relaxed each part of his body—his neck, his shoulders, and his hands—and tried to clear his mind. He'd given away more about himself than he'd intended, but he'd learned more than he'd expected about her as well.

"Let's get out of here," he said.

"Why? Don't you want to skate some more?"

"Not unless you do."

He led her out to the car. He went to turn it on, but she stopped him with her hand on his upper arm. "Why don't you like to talk about your family?"

His hand gripped the key, and he forced himself, once again, to loosen his grip. His chest tightened, and his gaze traveled from the key to her hand, up her arm to her violet eyes, unblinking and kind. *Crap.*

"There's nothing to say." He and his father never had conversations like this.

"You don't act like a man with nothing to say." If there was one thing he'd learned, it was to stifle all conversations about feelings. Except Dina tried to air them out.

The air in the car grew heavy and he needed space to breathe, but short of opening the car door, there was nowhere to go. He pulled at the chest strap of the seatbelt until there was more pressure on his other hand. Now it was between both of hers and she stroked it, like one would a frightened puppy.

He had nothing against puppies unless he was compared to one.

Swallowing, he tried to grin at her, but it came out as more of a grimace. "You've met my father."

"And I'm still here."

Good point.

"It's not your fault your mom left."

He rubbed his other hand, the one Dina didn't hold, across the top of his head. He needed a haircut. "You can't possibly know." Seriously, how did this woman know so much?

"It's never the kid's fault. Have you talked to your dad about it?"

He choked on a bitter laugh he tried to swallow. "He likes the conversation less than I do." Besides, if he'd poked that bear, maybe his father would have left too.

"It must have been hard for you to deal with."

He didn't know how to answer her, or if it required an answer. Instead, he focused on her hands wrapped around his. They were cool, but soothing. They didn't add to the heaviness. In fact, they centered him. "It's done."

She stared at him a moment longer, and he wondered what she saw. But she gave nothing away and finally, she let him have his hand back. He wasn't sure if he was disappointed or relieved.

Without a word, he started the car.

"Come to my place," she said. Her voice was low, but it wasn't a question. If it was anyone but Dina, he would have said it was a command.

Not in the mood for an argument, and really, what was there to argue about? He drove to her apartment and parked in front. She climbed out of the car and waited on the sidewalk until he joined her. Taking his hand once again, she led him into her quirky apartment.

Once inside, his mouth dried and for the first time, he didn't know what to do. He wasn't a moron when it came to women. He could read the signs, and Dina's clearly pointed to sex—from the way she'd touched him frequently, to the way her tongue slid across her lips, and the way she gave him such little personal space as she stood next to him.

She held her hand out for his coat and when he gave it to her, she held his hand a moment longer than necessary.

They'd had sex once and it was great. But he was trying to change, to show her and himself he was different. He wouldn't have sex with her again until they'd spent time getting to know each other better.

Returning to his side, she placed a hand on his arm. His muscle twitched, and her fingers tightened. Her gaze focused on his arm, and his focused on her. She pulled away and left the room.

He couldn't afford to get attached and have her leave him. It's why he never went for serious relationships with women. Casual flings? Sure. Him leaving first? Definitely. But Dina? Did she deserve someone like him? Probably not.

"You're thinking too hard." Dina returned with a bottle of wine and two glasses. She gave him the bottle to open and when their fingers touched, a jolt of electricity arced between them. Standing this close to her, he could see her individual eyelashes frame pupils wide with desire.

She wanted him. He wanted her. What was the

problem?

"I seem to think a lot around you." He poured the wine and clinked his glass against hers. The bell-like sound reminded him of Dina's laugh.

Was she always this blatantly sexual? Another reason why they needed to get to know each other better. She kept her gaze trained on him, took a sip, swallowed, and ran her tongue once again across her lips, and his groin tightened. Before he could force his brain to figure things out, she stepped toward him and took his glass out of his hand.

Oh, God. She pressed her body against him and rose on tiptoe to kiss him, creating a torturous friction. His hands, first suspended in some kind of midair limbo, dropped to her hips, luscious and firm.

Meanwhile, her hands brushed against his backside and squeezed.

He groaned, and when he opened his mouth she slipped her tongue inside. She tasted of chardonnay, she smelled of coconut and he was finished. So much for waiting. Lifting her up, he carried her across the room, toward her bedroom. She wrapped her legs around his waist.

Adam leaned against the wall and all of a sudden, her hands were everywhere—his hair, his neck, his back, his chest. She nibbled his ear and trailed kisses along his jaw. Blood rushed to his groin and he felt lightheaded, a buzz in his ears so loud he couldn't think. He needed to have her right here, right now.

And for once, she agreed. She fumbled with the buttons on his shirt, pushed the fabric off his shoulders, rubbed her fingers across his chest and drove him mad. He lowered her until her feet touched the floor. They pulled at each other's jeans at the same time. A moment later, both pairs were down. He ran his fingers beneath the waistband of her panties, dipped further and felt how wet she was for him already. He hardened painfully, his cock jumping as if of its own volition. She quivered against him and angled her hips.

"Are you sure?" he ground out.

"Yes."

The one word was all it took. He grabbed a condom from his wallet, hands shaking as he unwrapped it, and slid it on. Using the wall for support, he slid into her, trying to go slowly, but with her grip and rocking movement against him, it was impossible. She was tight, and her muscles clenched. His panting mingled with hers, and sweat dripped down his back. God, she felt good. His legs shook, and he braced himself as he plunged inside her, deeper still. He narrowed his focus until all he felt, all he smelled was her. She screamed her release and everything around him darkened until suddenly he fell over the edge. Red and yellow lights flashed like a hundred fireworks lighting up the night sky, and he roared.

When their breathing eased and his heart rate slowed, he lowered himself, with her still in his arms, to sit on the floor and pulled her into his lap. She smelled of sex and coconuts and her, and he inhaled deeply, leaning into her neck.

"Why didn't we do this sooner?" he asked.

She punched his arm. "Really?"

Smiling against her skin, he let her hair cover his face. God, he loved her curls.

Her fingers drew small circles against his back and a deep sense of peace settled over him.

"This is good, right?" he asked.

"This is very good."

****

"I wish I had better news for you," Jacob said.

Adam's every muscle tensed.

"I extended some feelers. People are hiring." He trailed off and tapped his pencil on his desk.

Adam frowned. It wasn't like him to be this uncomfortable. "Good. I can take it from here if you give me the contact info."

Jacob leaned forward and stared. "I can't. Because as soon as they heard my inquiries were for you, they suddenly lost interest. I tried not mentioning you, but they're all talking about how your firm bungled big-name cases. I'm sorry, Adam. You need to give it some time to let things settle."

Adam thrust himself out of his chair and stalked around the office, rubbing his hand over the top of his head. He wanted to shout. No, he wanted to kill his father.

"What the hell did he do to me?"

"I don't think it was your dad, Adz."

"Who else could it be?"

Jacob spun around in his chair. "What about the paralegal? Could she have told someone?"

Adam turned toward the window and looked out, images of his father, the paralegal, and his former office shuttling through his brain. "I don't know why she would. I mean I know the paralegals in our office talk, but between different law firms? I can't imagine it happening if she wants to get rid of me that bad."

"Your dad's an ass. Sorry."

Nodding in agreement, Adam turned. "I need a

new career plan."

"Well, if you can figure out who's spreading the news, maybe you can do something from another angle."

"The horse not only left the barn, but it left the state. It doesn't matter if I can find out who's after me. The news is out there. Shit, I am not letting them end my career!"

"I don't think you should ignore who might be trying to hurt your career. I think it's worth looking into."

"Oh, I'll definitely look into it, don't worry."

Jacob flipped a pencil through his fingers. "How are things with Dina?"

For the first time, Adam smiled. "Good." *Great.*

"Have you talked to her?"

He could play dumb and pretend he didn't know what Jacob meant, but he didn't think he could pull it off. "Not yet."

Jacob frowned. "How serious are you two?"

Adam pulled at his collar.

"Have you had sex yet?"

"Twice."

Jacob let out a breath, fluttering papers on his desk. "Oh boy. I hope you know what you're doing."

"If I tell her, she'll leave."

"If you don't, she might anyway."

"I can manage it."

Jacob walked with him to the door. "Go through your dad's employees and see who jumps out. And tell Dina."

Chapter Seventeen

Dina walked through the glass door separating the utilitarian conference room of the County Library from the public portion of the building and stopped. The person behind her rammed into her back.

"Sorry, Jack," she said to her colleague, moving out of his way and over to the table where Tracy poured herself a cup of coffee. The all-county librarians' meeting had gotten an early start this morning, and this was their first fifteen-minute break. "I swear I thought I saw Adam going downstairs to the Reference Room." She shook her head. *I must be imagining things.*

"Weird. Are you going to go look for him?"

"Maybe during the next break." She stretched her back. These meetings were always long, but informative. *It would be a really strange coincidence.*

"Uh oh, trouble in paradise?"

Dina made a face. "Of course not. We don't track each other's every move." She grabbed her paper cup and a small plate of fruit and returned to the faux wood conference table. Her pulse increased. Why was he in this library?

You'll never know unless you ask. At the next break, she descended carpeted stairs to the basement and walked to the back, her shoulders tightening as she approached the Reference Room. She pushed open the glass door. Sure enough, Adam sat hunched in front of a computer, a stack of papers next to him.

Smiling wide, she walked over. "Hey, I didn't know you planned to come here today."

He jumped, flipped the papers over, and turned.

Her curiosity increased.

Banking surprise, he smiled back, but his neck reddened, and the smile didn't reach his eyes.

"I didn't expect you to be here, either. I'm doing some research." He clenched his hand on top of the papers.

His law office didn't have a research department? "Tracy and I are here for a meeting. What are you researching? Anything I can help with?"

He spread his hand out. "No, I'll be done in a little bit. Want to do something when I'm finished?"

She admired his hands as she wondered what he researched. "I can't. I have a hair appointment for the reunion."

"Don't do anything to your hair." Adam's voice rose, and Dina's face heated seeing the people around them glare. He lowered his voice, but his tone was no less commanding. "It's perfect as it is."

"Really? I thought of getting it straightened. The curls are all over the place."

"Those curls are you. Don't change them." He looked fierce as he stared at her, his fingers flexing and straightening as if he ran them through her strands.

Dina fingered her frizz, not understanding why springy hair was his thing, but was touched he cared. "I still have to get it trimmed though."

"Not much."

"Seriously, you're crazy."

His green eyes glowed as if he looked deep into her

soul. "Don't let the mean girls change who you are."

His understanding pulled her up short, before a tingling created a trail of warmth. No matter what happened at the reunion, he'd have her back. If they promised to be silent, would the other people mind if she and Adam had sex right here? With a sigh, she pulled away. "I'll let you return to your research, whatever it is. Call me tonight?"

"Only if you text me a picture of your hair after your appointment."

"Only if you tell me what you're researching."

He shifted in his chair. "Law stuff. How's your meeting?"

Why was he suddenly eager to change the subject? "It's fine. What kind of law stuff? Must be pretty outside the box if you have to do it at the county library instead of your office."

He swallowed, shifting his gaze around the room. "It's…it's nothing. Don't worry. Want to come over tomorrow and watch a movie?"

"You're changing the subject, Adam. What's going on?"

He sighed. "Can we talk about this later?"

She nodded. "Come over tomorrow and we'll watch a movie at my place. I've got the perfect one."

****

The next evening when Adam entered her apartment, she held a DVD. "I came across this again, and it's amazing."

"*Mr. Smith Goes to Washington*?" Adam frowned as he read the back cover.

"Have you seen it?"

He shook his head.

"It's about a naïve politician battling corruption. It's great."

A strange look crossed his face. "Sure, if this is what you want to watch."

She ran her hand along his arm. Beneath the cotton shirt, tension hardened his muscles. "I thought you'd enjoy this, but if not…"

"No, it's fine. Sit with me."

She put in the movie and sat next to him. He put his arm around her and drew her close. She leaned against his chest. His fingers played in her hair.

"I like what you did with this," he said.

She'd cut about two inches off and had the rest of it shaped. She turned her face into his hand, kissing his palm. "I'm glad." Against her back, she could feel him exhale, as if he held his breath. Something bothered him, but she didn't know what. His list of secrets kept growing, and she wasn't sure how much longer she could wait. Maybe if she could relax him with the movie, they could talk.

It didn't work.

Dina wasn't sure if it was the specific movie, although his attention and focus indicated he liked it. Maybe it was the time of day, although a Saturday night didn't usually bother him. Perhaps it was her, yet he didn't once move or suggest she sit farther away. Whatever the reason, he remained as tense as when he arrived.

She wished she knew some obscure fact about keeping secrets from your girlfriend. Maybe it would help break the ice. Because he'd walled himself off from her, and it made her nervous.

"Good movie," he said, stretching.

"I love Jimmy Stewart. My grandmother used to watch his movies all the time, and I remember sitting with her on Saturday afternoons. Did you know the word 'Philadelphia' was misspelled on his Oscar?"

Adam laughed. "I'll bet you were adorable as a child."

"No, I wore these huge glasses, and I asked tons of questions and drove everyone crazy. Except her. She would answer anything I asked."

"Is she still alive?"

Dina shook her head. "No, she died a few years ago. What about your grandparents?"

"They died before I was born, although I was named after my mother's father."

"Did your mother ever talk to you about him?"

He took her hand. "I can't remember. There wasn't a lot of conversation in my house."

It explained a lot. Maybe he didn't know how to open up.

"What a shame. Talking keeps the bad things from festering and creating more stress."

"I seriously doubt it." He'd pulled away from her, looking wary.

She wanted to draw him close and reassure him whatever bothered him would be easier shared, but she didn't want to spook him.

"It's true," she said. "Kind of like the anticipation of something is worse than the actual event. Bringing it out in the open makes the burden lighter."

"Or it convinces you of the merits of what you worried about in the first place."

Somehow, she didn't think he spoke about the grandfather he'd never met. "But isn't it better to get it over with?"

His mouth whitened around the edge of his lips as he pressed them together so tightly they almost disappeared. "No." He rose and stalked toward the DVR, kneeling before it. He tried to look busy, but Dina could read him. He was fiddling.

"What's the worst that can happen?" she asked.

He kept his back to her, his muscles strained against his shirt.

At any other time, Dina's throat would have gone dry at the sight. However, knowing he was, in effect, straining against her attempts to know him better, made his muscles decidedly less attractive.

Adam rose and turned toward her, but kept his gaze focused somewhere behind her and to her left. He opened and closed his mouth several times before clenching his fist and focusing on her. He thrust his hand through his hair. "I know what you're trying to do. I know I need to talk to you, and I will, but I need time. Please, I need you to trust me. Can you?"

Her stomach twisted, and she swallowed. He hadn't done anything to abuse her trust, but how much time did he expect her to give? And what was important enough that he needed time to prepare? With a nod, she gave in. For now.

Chapter Eighteen

Adam called her on Monday, acting as if nothing happened. Acting, actually, like his Mr. Flashypants self. It was like he'd rebuilt the wall around himself and behind it, everything was fine. He kept his conversations light and avoided the painful topic.

Dina spent the week stuck in a fog. Her reunion was next weekend, and Adam was supposed to go with her, but if he thought she would bring it up, he had no idea who she was.

She didn't know what to do.

"Did you tell him how mad you are at him?" Tracy asked on Wednesday. They were on a lunch break at a sandwich shop down the street from the library. The small place was noisy and the tables were close together.

"No, because every time I figure out what I want to say, he changes the subject or teases me, or has to run."

"Don't be ridiculous, Deen. He should know how you feel."

"Yeah, but I also have a pretty good idea how I made him feel."

"So what, you're his girlfriend. If he won't be honest with you now, there's no future for you."

Dina stirred her soda with the straw. "I know you're right, but part of me doesn't want to mess with this. For the first time, I'm dating someone who likes me. Me. What if I screw it up?"

Tracy reached across the table and covered Dina's hand with her own. "If he's truly worth it, he'll understand."

"Okay, after the reunion. Despite what I said in the beginning, I'm really looking forward to having him go with me, and I don't want things to be tense there. It's already going to be nerve-wracking."

****

Adam shut off his computer and rubbed his face. He made a list of promising New York City law firms. He'd done a search of Ashley's name in relation to the firms and couldn't find any connections. If he couldn't use Jacob's connections, it didn't mean he couldn't find a job. The tricky part was the references, but maybe with some bargaining, his dad would consent to giving him a good one, if only to get his son out of the way.

His son. The words tasted bitter on his tongue. What kind of a man treated his son this way? The man who believed his firm's image was more important than anything. Adam thought he'd given up caring long ago, but his father's actions created a dull ache in his breastbone, and he couldn't get rid of it no matter how hard he tried.

Screw it. Lots of people didn't get along with their family and they survived. He would too. He had a plan—submit résumés, take Dina to the reunion, get a job offer, tell her he loved her, and come clean to her about being fired. Jacob was right—he did need to talk to her, if only because he was different from his father. But he'd look a lot less pitiful if he had a great job to prove his worth. She'd see him as a man who overcame adversity, not someone who was beaten by it.

He'd convinced her to go out with him through sheer force of will. Once his future was set, he'd convince her she loved him the same way. And her reunion would be the place to show her how indispensable he was. He needed to hold everything together for a few more days.

****

Dina's nerves crackled by the day of the reunion. Not only was she stressed about Adam and his secrets, but the thought of willingly putting herself in the same room as her high school classmates looked less and less appealing as the reunion approached. And now it was here. She was too nauseated to eat a real breakfast, but her stomach needed something in it to prevent its flip-flops. Settling for dry toast and tea, she curled up on her white upholstered window seat and looked outside. Steam from the teacup rose around her.

This early on a spring morning, joggers and dog walkers had the streets to themselves. Her toe tapping jostled her tea, and she squeezed her eyes shut. Exercise was what she needed to work through her anxiety.

After changing into leggings and a long-sleeved Smashing Pumpkins T-shirt, she plugged her ear buds into her phone, laced her bright orange running shoes, and left her apartment. Was she really ready to face the girls she'd gone to high school with? Shouldn't she be over her dislike of them by now? She took a deep, cleansing breath. Rather than walking toward the main street, she headed deeper into the residential part of town, admiring the converted Victorian mansions, and taking in the newly sprouting elm trees along the sidewalks. A few had leaves starting to emerge and the light bright green added hints of color to an otherwise

198

gray morning. She nodded toward passing joggers and dogs, and their owners, and by the time she returned to her apartment, she was calmer.

After showering, she puttered around her apartment. Feeling a bit like a squirrel who hops from tree to tree and acorn to acorn, she tried to focus on cleaning, but minor things like background humming noises from the refrigerator or passing conversations in the hallway distracted her. Deciding she needed something to take her mind off things, she called Tracy and asked her to come over, making tea in the meantime.

"What's wrong?" her friend asked when she arrived, baby in tow.

"This is stupid. I shouldn't bother going tonight." She twirled her hair around her finger, smiling at Mackenzie.

"Wow, this is really bad." Tracy handed her a cup of tea.

Dina's hands shook. She wrapped them around the mug to keep them still. The heat warmed them, and she inhaled the chamomile-scented steam.

"You should, for three reasons: Hot dress, hot guy, and payback."

She choked. "Seriously? I'm afraid no one will remember me or care whether or not I'm there, and it's probably a sign of some mental illness I'm still thinking about my high school horrors, and you say 'payback'?"

Handing her a napkin, Tracy perched on Dina's sofa. "Deep breath. Look, the ten-year reunion is all about payback. It's everyone's chance to prove themselves outside of their old cloistered high school world. You're going to walk in looking sexy and fabulous in your dress, with a gorgeous man on your arm, and everyone will come up to you."

"No one will come near me because they won't remember me, and I'll look stupid in front of Adam."

"No, they're all going to come up to you, especially because they don't remember you, in order to figure out who you are and how you got lucky. Trust me," Tracy said. "And besides, Adam likes you—I've seen how he looks at you. He won't care if the two of you are the only people in the room. In fact," she rose and moved toward the door, "I think he'd probably prefer you two being completely alone to undress you."

Chapter Nineteen

Adam's blood rushed to his groin when a goddess in white opened the door. He was pretty sure Dina was the goddess in white. Same intriguing violet eyes, but this time subtle green shimmery eye shadow accentuated them. Same curves that made him want to bury himself inside her, but this time white fabric hugged those curves and flowed around them at the same time. Her crazy outrageous hair was perfect. She'd pinned back her curls into a bun but allowed some of them to escape. They framed her face. He wanted to touch them. Instead, he clenched his fists at his side. He'd dated enough women to know better than to touch their hair when they'd spent time getting ready for an evening out.

All his worries about finding a job and proving himself to Dina disappeared. This night was about her. And she was stunning. She was also blushing, and he realized with a start he'd stood on her doorstep in silence for far too long.

"Hi," he said. Brilliant. "You look...beautiful." Equally brilliant.

She dipped her chin. "Thank you."

He held his hand out for her and when she placed her hand in his, the world shifted, like a household settling in before a storm. Peace encompassed him. He gripped her fingers and gave her a little tug. "Come on, we're going to have a great time."

She raised an eyebrow at him, and they walked to his car in silence. Once settled, he pulled onto the street and followed his GPS.

"Did you know Princeton was founded before the American Revolution?" she said. "The Lenni Lenape Indians—"

"Dina?"

She stopped, lips parted.

"Relax." He reached across the console and took her cold hand. Out of the corner of his eye, he watched her chest rise and fall, like she took her last breath of fresh air.

He stopped at a traffic light. "And you are going to be the star."

Her expression told him she thought he was crazy. "We'll see."

For the rest of the ride, she blurted out ridiculous facts about everything. The Greeks and Romans thought barbarians wore trousers. The first traffic light was installed in 1914. The British invented the first hair gel, Brylcreem, in 1929. No matter how many times Adam tried to engage her in what he considered "normal conversation," she always retreated to obscure facts. Finally, he let her ramble and admired the sound of her voice.

An hour later, when they pulled up at the hotel in Princeton, Dina remained seated after he'd turned off the engine. She stared out the window at the façade of the building. Maybe she watched the people enter. Could be she plotted the perfect angle to make her escape.

"Dina?"

He craned his neck to look—at her eyes, glassy and focused inward; at her hands, clasped tight in her lap; at her mouth, compressed into a firm line.

"Dina."

Like someone awakening, she opened her hands and sighed. "I'm ready."

"It's going to be fine."

She gave him a bright smile. It didn't reach her eyes. "We should go inside now."

He reached for her hand. It was still icy cold, and he rubbed it. He hated that she felt so out of her element. Although he homed in on the softness of her skin and the delicacy of her bones, he suspected right at this very moment, she didn't notice his touch. With a sigh, he pulled away and opened the door.

Inside the hotel, they retrieved nametags from the registration table in the black and tan lobby. None of the three women who manned it showed recognition when Dina picked up her tag, nor did they interrupt their conversation with the guests who stood behind him waiting for their turn. But it wasn't too unusual. Not everyone remembered their entire class, even if they served on the reunion committee.

Following the sound of the music, they entered a ballroom with high ceilings and enormous crystal chandeliers. Gold tablecloths covered round tables with centerpieces of green balloons. A "Welcome Class of 2007" banner, also in green and gold, hung over the DJ station at the far end of the room. In the center was a dance floor, where couples mingled. To the left was a mirrored wall, lending enormity to the room. Wait staff zigzagged through the crowd, offering hot hors d'oeuvres. A banquet table on the right was filled with cold appetizers, and a crowd surged to the bar.

"Would you like a drink?" Adam asked.

When she nodded, he cupped her elbow and led her forward. She scanned nametags, with only an occasional discreet frown indicating her reaction.

"See anyone you recognize?" he asked as he handed her a gin and tonic with lime.

Dina shook her head. "Not really. Like I said, I didn't really have any close friends in high school. These people all look familiar but not, if you know what I mean."

What he knew was that it had to have been isolating and heartbreaking to go through high school without a single friend.

"Pick a person," he said.

"What do you mean?"

"Pick someone for us to talk to."

"That's crazy."

"Okay, I will." He started to walk toward a cluster of people, and she grabbed his arm. Only the fact that he'd anticipated her reaction, and kept his drink in his other hand, prevented him from sloshing his beer everywhere.

"Wait! Please don't," she said.

He turned to her and stepped close enough to see worry etched in her violet eyes. "The first time is the hardest. Afterward, it gets easier."

"But they won't remember me."

His eyes softened. They might not have known her back then, but they'd know her now. "So what? We'll introduce ourselves, talk about our jobs, say how nice it was to see them and move on. It's easy."

"It's embarrassing."

"Okay, let's play a game. Pick someone."

When she looked at him askance, he held his hand out to the room. After a quick scan, she pointed to a couple nearby. The red-haired woman and the brown-haired man were well dressed, if ordinary, with him in a suit and her in a black sheath dress. They each held a soda in their hands.

"Do you know them?" he asked.

"I can't see their nametags, but I don't think so."

"Perfect. What do you think they're doing now? I mean career wise."

"Doctor and lawyer?" she asked.

He shook his head. "Accountant and teacher. Now we find out who's right." Before she could protest, he pulled her toward them and held out his hand. "Adam Mandel. This is Dina Jacobs. Nice to see you here."

"Cory and Steve Tindal," Steve said. "Did you attend school here?"

"I didn't, but Dina did."

Steve undressed Dina with his eyes, while Cory sported a blank look on her face. Adam wanted to punch them both.

Dina squeezed his hand. She looked stunned but managed to ask if they knew who was on the planning committee, asked if they still lived in the area and if they kept in touch with any other classmates. "So, what are you doing now?"

"Well, I graduated from Penn State, and I'm a lawyer," Cory said. "Steve's in real estate. You?"

"Harvard undergrad and University of Illinois with a Masters in Library Science," Dina said.

Adam's chest swelled with pride as she readily admitted her intelligence. From the looks on Cory's and

Steve's faces, they were impressed. Dina softened next to him.

"It must be why I don't remember-you," Cory said. "You must have been in all the honors and AP classes."

As they moved on from the couple, Adam snagged two eggrolls from a passing waiter.

"It wasn't actually too bad," Dina said before biting into the crispy hors d'oeuvre. "Especially since I was right about Cory."

"I'll get it right next time," he said. "Who should we target next?"

They met a second couple, who remembered Dina and were nice to her, and a foursome that was friendly, before Dina stopped in her tracks. "Uh, let's go over there." She pointed away from a clump of women.

"What's wrong with that group?"

"I think I recognize them."

"And it's a bad thing?"

"I'm not sure."

"They just saw you, so we're about to find out." He put his arm around her and faced the woman walking toward them. If Barbie were a living person, this woman would be her. Blonde, straight hair, big boobs, tiny waist, endless legs. But he wasn't attracted. At all.

"Oh my gosh, I love your dress," Barbie said with a squeal. "Where did you get it?"

Dina gave her the name of the store, and Barbie scrunched her nose. "I've never heard of it." She leaned toward Dina's nametag, and he'd swear she mouthed the words as she read them.

"Dyna Jacobs? I'm not sure…"

"It's Dina with a long E. We were in a marketing class together sophomore year." Tension entered her shoulders.

"Oh, Dina! Now I remember you. Meg, Stacie, come here! It's Dina Jacobs."

Her voice could grate cheese. Adam winced. All around them, heads turned while Meg and Stacie minced over.

"Dina? I don't remember any Dina," Meg said, her brassy red hair-from-a-bottle overflowing her shoulders and emphasizing the swell of her breasts in a low-cut black tube of a dress.

"Yes, you do, girls," Barbie said. "She was in marketing with us."

"I was drunk in marketing," Stacie said. When she rubbed against Adam, he stepped to the side. "I'd remember you, though." Stacie eyed him up and down. "Come join us."

He stepped back and put his arm around Dina's shoulders. "Love to, but we have something to do. Nice meeting you all."

With a firm grip on her upper arm, he led Dina across the room. They stopped at the banquet table, where Adam turned to Dina. He wondered how he could ever have thought someone like Barbie or any of those other vocabulary-challenged women could be appealing. Everything he wanted in a woman was right in front of him. Class, humor, beauty, and brains.

"Wow."

Dina shook her head. "I told you. There was a group of them—those three were part of it—who drank and partied and were…um…in the service of Venus with anyone who breathed…"

His lips twitched.

"What?"

His chin trembled.

"Adam, what?"

His eyes watered.

"Are you okay?"

Eyes streaming, he burst out laughing. Concern, confusion, and annoyance flashed across her features. By the time he controlled himself, she stood in front of him, arms crossed beneath her breasts, toe tapping. She reminded him of the stereotypical sexy librarian. "The service of Venus?" he gasped on a laugh.

"It's an old term to describe you-know-what, and we're in public."

She was right. They were in public. But he didn't care. For once in his entire adult life, he didn't care what others thought. He reached for Dina, and his fingers brushed the undersides of her breasts as he grasped her forearms. His breath quickened, and he drew her in. When their bodies touched, he looked at her upturned face. She made him feel good about himself. She made him less afraid. She gave him hope. To hell with his plan.

"I love you." Saying the words didn't scare him anymore. They filled him with peace. "I love you, Dina."

****

She must have misheard him. Voices mingled with the sounds of the music, making it hard to hear. "What?"

"I love you."

She didn't mishear him. "Did you know when two lovers stare into each other's eyes, their heart rates synchronize?"

Adam's body vibrated against hers as he laughed

silently. "Relax, sweetheart, I love you."

He must be crazy, because who declared their love for someone at a high school reunion? She watched surreptitious pointing from Stacie and some of her friends. Did they hear what he said? Did they think he was crazy? Except…he didn't look crazy. He looked like Adam.

At the same time, he didn't. He looked sure and settled and solid. Not like Mr. Flashypants. More like Mr. Dependable.

Her heart raced in her chest, and she swallowed. Her mouth was dry and her arms, where he held on, were warm and cold.

"You do?"

He chuckled. "Most women wouldn't question the first time their boyfriend declared his love for her."

"Most boyfriends don't declare their love at a reunion." Surrounded by women so much more beautiful than she was. She took a quick glance around. The number of women staring at her surprised her. Was it hard for them to believe a guy like him could like— no, love—a woman like her?

He let go of her arm and caressed her jaw with his finger, making her forget about everyone else, before tipping her face to meet his gaze. "Most boyfriends are not in love with a woman who calls sex 'the service of Venus.' "

She melted a little. "You keep saying that word."

"I've said a lot of words."

"The 'love' one."

"Is there some archaic vocabulary you'd prefer me to use instead?"

"No, I like it."

He hugged her to him, and she inhaled his clove scent. The music and flashing lights and conversations melted into the background.

"Good," he said. "Because I do love you, and I don't say it without meaning it."

Her heart fluttered in her chest. He loved her. She loved him too. Should she tell him now? Would he think she said it because he said it to her? It was too important for it to be handled trivially.

He brushed his lips against hers, stopping all thought of conversation. In fact, all thoughts flew from her brain as he deepened the kiss, sending trails of heat to her belly and making her breasts tingle. Before she could do more than kiss him back, he pulled away.

"We'll have to continue that at another time," he said. "Are you hungry?" Taking her hand in his, he turned toward the buffet table and handed her a plate.

She blinked, trying to focus on something other than his lips. Or his butt, which faced her as he spooned a variety of foods and sauces onto her plate. Sauce. Most of the food was accompanied with sauce, and she wore white. Lovely. With a sigh, she took the plate and held it gingerly, scanning the room for an empty table. Preferably one where they could talk more about this "love" business.

"Let's sit there." She pointed to a table next to the dance floor. They ate with fingers entwined. She didn't taste the food, didn't know what she ate, but focused on how to tell Adam she loved him.

When she'd decided just to come out with it, two more couples joined their table. She sighed, not in the mood to be friendly.

Adam squeezed her hand and leaned forward. "Hi,

I'm Adam Mandel and this is my girlfriend, Dina Jacobs. Great reunion, isn't it?"

The women shrugged, and the guys looked at each other before the larger man with a square head answered. "I guess it depends on what you want to get out of it." The skinny guy put his arm around his date.

"So, did you all graduate from here?" Adam asked. Another reason she loved him—he tried so hard for her.

The women turned to Dina. "We both did," the date of the blockhead answered. "I'm Cheryl and this is Ann. We're friends with Stacie. You were in marketing with us, right?"

Dina nodded, realizing Cheryl spoke more to her with those three sentences than she ever had in four years of high school. It was weird. It was weirder she wasn't looking at Adam, the person who had asked the question in the first place.

"What are you doing now?" Dina asked.

"I'm an office assistant at an investment firm," Cheryl said. "You?"

"I'm a librarian."

Cheryl nodded. "You always were really smart." There was no scorn on her face. Instead, Dina detected admiration. She looked at Ann, who looked…sympathetic?

"And you?" she asked Ann. "What are you doing?"

"I'm a teacher, can you believe it? I used to hate school."

Dina smiled. "That's great. We all change."

In fact, Dina had a hard time detecting the vapid, nasty girls in these two women and her judgment softened.

The music switched to a slow song, and Adam

leaned toward her. "Want to dance?"

"Yes." She rose and the other women whispered to their dates. She assumed they would join them on the dance floor, but instead, Cheryl and Ann called her name.

"Wait, Dina, we're going to the ladies' room. Want to join us?" There was an intensity in their expression Dina didn't understand. She turned to Adam, who shrugged. "Go ahead."

"But I'd rather dance with you."

He touched her cheek. "We can dance to the next song." He sat while Dina followed the women to the ladies' room, if only for curiosity's sake.

The door barely swung shut when they pulled her into the room and off to the side.

"The guy you're with," Cheryl said. "How long have you two been dating?"

In the mirror, Dina's shock at the question reflected back at her, but it wasn't nearly as strong as her actual feelings.

"About six weeks or so." She turned to go, but a manicured hand on her arm stopped her.

"Does he work at some law firm named Mandel and something?" This time it was Ann who spoke.

She stiffened. "I don't think it's any of your business." Dina's face heated.

Cheryl and Ann drew her over to the side. "Listen," Cheryl said. "I know you don't remember us. But you were always sweet, and you should know who you're involved with. Did you hear what he did to Ashley Peters?"

They thought she was sweet back then? "What are you talking about?"

"He works at the same firm as Ashley Peters," Ann said. "She was part of our group in high school."

"So what?" Dina asked. The whir of the air dryer gave her a headache. Or maybe it was the mixture of perfume, hairspray, and scented lotion. She rubbed her temples, wishing she could rub the women away instead. She had a man to tell she loved him.

"Do you know what he did to her?" Cheryl said.

****

Sitting at the table waiting for Dina, Adam watched the crowd part and a model-thin woman in a slinky black dress and sky-high heels stalk toward him. His stomach dropped.

"It's you!" Her loud voice caused people to turn and stare. "What are you doing here?" She stopped close enough to him he could see her tremble. Her skin was pale, her ruby lips outlined in a thin white line of anger.

Adam gripped his drink so hard he was certain the glass would shatter. Forcing himself to act calm, he placed his glass on the table and wiped his lips with a napkin before folding it and placing it next to the glass at a precise right angle.

"Ashley," he said. "What are you doing here?"

"I belong here," she snapped, getting close in his face. "The question is, why are you here?"

"I'm here with my date." He didn't name her. The last thing he wanted to do was embarrass Dina. Ashley glared at him, before looking around at the gathered crowd.

"Pfft. I bet you tried to impress her with your position at your daddy's law firm. Maybe I should tell her about the real you. About how your father—"

213

He moved closer and spoke in a low voice. "Ash…" She lurched away. Her drink sloshed over the side of the glass and splattered on the floor.

A buzz started in the crowd, or was it in his mind? He blinked. A sea of faces stared at him, while two guys walked over and flanked Ashley. A third approached him.

"Listen, buddy, you need to leave her alone," guy number three said. He had the beer belly of a former football player and a buzz cut, with a thick neck and small eyes.

"I'm not doing anything to her," he said. "Never have."

"Never does anything for me, either. He used to leave work to go party, gave me all his busywork, and blamed me when he forgot to do something," she said.

The crowd should have gotten bored by now and returned to their food, drink, and dancing. But it looked like he was the latest entertainment of the evening.

Shit. Dina. He didn't want her anywhere near this. She'd be mortified. He was supposed to have helped her deal with tonight and instead, he caused a scene. Beads of sweat popped on his brow, and he reached for the napkin he'd slipped into his breast pocket.

The crowd parted again, and the women approached. As they got closer, he recognized Cheryl and Ann, the two women who'd asked Dina to join them in the bathroom. She looked pale. Was she sick or did the two women say something to bother her? He backed away from Ashley and hurried over to Dina.

"You okay?" He cupped her cheek.

"I'm fine," she whispered.

She didn't look it.

Ashley joined them, as well as the various men associated with her. Dina was upset or sick, and he wanted to back up time by about fifteen minutes. He didn't want her knowing about Ashley.

Unless she already did.

If only he could read her expression. Or her mind.

He focused on Dina and kept his voice low. "Ashley is the paralegal who works in my office. She clearly isn't happy I'm here." He glanced over at Ashley, who gave him a murderous look. "I had no idea she went to school with you, much less graduated at the same time." He looked out at the gathered crowd. He was here for Dina. "I'm sorry my presence has created a scene. Dina, would you like to go?" His voice sounded raspy to his ears, as if he'd dragged it over an artificial turf. All he wanted was to get the two of them out of here, or at least away from these people.

She shook her head no. She didn't want to go with him. His body heated with shame. He reached for the bar, forgetting he'd stepped forward when the guys came to him. He stumbled and righted himself. Fine. He was here for her, to make the reunion easier.

"I didn't mean to ruin your reunion. I'll go find a coffee shop and wait until you're ready to leave. You can text me, and I'll give you a ride home." He tossed a quick look over his shoulder, trying to find a clear path to the door, but guests surrounded them and there was no easy way out.

Cool pressure on his hand startled him, and he looked down.

Dina. Her eyes filled with an emotion he couldn't quite read. "I don't want to leave. I don't want *you* to leave. I want to dance with you."

Chapter Twenty

The DJ started the music as soon as she walked out onto the dance floor with Adam. "I Gotta Feeling" drowned out the voices, but it couldn't eliminate the images flashing through her mind—Ashley's anger, Adam's desolation.

The hollow look in his eyes replayed more often than the other images. And it made her push away her own fears and ask him to dance. But she still wondered why Cheryl and Ann were so desperate to warn her about him, and why Ashley was so angry. Because despite Ann and Cheryl's attempts, she'd refused to let them spout gossip about Adam or Ashley.

Possibly because they were the only people on the dance floor, the DJ switched to a slow song. Now there was a reason to look as if they held each other up. Adam had never been this stiff. It was like dancing with a stone statue. His hands grasped her waist and although it wasn't painful, he gripped her like he thought she would run away.

This man who loved her was afraid she'd leave him.

With her cheek against his chest, she felt his heart pound. She ran her fingers along his nape, trying to ease some of the tension. "Relax," she said. "We're dancing. Don't let them get to you."

"Dina, I—"

"It's okay. They ruined my entire high school experience. I won't let them ruin tonight."

He pulled her close—or maybe his body relaxed enough to make her feel like he did—and rested his cheek against her hair. The contact sent shivers down her spine. He swallowed—once, twice, three times—and she focused on keeping them moving to the music and running her fingers through his soft hair.

Out of the corner of her eye, other couples joined them on the dance floor, the lure of the music too much to resist. Yet they kept a safe distance away from them, as if afraid of catching something.

The DJ changed the song to "Hips Don't Lie," and although everyone around them picked up the speed, Adam found a slow tempo hidden in the song and kept them dancing to it. All around them, bodies undulated to Shakira's song, yet she and Adam swayed to their private version of the music.

But when the song ended, Adam took a deep breath and pulled her off the dance floor. They grabbed their things from the table and walked toward the exit. Once again, her tormentors/rescuers confronted them.

"Dina, remember what we said," Ann said. Why was this woman, who never spared two thoughts for her in high school, looking out for her now?

"I'm fine, Ann."

Adam ignored them, walking toward the exit with single-minded purpose, and Dina increased her pace to keep up. At the door, she turned to take a last glimpse of the banquet room. The decorations were festive, but the people inside were no more familiar to her now than they were when she was a student ten years ago.

She'd come, she'd seen, and now she was leaving.

Adam handed her his keys when they reached the parking lot. "I drank more than I should have."

She frowned as she removed her heels and entered the car. He didn't appear drunk. Why else would he let her drive his car? After taking a quick glance at him in the passenger seat—eyes closed, head back, legs stretched out, she focused on the workings of his fancy car and the road as she navigated them home.

The ride was silent. She wanted to discuss what happened, but if Adam needed to sleep off the alcohol, there was no point in trying to have a reasonable discussion. Her questions, which increased in number with every mile marker they passed, would have to wait.

Why did Cheryl and Ann warn her about Adam?

What really happened between Adam and Ashley?

How could she ask Adam?

He opened his eyes when she pulled up to her apartment, and they climbed out of the car.

She reached for him, but he took a step back, holding his hands out for the keys.

"I know we've got a lot to talk about, but I want to make sure I say it right, and I'm too tired to do that right now. Can we talk tomorrow?"

She nodded and gave him his keys.

He looked over his shoulder as he climbed back in his car. "We'll talk later."

"Soon."

But he pulled away without acknowledging what she'd said.

****

Adam paced the confines of his spacious apartment. The room, which he once thought large, made him claustrophobic. Floor-to-ceiling windows, white walls, and the clean lines of expensive leather and marble furniture the saleswoman had picked out were all supposed to convey light, air, and space. Yet with one evening at a reunion, one scene at a table, one conversation among many, now he couldn't breathe.

He shivered and jacked up the heat on the thermostat, but he couldn't shake off the cold seeping into his bones.

Ashley had gotten to her. Well, maybe not Ashley, but her minions. He had no idea what they'd said to her, but based on their expressions and Ashley's anger, it couldn't be good. Not only had they gotten to her first, but they'd probably gloated to her that his own father had fired him. He should have told her about what happened between him and Ashley ahead of time.

His reputation—both professional and now personal—was in tatters. Why would anyone, much less Dina, want to be with him? For as much as their relationship had progressed, he still hadn't told her the truth about his job. Instead, she'd had to find it out from someone else. What were the odds Dina had gone to high school with his adversary? His stomach tightened, and bile rose in his throat.

Dina valued honesty and he'd lied, even if only by omission. The silence in his apartment stifled him. Even his neighbors were silent.

Dina would leave him. After his mother had abandoned him and his father as well, he'd vowed never to be in the position of letting someone leave him again. If he were half the man he wanted to be, he'd show Dina the way out.

****

Dina frowned at her phone. She'd texted Adam twice—once in the morning and once this afternoon—and he didn't respond to either text. After his desolation last night, she was concerned. Maybe he was sleeping it off? But it was four o'clock. Even someone who'd had too much to drink would be awake by now.

And Adam didn't seem drunk.

When her buzzer rang, she pressed the speaker button. "H...Hello?"

"Dinaaaa!"

Her hands trembled as she allowed him entry into her building and held open the door. His tread on the stairs was heavy. "Adam. Are you okay?" she asked when he reached her apartment.

"Suuuuure."

She cringed at the way he spoke and stepped aside. It reminded her of the last time he'd gotten super drunk. "You don't sound it."

He walked in, shoulders stiff. "Like you'd expect anything else?"

Her stomach was like lead. "What are you talking about?"

"Come on, Dina, don't pretend you don't know."

Her throat tightened, and the room tilted. Reaching for something to grab onto, her hand found the arm of the sofa. "You don't make any sense." He'd just told her he loved her. She swallowed and dug her fingernails into her palms. "Why are you here?"

Adam's humorless laugh echoed in the apartment. "You're the one who texted me all day."

So he'd gotten her texts and ignored them. "We said we would talk about last night."

"There's no need."

Sweat dotted her forehead. "Adam, what's going on?"

"I'm never going to be the man you need."

"What?"

"Last night. Despite everything they told you about me, you came back to me, came to my rescue, danced with me. Even now, you stick with me. You have this idea that you're going to change me, make me into this honorable guy who sees past shallow trappings, who's honest. But I'll never be that guy, and there's no way I can live up to your expectations."

"What are you talking about? I don't do that!"

"Come on, Dina. You and I are just too different. You were right when we first met. You're not my type, and I'm not yours. I'm just like the mean girls from high school that you dreaded being around so much. You came out of the bathroom with them, looking like you wanted to throw up after spending time listening to their gossip. Except it was the truth. Truth that I should have told you. You deserve way better than me."

"I don't understand what you're talking about. They didn't tell me anything."

His voice lost all the "drunk Adam" tone and hardened. "Don't pretend anymore you don't know about Ashley and that my father fired me. Don't pretend it doesn't bother you that you had to hear it from someone else. Go find someone more like you. It never would have worked with us, Dina. We're just too different."

He slipped out of the apartment.

"Adam, wait!"

But his footsteps pounded down the stairs. Tears welled and overflowed down her cheeks.

He'd broken up with her, even though he'd told her he loved her.

Chapter Twenty-One

For the third time after breaking up with Dina, Adam vomited. He'd broken up with the one girl he loved. And he was a bastard.

At least he left first.

His stomach gurgled and flopped and once again, he hunched over the toilet in the public restroom of the third largest law firm in Manhattan. The cold porcelain did little to ease his torment. This was worse than being drunk. At least he'd feel better once the alcohol was purged from his system. But this? There was no way to purge his vile behavior from his system.

Flushing the toilet, Adam washed his hands, adjusted his tie, combed his hair, popped a breath mint, and shot his cuffs. Stepping out of the restroom into the black and gray marble lobby, he strode to the elevator and punched the button for the fifth floor. When the doors opened, he stepped into a carpeted reception area and approached the desk. An older woman with perfectly coiffed white hair looked at him over reading glasses perched on her nose.

"May I help you?"

"I'm Adam Mandel. I have an interview with Matthew Stevens."

"I'll page him."

She pointed to the buff leather sofa, but Adam paced instead. He should be thrilled his headhunter found three law firms looking to hire junior partners in his area of expertise, but after the previous two interviews weren't successful, he didn't hold out much hope.

The door opened. "Adam? I'm Matthew. Come on in."

Adam followed the older gentleman through a labyrinth of hallways until they reached a corner office. Unlike his father's, which was dark and stately, this one was airy with floor-to-ceiling windows and filled with the clean lines of a glass table that served as a desk, sleek modern furniture, and geometric patterned rugs. He sat in the black leather mid-century modern chair Matthew pointed to and leaned against its back. The pseudo-relaxed pose was supposed to hide his anxiety.

"So, Adam, I took a look at your résumé, but I'm a little concerned about something."

Adam's stomach knotted. He knew all the right the answers, but he'd hoped to get further into the interview process before using them. "What are you concerned about?"

"The reason you left your father's firm. I've heard the whispers. Can you explain?"

Adam leaned forward in his chair and met Matthew's gaze square on. He held up his hands. "The very first time, months ago, I botched something I worked on. It was my fault. But the other two you heard about? I gave everything to my paralegal to file. I have no idea how the filing didn't happen. She says I never gave anything to her, but she's wrong. I've learned my lesson and in the future, I'll either file the motions myself or confirm someone else definitely filed them, even if it means staying in the office all night. I know you have no reason to believe me, but I'm telling you the truth."

"Why did your father fire you?"

The million-dollar question. He shrugged. "When your name is on the door, the only way to convince a client a mistake won't happen twice and to reassure the rest of the office staff is to fire the lawyer who supposedly screwed up, even if the lawyer is innocent." *Or your own son.*

"Okay, let's look at your experience."

They spoke for the next thirty minutes about cases Adam had tried, goals he had and what the firm looked for in a junior partner. When Matthew rose to shake his hand, Adam got to his feet.

"Thank you for taking a chance and interviewing me," Adam said.

"I'm good at judging people. How you told me about some of your cases, your manner in relating it all to me makes me think there's more to the situation you've found yourself in than meets the eye. And it can't be easy working for your own father. Let me get back to you in a few days."

Adam left the interview feeling better. As he walked to Penn Station to catch the train, he thought once again about Dina. He had talked about what happened to his potential employer. Why couldn't he talk to her?

Because no matter what he said, she'd never forgive him.

Chapter Twenty-Two

Lunch breaks were the worst. Dina spent the entire hour staring at the door of the library, expecting Adam to walk in and beg her forgiveness. For the fourteenth consecutive day since they broke up, Dina took a walk through Morristown. She walked, trying to focus on anything—items in store windows, how cold it was when the wind blew, pity for the homeless woman sitting in the middle of the green—other than Adam.

But today, she couldn't stop her mind from picturing a reunion. She'd come out of a store or restaurant and bump into someone who would be Adam, and he'd grovel until she forgave him. She wouldn't, but it was nice to imagine the groveling part. A passing car honked, and she jumped, thinking it was him. It wasn't. Startled out of her reverie, her stomach dropped—she'd walked to Adam's office. Or should she say, his former office. Spinning around to go the other way, she banged into someone.

"Watch where you're going," a deep voice said. It sounded familiar.

When she looked at his face, she blanched. It wasn't Adam. She'd bumped into his dad.

"S...sorry." The smell of Mr. Mandel's cologne transported her back to dinner at his house, when Adam was solicitous of her as his dad humiliated him. Her stomach churned.

He stepped back and frowned. "You're Dina, right? My son's girlfriend."

Oh God, he remembered her. "Sorry for bumping into you."

"How are you?"

She swallowed. She wasn't sure she could have this conversation, not without dissolving into a puddle on the sidewalk. "We're not together anymore."

He raised his eyebrows. "Really? You were a great influence on him."

She bit her lip.

"You're too good for him," he said. "I knew it from the moment I saw you. I hoped it would work out, or he could change, but I had my doubts."

The conversation would have been awkward if she still dated Adam, but now that they were broken up, it was worse. What kind of father spoke ill of his son to the ex-girlfriend? The physical resemblance she'd noted vaguely at dinner was highlighted now in the harsh sunlight. The space his father's and Adam's bodies took up was similar and their tone of voice, while not exact, was close enough to make her ache. All she wanted to do was forget Adam, and his father made her want to defend him.

Her blood pressure rose. Adam did not deserve her defense. Not after the way he treated her. How dare his father make her feel this way?

"Adam is a grown man. He's capable of doing whatever he wants on his own. He doesn't now, nor has he ever, needed me. As for your doubts, he deserves more from you."

She turned and walked away, but not before seeing a glimmer of admiration in his father's eyes.

****

Adam sifted through his email. Still no word from any of the firms he'd interviewed with. The knot in his stomach tightened. No callbacks, no questions, nothing. He supposed it was better than a slew of rejections, but there was little solace in the thought, since he still didn't have a paycheck. The thought of approaching his father for a loan made his shoulders ache from tension.

However, if he didn't get a job soon, he might have to. Bile rose in his throat, and he swallowed the bitter taste.

He looked on his computer at his bills coming due. He had enough saved in the bank for this month and possibly next, but sweat gathered on his upper lip as he looked at his list of expenses: rent on his "luxury" apartment, his BMW lease, and law school loan. Those were the biggies. But there were his everyday expenses: food, phone, and cable. And others he couldn't think of right now. His friends expected him to socialize a certain amount, and while he'd cut back after his breakup with Dina, they wouldn't let him continue to live the life of a hermit for long. And a guy needed to eat. He started to get nervous.

Should he look for a different kind of job to tide him over? It would keep him from having to ask his father for money, but what would he do? Bartend? He'd seen help-wanted signs at plenty of the bars he frequented. The places did great and were always packed, which meant good tips. But it was one thing to be a patron. It was something completely different to work there and serve his friends and acquaintances.

Temp work? He wasn't qualified for much, and what if they placed him in the office of a former client?

God, the embarrassment would be awful.

No, he'd wait it out a little longer. If he didn't get a job offer in two more weeks, he'd reevaluate his options.

His ringing phone pulled him out of his worries about the future, until his caller ID flashed. His father. Crap. He was tempted to let it go to voicemail. However, the slight but improbable chance he called to offer him his old job made him answer.

"Adam, we need to meet."

Should have let it go to voice mail. "About what?"

"Things I'd rather not discuss on the phone."

Great. A crick formed in his neck. "I'm busy, Dad. I'll give you a call when my calendar clears up."

"No, we'll set something up now. Your calendar can't be full because you're not working for me, and I haven't heard of anyone else hiring you yet."

Score one for good ole dad. "When?"

"Sunday, lunchtime. The house. And come alone."

Adam hung up the phone and banged his head against the wall. Just when he thought things couldn't get any worse.

****

Dina burrowed beneath the quilt as she sat on the hearth in front of the lit fireplace, hands wrapped around her steaming teacup, and still she couldn't warm up.

"Deen, come over here." Tracy juggled the baby on the sofa. "You're going to catch on fire."

She stared into the flames. The yellow edges reminded her of Adam's hair, and tears leaked from her eyes. Dammit, she should be done crying over the jerk.

"Why did Adam's dad upset you?" Tracy asked.

Dina had dragged herself to work after her lunch break and hid herself in one of the storage rooms for most of the rest of the day. When Tracy found her, she pulled her up and brought her to her house. Joe took one look at Dina, grabbed his jacket, and left the house, with a quick kiss for Tracy. Dina didn't want to talk about it, gave Tracy only the barest of details, but she was her best friend and deserved to have her questions answered. With a sigh, she turned.

"Because he made me feel sorry for Adam, and I don't want to feel sorry for him. I want to hate him, and I do…mostly. Only, for a lawyer, he's not being logical." Dina brought the tea to her lips. The liquid burned her throat, but she didn't care.

"And for a guy, he's being a dick," Tracy said.

She sputtered and choked on the tea already half-swallowed. Her eyes watered further, and Tracy rushed forward to pat her back.

"I'm sorry, I didn't mean to make you choke."

Dina rested her head on Tracy's shoulder and stroked the baby. "It's actually the best thing anyone has said to me since he broke up with me." She played with the baby's feet in their footy pajamas.

"Would be nice if we could turn a switch in our brains," Tracy said. "But you're a good person. Of course you care. Plus, you love him."

She swung around to face Tracy. "What? I don't love him." She had thought she did. She'd tried to figure out the right time to tell him. But he'd broken up with her, and those feelings died. It proved she didn't really love him, didn't it?

Tracy gave her a look like she didn't believe her. "Or, because you really do love him, you feel sorry for him. I don't think you'd feel emotional over a guy you didn't love."

Dina turned to the fire. It wasn't fair. She'd finally fallen in love—head over heels, every cliché ever written about, in love—and it was with Adam. Golden-haired, way above her everything, Adam. And what amazed her more? He had loved her back. In fact, since she had never told him her feelings, he loved her "first." She should have swooned. She should have at least gotten to hug herself. Instead, she'd missed out on everything because of Ashley.

And this was what Tracy chose to focus on?

"You're not making me feel better. I loved him. Big deal. It's moot at this point, because he hates me. And I'm angry, and he and I are finished."

Tracy put the baby in her playpen and gave Dina a hug. "I'm sorry, sweetie. Whatever you're feeling for him is justified. And you're right, he's the one who's in the wrong here, not you. Also, he has no idea what he's missing. His dad is a bigger ass than he is. Don't let his behavior make you question yours."

Dina's phone rang, and Tracy reached for it. "Want to answer it?"

She shook her head. There was no one, other than Tracy, whom she wanted to talk to.

"I think we need a girls' night out," Tracy said.

"No, I don't want to go anywhere right now."

"I know, and I can't with Peanut, here, anyway. But Saturday night you and I are going out. There's a film festival at the university. We'll go and forget all about Adam and his dad."

"Okay." Dina gave Tracy a hug and kissed the baby. She wouldn't cry. Not again. She would think of something else—anything else—and somehow get over Mr. Flashypants.

Except as she made her way home, she couldn't get over Adam's lack of logic. Once under the covers, she stared out the window into the darkness and tried to figure it out. He wasn't being logical, even though his profession required him to be. She bolted upright. He was being emotional.

Why?

Chapter Twenty-Three

By the next morning, Dina still couldn't figure out what Adam was afraid of, but her phone rang two more times from an unknown number while she was with Tracy. Whoever it was didn't leave a message, which meant it was a telemarketer. A very annoying one.

When the phone rang a third time, Dina grabbed it and barked, "What?" as she walked from her parking spot toward the library.

"Dina? Oh, I'm glad I caught you," the female voice on the other end said.

"Who is this?"

"It's Cheryl McAdams. From high school. We were at the reunion together."

"How did you get my number?"

"I asked the reunion chair. Listen, I really need to talk to you and Adam."

Fat chance. "I'm sorry, I'm on my way into work."

"Are you free tonight? We could meet for dinner."

"I really don't think…"

"Please, it's super important. It's about Ashley."

No way. "I have no desire to waste any more time on her, Cheryl. Please stop calling me."

"Even if she lied?"

Dina caught her breath and choked. Her nose ran, and she dropped her phone into her bag as she rummaged for a tissue. Ashley lied?

Wiping her nose one last time, she put the phone to her ear. "What are you talking about?"

"Oh good, you're still there. I heard this horrendous noise and I called and called your name and you didn't answer and—"

"Cheryl!"

"What?"

"Ashley lied? How do you know?"

"Oh, right. Sorry. Yes, but this is too important to discuss over the phone. Please meet me for dinner tonight."

Dina's glance shifted between the library door and her car. If she had to meet her in person, she wanted to do it now, so she didn't have to spend the entire day wondering about their conversation. Because although she and Adam were no longer together, her curiosity was too strong for her not to pursue this.

"Okay."

They fine tuned the details and Dina went into work, confident she'd get nothing done today. She was right. In spades. By lunchtime, she'd filed three books in the wrong place, looked up the wrong information for her research project, and repacked the books she was supposed to unpack.

Brian, her boss, came to her as she searched for her lunch in her bag. The crinkling paper muffled his footsteps, and she jumped. "Dina, everything okay today?"

"I'm sorry, Brian. I'm distracted today. I'll get a grip, I promise."

"Everyone has an off day once in a while, but you've been off now more than usual. I'm concerned about you."

She ran a hand through her hair and it caught in her frizz. Wincing, she untangled her fingers and massaged her scalp. "I know. I'm sorry."

As he walked away, she sighed. She needed to find a way to get over Adam. Maybe her conversation tonight with Cheryl would help. She paused, her sandwich halfway to her mouth. Cheryl invited her and Adam to dinner. Should she call him and ask him if he wanted to go?

No, she'd sound desperate.

But it was about Ashley, who ruined his life.

Except she didn't know specifically what, other than she lied, which, if she were honest with herself, didn't mean much. She could have lied about anything.

It was probably better to wait until after she met with Cheryl and listened to what she had to say before she decided whether or not to tell Adam. It might not be important, and it was silly to involve him for nothing.

****

That evening, after a less productive afternoon than morning, Dina walked into the sushi restaurant to meet Cheryl. It was a favorite of hers, and when Cheryl expressed a willingness to come to Morristown, Dina gave her the name and location of the restaurant. She was about to give her name to the hostess when movement caught the corner of her eye. Cheryl sat in a corner booth and waved her arms, trying to flag her down. Gritting her teeth, Dina thanked the hostess and walked over.

Cheryl gave her two air kisses before she sat and pointed to the empty seat across from her. Stashing her purse next to her, Dina sat and took the menu from the waitress who appeared at the table, though she already knew what she wanted to order. It gave her hands something to do if nothing else.

"Oh, you really do look like a librarian," Cheryl said. "It's adorable."

Not quite sure what to make of her statement, Dina nodded. "Did you know Casanova was a librarian?"

"Uh…wasn't he some sort of lover?"

"He was also a scam artist, alchemist, spy, and church cleric."

Cheryl looked at her askance, and Dina could feel a flush creep from her chest to her face. Why did she try to have a conversation with this woman? She had no desire to be friends with her—they were completely different types of people. If she were smart, she'd keep her mouth shut—except to eat—and let Cheryl say her piece. She could leave and be done with this ridiculous dinner.

"I guess being a librarian gives you access to all kinds of information," Cheryl said after a few moments passed with agonizing slowness.

"Pretty much everything is good here," Dina said. "My favorites are the dragon roll and the spider roll."

"I don't really like eel—too rubbery. Oh, they have California rolls! My favorite!"

And now she knew exactly what kind of sushi "lover" Cheryl was. As soon as they'd ordered, Dina waited for Cheryl to tell her why they were here. She tried not to fidget, but she couldn't stop her foot from swinging like a clock pendulum on steroids. When the toe of her shoe made contact with something solid, she hoped, for a nanosecond, it was the table leg.

"Ouch!"

Oops. "I'm sorry," she said. "I guess I'm anxious

to find out what you wanted to tell me."

Cheryl grimaced as she rubbed her leg through her black wool trousers. "It's okay. Yeah. So, you know how Ashley accused Adam Mandel of not actually giving her the forms she needed?"

"No, I stopped you before you could tell me any details."

"Oh right." She filled her in. "Well, she made it up. All of it."

"Why?" Dina leaned forward, trying to cover her amazement that someone could do something so terrible. "Why would she?"

"Apparently, Adam is competing with someone else at the firm for junior partner. The guy—I don't know his name—is nervous because Adam's dad is the head of the firm. Ashley has a thing for him. She messed up Adam's cases to help the guy. I guess this isn't the first one she didn't file on time. She mentioned doing it a couple months ago and then again this time."

"Oh my God, I can't believe she'd play with someone's reputation and career! You know he got fired, right? From his *Dad's* firm!"

"She's a witch and she cares only about herself and her own interests. Well, and the other guy, although knowing her, it probably won't last."

Dina waited as the waiter delivered their sushi, but she couldn't bring herself to eat. Her stomach roiled at the destruction Ashley caused.

She squinted at Cheryl. "Why are you telling me this? I thought you were friends." Her heartbeat increased as she waited for her answer.

Cheryl's expression hardened, and Dina caught a glimpse of the mean girl she remembered from high school. "She tried to steal my boyfriend."

"But I thought she was into the other guy at the firm?"

Cheryl waved her hand in the air. "With Ashley, there's always someone. Multiple someones."

If this was the big league, Dina wanted no part of it. She wanted to stay in her own world, where people acted like adults, where girlfriends trusted their boyfriends and vice versa, where communication and not deception solved problems. But she couldn't say it to Cheryl.

Dina nibbled her sushi as Cheryl went into all the evil ways Ashley tried to steal Cheryl's boyfriend. Dina nodded and made sympathetic noises, but wasn't required to do more, which was good since Cheryl left her little time to speak. Finally, when she took a break to breathe and pop the last California roll in her mouth, Dina returned the subject to Ashley's accusation.

"But why are you telling me this? Why not go to the law firm or Adam?"

"He's your boyfriend. You should be the one who gets to do it."

Cheryl was being her version of nice to her? Dina wasn't sure if she should be thankful or wary.

"But they're never going to believe me. It's hearsay."

Cheryl grabbed her phone and tapped the screen a few times. "I'll send you a screenshot of a text Ashley sent me."

Dina's phone binged. When she opened the text, she gasped.

Don't forget, ladies, lying and manipulation are the norm in the law profession—I should know!

There was more, but red spots appeared in Dina's vision and prevented her from reading any further. Her anger at Ashley's careless disregard for the truth and for Adam threatened to overwhelm her.

"Hey, relax." Cheryl reached for her hand. "We'll pay her back, don't worry."

Cheryl spent the rest of dinner discussing all the ways she'd retaliated against people who wronged her—her mother for being uninvolved in her life and whom she now refused to visit; her ex-boyfriend who'd cheated on her and whose current girlfriend she mailed old photos to; her old boss, for whom she'd moved around all kinds of files when he let her go; and of course, Ashley.

By the time Dina left, she was in desperate need of a shower. She didn't want to be as spiteful as Cheryl, and she had no desire to continue any kind of a relationship with her. But if she passed along this information, she'd probably have to see Cheryl again to obtain proof or something. And would she seem like she couldn't let Adam go by bringing this information to his attention? Would she be showing him how much his accusations hurt her and would it be the assumed motivation?

****

Whatever Dina expected her Rabbi's office to look like, it wasn't this. Pale gray walls with bright white trim, a large window with multi-colored beads instead of curtains, and a glass topped chrome table instead of a desk. White bookshelves covered two of the four walls, filled with Judaica books, modern textbooks and a variety of other books Dina itched to explore. Interspersed with the books were modern art paintings and black and white photographs of Israel. The one free wall featured colorful Jewish prints and her rabbinical ordination certificates. The overall effect was one of friendliness and approachability, which shouldn't have surprised her at all. Because the Rabbi was friendly and approachable, which was why Dina requested a meeting with her.

Only now, with the prospect of having to discuss the situation, Dina had second thoughts. She sat on one of the two raspberry-colored leather chairs and clasped her hands together to keep them from trembling.

"It's nice to see you, Dina." Rabbi Ackerman leaned forward and smiled. "And I wanted to thank you for the book recommendation you gave me Friday night. I ordered it on Sunday and started reading it yesterday. It's excellent!"

Dina's face warmed and her hands stilled. "I'm glad you enjoy it. You know, if anyone ever wants to start a book club at the temple, I'd be happy to help."

"A book club would be wonderful. But I don't think it's the reason you wanted to talk to me today."

Dina gripped her knees and forced herself to relax. "No, it's not. I have a dilemma I hoped you might be able to help me with." She outlined what happened with Adam, being careful not to name names, and finished with her conversation with Cheryl.

"My problem is I don't know what to do with the information."

"Why not?" the Rabbi asked.

"Because he and I aren't together anymore and honestly, after the way he treated me, I don't want anything to do with him."

"I can understand, Dina. But you know information

will help clear his name."

"He's not under arrest and believe me, these women are gossipy. The information will get back to him anyway."

"Why are you here?"

Dina shrugged. "I guess I feel guilty doing nothing. I don't want to be spiteful, but I don't want to come across as this desperate girl trying to get back together with him."

"Do you really think he'd take it that way?"

"I don't know. Women throw themselves at him all the time."

"Did you?"

Dina's mouth dropped. "No. If anything, I tried to avoid him."

"And yet he still went out with you."

She blinked her tears away. "It doesn't matter now."

The Rabbi nodded sympathetically. "Look, I suspect you have plenty of girlfriends who can give you relationship advice. How about I give you advice from a Jewish perspective. I am a Rabbi, after all." She winked at Dina.

For the first time since she walked into the Rabbi's office, Dina relaxed.

"In Deuteronomy, it tells us 'Righteousness, righteousness you shall pursue.' Because the word 'righteousness' is repeated, some say we may not use unjust methods in pursuit of a just cause. Kind of like the end doesn't justify the means."

"So leaving it to others to allow word to filter back to Adam would be wrong?" Dina asked.

Instead of answering, the Rabbi continued,

"There's another story, in Leviticus, where Moses chastises Aaron for not following his instructions. Aaron suggests perhaps Moses didn't quite understand what God told him, and Moses agreed Aaron could be right. When we study this text, Moses admitting he might be wrong is huge, because if he's misinterpreted God's words here, where else might he have done so? By admitting he's not perfect, he gives the Hebrews an opportunity to go against him. But Moses realizes his duty is to tell the truth."

"So I have to tell him."

"I think you do. And I think you knew that deep down."

Dina sighed. "I did. I hoped there was a way around it."

Sitting back in her chair, the Rabbi thought a moment. "Well, there is one thing. His father is the one who fired him, right?"

Dina nodded.

"So could you bring the information to his father? Of course, you'd have to be sure his father would tell him; otherwise you'd have to tell Adam anyway and you'd be exposing a fault in his father to his son, which isn't very righteous."

"His father is many things, but I can't imagine he wouldn't tell his son the truth."

As she left the Rabbi's office, she thought about their conversation. Adam's father wasn't the nicest man, but he wouldn't want his company to suffer. He'd want to expose the truth so his reputation would be pristine. All she'd have to do is meet with him, expose Ashley's lies, and frame it as a matter of honor to tell Adam. They'd both win. Adam's father would know the truth, as would Adam, and she wouldn't have to see him.

It was perfect.

Chapter Twenty-Four

Dina paused in front of Adam's father's house. Her "perfect" plan might not be perfect after all. She'd called his father at work and asked to meet with him, telling him she had news to share. It was too important to discuss over the phone. Instead of picking a time during the week as she'd expected, he'd invited her over to his house today, Sunday, at eleven o'clock. Reluctant to go to his home, she tried to offer alternatives, but he was adamant. Here she was. At least she was guaranteed not to run into Adam.

The house intimidated her. The man intimidated her. This lifestyle intimidated her. Every fiber of her being wanted to turn around and leave, forget about what she knew and go to her cozy apartment to curl up with a book.

But she was righteous and had a duty to tell the truth.

Dammit.

Finding her backbone, she pushed the door chime and listened to it echo throughout the house. Mere moments later, the front door opened, and the same formal woman stood in the doorway. There was no sign of recognition, no welcoming gesture. *I guess hired help is paid to be neutral.*

"Hi, I'm Dina. I'm here to see Mr. Mandel."

"Come in." She motioned for Dina to follow. This

time, she wasn't led into the living room. She was shown to a room off of the foyer. Decorated in shades of blue and cream, with white orchids on the table and a small Queen Anne sofa, it showed a more feminine touch. Dina sat on the sofa and gazed at the Monets on the wall as some of her nerves dissipated.

"This was my wife's favorite room," Mr. Mandel said.

Dina startled at his silent appearance and rose to greet him. "I can see why." She held out her hand to shake his. "It's lovely."

"My son never sets foot in here."

She did not want to talk about Adam any more than necessary. "I'm sure it's a reminder she left. Thank you for seeing me today."

He sat in a blue and cream striped wingback chair, across from her, and the woman who'd answered the door brought in a tea service. When Dina nodded to the silent question, she poured tea and handed Dina the sugar, before arranging a cup for Mr. Mandel.

When she'd left, he leaned forward. "You said you had news for me?"

The bone china teacup rattled as she placed it on the saucer, and she wished there was alcohol added to it to steady her nerves.

"I have proof Ashley lied about everything."

"Ashley…?"

"The paralegal who accused Adam of never giving her the motions she was supposed to file." Did he really not remember who she was?

"You know her?"

"I went to high school with her, although I never knew her, other than by reputation."

"What's your proof? Because I was never able to find out any information. The paralegals in my office presented a united front and defended her."

She told him about the reunion and about Cheryl and Ann and Ashley and all the rest of the "mean girls." She recounted her dinner with Cheryl and finally, she handed him her phone.

"The screenshots are of texts Ashley sent her group of friends. Ashley is currently trying to steal Cheryl's boyfriend, and this is Cheryl's way of getting payback."

"And these girls are your friends?" His disdain showed on his face and though it was undeserved, Dina winced.

"No, they never were. I didn't have friends in high school. I was too smart to fit in. They used me to try to pass their classes, and they're using me now to get revenge."

"Why are you helping them?"

She met his gaze and refused to cower. "Because in this instance, the truth is more important than anything else. I'm not a part of them, I never was. And I won't participate in their payback. I'm simply passing along information you need to hear."

"What about what I need to hear?"

The voice made her drop her teacup, which shattered in the saucer and spilled tea on the table before dripping onto the Aubusson rug. Mr. Mandel yelled for the maid, but Dina froze, staring at Adam.

He wasn't supposed to be here.

He never visited his dad. It was the only benefit she'd seen to meeting at his house. Her body temperature plummeted before ratcheting up and making her sweat. She opened her mouth, remained silent, and closed it again.

The maid entered with a rag and cleaned up the mess. Adam remained in the doorway, leaning against the jamb, feet and arms crossed. Only the tic of his jaw told Dina he wasn't as relaxed as he pretended to be.

When all traces of the spilled tea had been erased, Mr. Mandel settled in his chair and focused his gaze on Dina, seeming to ignore Adam. If only it were as easy for her.

"Why?" Mr. Mandel asked.

Dina frowned, trying to keep her focus. "Why, what?"

"Why are you giving me this information?"

"Because it's the truth. Adam didn't shirk his duties or lie. It wasn't his fault on either of the accounts. She made it up. And with the proof, you can give him his job back."

"What's in it for you?"

The question came from Adam, and she tried to control her breathing before she answered. "Nothing."

Mr. Mandel stared at her like she was a brand new species of insect. She refused to squirm.

"Thank you for bringing this to me," Mr. Mandel said. "Can I get a copy of the texts?"

"You can have them. I don't ever want to see them again." She sent him the screenshots and when he confirmed receipt, she deleted them from her phone. "If you'll excuse me, I have to leave. Thank you for the tea, and I'm sorry about the mess."

As she passed through the doorway, Adam grabbed her arm, but she yanked it away.

"Don't touch me."

"Dina."

Hearing her name on his lips was like a knife through her chest. Without waiting for him to say anything else, she rushed out the door and drove away.

****

"What the hell did you do?" Adam shouted to his father as he watched Dina leave him. Dammit. He'd set this whole thing up so he could be the one to leave. And now his father interfered. The familiar hollow feeling filled his chest and bands of pressure squeezed, making him picture an empty bag with a tie around it, slowly squeezing all the air out of it.

"What did *I* do?" his father asked. "There you go again, blaming all your problems on everyone but yourself. Why don't you ask her yourself?"

His father strode out of his mother's parlor, into his office and grabbed a bottle of scotch off the sideboard. Adam hated this room as much as his mother's parlor, except he'd enter this one. He followed his father and watched him pour a shot into a Glencairn tumbler and toss it back. He could feel the burn in his own throat, but he didn't drink it. Not until he got answers from his father.

"What was Dina doing here?"

"I believe you overheard at least part of what she said. She told me she had something to tell me."

"And you happened to invite her over right before the time you'd told me to arrive?"

"Two birds, one stone."

"What the hell is that supposed to mean?" Adam paced the room, too agitated to sit still.

"It means you need to fix things with Dina, and she was going to be here."

"I need to…who the hell gives you the right to butt

into my business?"

His father loomed over his desk, fists planted on either side of the leather blotter, a frown twisting his face. "I am your father, and you are royally screwing up your life. It's high time you settled down and made something out of yourself."

"I was *making something* of myself just fine until you fired me on unsubstantiated accusations."

For the first time since Adam arrived at the house, a look of discomfort passed across his father's face. He'd learned from years of experience, the best way to best his father was indirectly.

"The accusations hurt the firm."

"The accusations were false, as Dina proved." He glowered at his father and watched his face suffuse with color.

"I had no way of knowing."

"Yet somehow, Dina was able to find out?" Adam staggered. "How could she have known, Dad? Unless she worked with Ashley all along." The last sentence came out in a hoarse whisper, and he sank into the chair across from his father's desk.

"If you believe Dina worked with Ashley, you're dumber than I ever thought you were," his father said.

Adam remained silent.

"You're kidding me." His father rose from behind his desk, came around and leaned against it, mere inches away. "Adam, think about it. Can you really picture her and Ashley working together? This is Dina. The girl who spouts obscure facts Ashley wouldn't recognize in an encyclopedia, and covers more skin than Ashley ever has in her life. Come on!"

"They went to high school together. Ashley used

Dina to get good grades. Who knows what else they've done?" But Adam recognized the absurdity of his statement. He dropped his chin to his chest. "Okay, scratch it. Dina's not that type of woman."

"Damn right. And you owe her an apology for even thinking she was."

He was right. "What about what you owe me?"

"I owe you one as well. I'm sorry. I couldn't face the idea of the firm suffering."

His father never showed this side of himself and Adam rose, sticking his hands in his pocket and shrugging off the unexpected emotion. "It's fine. I'm used to it."

"Adz."

Adam stiffened at the unused childhood nickname. He hadn't heard it from his lips since before his mother left.

"Don't let my mistakes ruin your life, son."

"It's a little late for your advice, when your own father fires you."

His father's gaze bore into him. "I'll take care of reinstating you and making things right at the office. But I'm not talking about your job."

"What gives you the right to think you have a say in anything else?"

A brief flicker in his father's eyes was the only indication he'd scored a hit. "She did come to me with the information."

And that was the million-dollar question. Why hadn't Dina come to him?

"Don't push her away, Adam. Not for me, but for you. She's the best thing to ever happen to you. Find a way to make it work."

He couldn't listen to his father anymore. Too many things zoomed around in his brain—Ashley and her accusation, Dina, how the hell Dina knew the truth, why she'd gone to his father instead of him, his mother, his father calling him 'Adz.' He needed to get out of this house, where memories threatened to overwhelm him.

Striding out of his father's office, he raced to the front door, but his father stopped him in front of his mother's parlor.

"I miss her too, you know."

The raw emotion in his father's voice struck him like a physical blow. Daring a glance at him, he looked in awe at his father's moist eyes. He couldn't handle his father or the implications of his statement. He needed to escape. Throwing the front door open, he ran to his car, gunned the engine, and sped down the paved driveway. The thrum of the engine echoed the racing of his pulse. He hugged the curves in the road, watching trees pass in a blur, knowing he drove too fast but not caring. When he reached the straightaway, he slowed, taking deep breaths as if to slow his car as well as his heart.

He needed to talk to Dina.

****

Dina lay curled in a ball on her bed, the shades drawn. She'd spent an hour sobbing to Tracy. Her throat was parched, and her limbs were heavy. She had the "Adam Flu." And she was pissed.

He was an ass. There was no reason for her to feel this bad after clearing his name with his father. The truth was supposed to set her free, or some such crap. It was supposed to make her feel better.

It didn't.

Maybe if Adam hadn't shown up. But he did, and the sight of him shredded her heart.

Her intercom buzzed, and she roused herself enough to stumble out to the kitchen. Tracy was a sweetheart to come over.

"Hello?" Her voice was hoarse.

"Dina, let me in."

The masculine voice was not Tracy. For a millisecond, she tried to convince herself it was Tracy's husband.

"Go away, Adam."

"Dina, I want to talk to you."

She leaned against the wall. "I don't want to talk to you. Go away, Adam."

"Please."

"No."

She returned to her bedroom and burrowed under the covers as she listened to the intercom continue to buzz. There was nothing to talk about.

After five minutes of near continuous buzzing—she could imagine him leaning against the button like some crazy combination of debonair movie star and petulant toddler—the noise ceased. Dina raised her gaze. The silence disturbed and relieved her at the same time. Exhaling, she made herself more comfortable among the light blue and yellow throw pillows and soft white comforter.

And then the knocking started.

"Oh no," she said. "Oh no, no, no, no, no!"

She threw off the covers and stormed to her front door. Through the peephole stood Adam. Which of her neighbors was she going to have to kill?

"Go away, Adam!"

"Dina, I need to talk to you. Please let me in."

"No."

The knocking turned to pounding, and as she leaned against the door, the wood vibrated against her back.

"Dina, come on."

"Adam, if you don't stop, I'll call the police."

Her phone buzzed in her pocket, and a text from Tracy appeared.

are you okay

adam is here. he wants me to let him in

The knocking ceased, and Dina waited, sure it would resume. But after a few minutes, his footsteps receded. Her phone buzzed again.

I told him to stop

so did I. how'd you do it?

I have my ways. do you want me to come over?

no, I'm okay now

call me if you need anything

Now he was gone, and her anger subsided, Dina started to shake. She was tired, hungry, sad, and a host of other emotions she couldn't name. She paced the confines of her small apartment, overcome with a desire to leave, which warred with her fear of running into Adam. He'd come to her apartment and managed to get inside. Tracy somehow convinced him to leave, but what if he waited for her outside?

She raced to the window and peeked outside. Neither he nor his car was in view, and she backed away. She had no idea how Tracy convinced him to leave, but he was gone, and it was time to go on with her own life.

And somehow find a way to get over Adam.

Chapter Twenty-Five

Getting over Adam would be a lot harder than Dina expected. The following morning, Dina woke to four text messages from him.

Dina, it's Adam. can we talk?
please, I really need to talk to you
I know you're angry and I'd like to make it right
Dina, I'm sorry

She turned off her phone and got ready for work.

Tracy took her out to lunch and while they waited in line at the bagel store for their sandwiches, Dina turned on her phone. Another three messages from him, which she deleted without reading. The yeasty bread smells mingled with garlic and lox, and her stomach growled.

"Do you want me to tell him to stop texting you?" Tracy asked.

"I'll ignore them. He'll get tired and stop eventually."

"And you're sure you don't want to hear what he has to say?"

She leveled a glare at Tracy. "Do you know any reason why I should?"

"Nope, just checking."

"Then no. And I still need you to tell me how you got him to leave my apartment."

"I told him if he wanted his reputation fixed,

getting a complaint filed with the cops wasn't the way to do it."

Dina stared at her for a few seconds. She suspected there was more to it, but she didn't have the energy to push. And this was Adam. He was always concerned about his reputation. Besides, she was tired of focusing all her attention on him. She wanted a distraction.

"I want to go to the movies," she said after placing her order. "Want to go with me?"

"Sure, what are we seeing? And when? Because I need to make sure Joe is around for the baby."

"Something funny. I need to be entertained."

"Okay," Tracy said. "I'll have tuna on a blueberry bagel," she said to the guy behind the counter. "Look at what's playing and let me know."

"I can't believe you ordered that," Dina said. "Blueberry with tuna?"

"Don't knock it 'til you try it. It's really good."

Dina shuddered. "No thanks, I'll leave it to you. And I'll pick a movie tonight and let you know."

As they sat to eat, Dina's phone buzzed again, and she shut it off.

"You're sure?" Tracy eyed the phone.

"He'll get bored. It'll pass."

"Okay. In the meantime, I should probably plan on only using your home phone to reach you, huh?"

Dina nodded. "For the time being."

****

The next morning, a pot of basil, tied with a yellow ribbon, arrived for Dina at the library. She frowned as she pulled the card from the envelope.

"If it be a sin to covet honor, I am the most offending soul."—Adam

"Mmm, it smells good," Tracy said as she walked by. "Where'd you get it?"

"Adam."

"He sent you basil?" She started to laugh. "So he went from stalking your apartment, to texting non-stop, to sending you an herb?"

Dina started to giggle. "It's strange."

"There has to be a reason. Let me think about this one."

"Trace, there's a card, too."

Tracy's mouth dropped when she read the card. "Did you know he was this odd when you dated him?"

Dina blinked. "No."

"Don't cry, sweetie. Let's enjoy the game." Tracy picked up the pot and brought it to her desk.

Without the overpowering scent of basil, Dina was able to breathe again and after a few attempts, she focused her thoughts on organizing the children's programs for May. When her stomach started to rumble, Tracy returned with the pot.

"I figured it out. He's actually pretty clever, you know."

"Do I want to know?"

Tracy put her hand on her shoulder. "It's up to you."

Dina sighed. "Fine, tell me. Why is he sending me herbs?"

"Not 'herbs,' a specific herb. Flowers and herbs and trees all have specific meanings. Basil means 'good wishes.' Colors do too, and yellow is for apologies. The Shakespeare quote is also an apology."

"Yeah, I got that."

"He put a lot of effort into this one."

"Still doesn't change my mind." Dina rubbed the yellow ribbon between her fingers.

"I never said it should. Do you want this, or do you want me to keep it?"

"You keep it." Memory of all the gold flowers he'd sent her for her reunion flashed through her mind, and she shuddered. It was thoughtful, but over the top. And thinking of them made her remember the disaster of the reunion.

"Want to grab lunch?" Tracy asked.

"No thanks, I brought my own today. Besides, I can't focus on work very well, and I need to get stuff done. These piles aren't going away nearly as fast as I'd like."

"Okay, see you later."

When she finally left work and returned home, another plant sat outside her apartment door. This time it was a bouquet of carnations. Pink ones, tied with a blue bow. She picked them up and dialed Tracy as she unlocked her door.

"He did it again," she said without saying hello.

"What did he do?"

"Left me a bouquet of flowers outside my door."

"Really? What kind? Color? Tell me!"

"You don't need to sound excited about it."

"I'm sorry, Deen. I'm putting aside my feelings for him and separating them from my fascination with this game he's playing."

"That's part of the problem. It's all a game to him."

"So have fun with it."

Dina sighed as she unwrapped the bouquet, filled a vase and put the flowers in the water. "They're pink carnations tied with a blue bow."

"Is there a card?"

"Oh, I forgot to look. Hold on." She sifted through the wrapping until the hard edges of a card dug into the pads of her fingers. "Yeah, found it."

She pulled it out of the envelope. "This one says, 'A fool thinks himself to be wise, but a wise man knows himself to be a fool.' "

"Oh, As You Like It!" Tracy said. "I love that play! Okay, I'll research the flowers and let you know. Unless you want to…"

"Nope, all yours."

"Okay, gotta run, baby's crying. I'll call you later."

Maybe it was the basil, but she had a sudden desire for Italian. She made herself pasta with a red sauce for dinner, along with a salad. She finished when Tracy called her back.

"Carnations mean 'alas for my poor heart'—kinda dramatic, don't you think? Pink means love, obviously, and blue is the color of trust and peace."

"Ha! And I don't mean it in a funny way. He wants me to believe he loves me, and I should trust him? He's insane."

"But creative, Dina. You have to give him credit."

"Somehow I think you're silently rooting for him."

"No, but I'm making notes for Joe. He could learn a thing or two from Adam."

"Careful what you wish for, Tracy."

"I know. And I'm looking forward to tomorrow."

"Oh my God, you think this is going to continue?"

"Of course I do!"

"How long?"

"Depends on how long it takes for you to talk to him."

"Oh brother."

Tracy was correct. For the rest of the week, twice a day, Adam sent Dina bouquets. On Tuesday, he sent her chamomile with "No legacy is so rich as honesty," and white clover with "The course of true love never did run smooth." Tracy researched the meanings—chamomile for 'patience' and white clover for 'think of me'—while Dina researched how to make chamomile into tea.

On Wednesday, daffodils with a pink bow and "I hold the world but as the world, Gratiano; A stage where every man must play a part, and mine is a sad one," arrived. That night, there was a delivery of daisies in pink tissue paper and "Love all, trust a few, do wrong to no one."

Thursday brought ferns and forget-me-nots—obviously he was going through the alphabet, she thought to herself. The cards got more dramatic, too. "Love to faults is always blind, always is to joy inclined." She was tempted to send him a text with the rest of the quote: "Lawless, winged, and unconfined, and breaks all chains from every mind," but she didn't want to encourage him. She choked when she read the second card, "No legacy is so rich as honesty."

By Friday, when he'd sent her holly for hope and white jasmine for sweet love, she'd had enough. Especially when she read the cards, "Now, God be praised, that to believing souls gives light in darkness, comfort in despair" and "O God, O God, how weary, stale, flat, and unprofitable seem to me all the uses of this world!" Creativity was one thing, but she started to think he mocked her.

Later that night, she was sure of it.

****

"Jake, it's not working." Adam paced his apartment and ran his hand over the crown of his head. When Dina refused to answer his calls or his texts, he'd called Jacob in desperation and told him everything. His advice was to woo her. He'd spent the past week wooing her and still she didn't call.

"What have you tried?"

Adam filled him in.

"You need to apologize to her, Adam."

"I would if she'd talk to me."

"You need to force the issue. Unfortunately, you've given her the message you don't trust her. It's hard to overcome. You've shown her you want her back, but you need to show her why."

Adam swallowed. "She knows I want her back. What more do I need to do?"

"You need to open yourself to her." Silence stretched across the line. "She's not your mom."

His breath hitched, and his stomach dropped to his knees. "I know."

"Do you? Because it sounds to me like you pushed her away before she could leave. And you haven't done anything to convince her you made a mistake."

"I sent her flowers. And herbs. With meanings."

"Which she probably understood because she's brilliant. You've appealed to her mind. But you need to appeal to her heart, Adam."

"Her heart? I don't know how she feels about me." He'd told her he loved her, but she'd never responded.

"Ask her."

"And what if I don't like the answer?"

"At least you'll know. Knowledge is much better

than fear, Adam. Trust me. And her."

Adam hung up the phone and continued to pace. He didn't know if he could do it. Trust her? He'd trusted his mother, and she'd left him. Jacob might say Dina wasn't like his mother, but how could he be sure? He passed his bookshelf, where a photo sat of his mother, holding his four-year-old self on her lap. They both smiled for the camera. He picked it up and examined it. The gold frame had intricate designs on it, and the swirls somehow reminded him of Dina's apartment, which was weird, because nothing about the apartment was similar to his mother's decorating style. She loved perfectly matched antiques, orderliness, and calm. Dina's apartment was boho chic, with mismatched everything. It all somehow coordinated and conveyed warmth.

His mother's smile didn't reach her eyes. When Dina grinned, her nose crinkled, her frizzy hair vibrated, and her eyes shone. Her entire body softened.

Did he ever make his mother happy? He assumed so. She wasn't a bad mother. She just turned into an absentee one. But he remembered them playing on the swings, making bubble people during his bath time, snuggling together when she read him a story. He also remembered trying to impress her so she'd stay longer—she always had to go somewhere or do something, and he would beg for one more story, show her one more amazing rock he'd found, or ask for one more hug. But she'd always left soon after.

With Dina, he never felt underlying fear. When he was with her, she showed how much she liked being with him. He never worried about having to impress her or begging her to stay. He never wondered if she'd let him see her again.

Dina and his mother were completely different people. And it was time he gave her what she deserved. His trust.

Chapter Twenty-Six

That night, after watering the white jasmine, she'd rushed to get dressed and raced to temple. Walking in five minutes late, she tried to slide into her seat unobtrusively while the Rabbi read one of the opening prayers. A movement to her left caused her to look up as Adam slid into the adjacent seat. Her mouth dropped.

"What are you doing here?" she hissed.

He leaned forward, pulled out the prayer book and opened it to the correct page. Handing it to her, he reached for another book for himself before answering her.

"Attending services."

"I don't want to talk to you."

He looked over at her and held her gaze for a moment. "Then don't. It's rude to talk through services anyway."

God, he infuriated her. She'd move, but it would call attention to her and to him, and she'd already walked in five minutes late.

For the rest of the service, Dina couldn't focus on anything but Adam—his proximity to her, his smell, his deep voice slightly off-key. When they *davened* in prayer and bowed before the ark, she noticed the tips of his shoes, highly polished, like him. When they stood, his shoulder brushed against hers, as if he knew how hard it was for her to be away from him.

When the service finally ended, he turned.

"Shabbat Shalom, Dina."

It was the traditional thing to say to each other on Shabbat. It would be rude not to respond.

"Shabbat Shalom."

He turned and walked out of the sanctuary and into the social hall for the *oneg*. She followed him, despite her desire to make a run for it. Unfortunately, Rebecca and her family weren't here tonight and the Rabbi saw her. If she left, it would be obvious. She sighed and took her cup of wine to say the prayers. When they finished, Adam took her empty cup and threw it away for her, though she didn't ask him to do it. After the prayer over the challah, the Rabbi approached.

"Hello, Dina."

"Shabbat Shalom, Rabbi."

Adam leaned forward. "Shabbat Shalom, Rabbi. I'm Adam."

The Rabbi looked between the two of them. "Nice to meet you, Adam. I think I've seen you here before with Dina?"

Dina's cheeks heated.

"Yes. She's angry at me right now, and we're not together, but I hope to change her mind."

Dina couldn't prevent her jaw from dropping.

The Rabbi's eyes twinkled with amusement. "I like your honesty," she said, with a wink at Dina. "But perhaps you should talk to her instead of me."

"I intend to," he said, pinning Dina with a look promising he'd get his way. "But in the meantime, I'll wait."

"Going to be waiting a long time," Dina muttered under her breath.

The Rabbi chuckled. "Well, as it says in *Pirkei Avot*, 'Do not be contemptuous of any person, and don't remove yourself from anything, for every person has his moment and everything has its place.' Good luck, Dina."

The Rabbi walked away, leaving Dina and Adam alone.

"I don't appreciate your speaking about me to my Rabbi," she said to Adam, looking straight ahead, and counting the stripes in the wallpaper on the far wall. Anything to avoid his gaze.

"You used to not like when I kept our relationship quiet," he said. She could feel the air around her constrict as he took a step closer to her, an almost physical charge zinging between his chest and her arm.

"I am not getting back together with you." She opened and closed her hands at her sides as she wished for something to do with them, other than strangling him. There were too many witnesses.

"I want to talk to you."

"You already are. And I'm not interested in having a conversation with someone who doesn't trust me."

"I'll wait," he said and took a step back. A chill wrapped around her like a shawl, and for a brief moment she wanted to pull him closer. But it would be ridiculous. Because she was still angry at him.

A man Dina recognized as someone from Brotherhood approached.

"Hi, I'm Dave," he said to Adam and held out his hand as he nodded to Dina. "Welcome to Temple Tikvah. Are you interested in Brotherhood events? We have a breakfast coming up in a week."

Adam shook Dave's hand. "Oh yeah? Sounds

great. I'd love information about it. I'm Adam Mandel, by the way, a friend of Dina's."

"Nice to meet you. Dina, the breakfast is actually open to everyone, if you'd like to join us."

She plastered a smile on her face. "Thanks, I'll think about it."

As Dave walked away, she stalked toward the door, wishing the carpeted floor was bare so her footsteps would broadcast her anger. This was ridiculous. She couldn't take any more of it.

Adam rushed to keep up with her, his long legs making it easy.

"Leave me alone, Adam. You've had your fun."

He jumped forward until he could block her way. She thought about skirting around him, but he folded his arms and looked at her like he'd like nothing better than to pick her up and dangle her in the air if she tried to get away.

"I'm not having fun, Dina. I'm trying to apologize. But you won't let me."

"No, you're not. You're trying to make an impression—with me, with those ridiculous flowers, with my Rabbi, and with everyone at my temple. But what you don't get is I'm not interested. I'm done. You need to stop and leave me alone."

She removed her heels and ran out of the synagogue, leaving Adam in the shadows.

****

On Monday, Adam passed the library on his way to his father's office. He remembered Friday night in the synagogue. For a man who'd refused to allow a woman to ever walk out on him again, he sure failed when it came to Dina. Because she'd walked out on him twice so far.

Each time she left, the invisible bands around his chest tightened. And this latest time left him with the knowledge not only wasn't there anything he could do about it, most likely, he had to suffer through it several more times, because as he'd said to her Rabbi, he hoped she'd come back to him, and he would be patient. And you didn't lie to a Rabbi.

He parked his car in the parking garage, in the spaces designated for visitors to his father's firm and swallowed the bile that rose in his throat. His father's secretary called him to this command performance, in a suit, no less. He pulled on his blue silk tie before readjusting it in the rearview mirror, left his car, and took the elevator to the firm's floor. There was no need to give his name to the receptionist, but he did anyway. Nothing stopped him from walking in like he belonged—except he didn't. He waited for direction and tried to keep his toe from tapping or his fingers from fiddling with his tie.

A moment later, his father's secretary opened the door. "Come on in, Adam. Your father is in the conference room."

Adam followed her down the warren of hallways to the glassed-in conference room. His father sat at the head of the teak table. Senior partners sat around it. Partners and junior partners stood behind them. Adam swallowed as his throat went dry. When Diane opened the door, there was no other recourse than to enter. James was there as well.

Fan-damn-tastic, I've been invited to watch my father promote James to junior partner. Thanks, Dad.

He leaned against the wall, hoping not to be

noticed.

His father rose, and the room grew silent.

"About a month ago, a former paralegal claimed— for the second time—my son did not give her a motion to file. Two different cases, two different outcomes, neither of them good. Despite my son's protests otherwise, she swore he'd never given her the material. She also said he threw her under the bus—blaming her for his mistake. As a result, the entire paralegal department banded together in her defense. She had a plausible story, he had a problematic reputation and while there was no way to verify her claim, there was no way to refute it, either. And I, as the head of this firm, fired my son. I put the well-being of this place above my love for my son." He paused and cleared his throat before he continued, "Something for which I will be forever ashamed."

Adam's pulse pounded in his ears. It was the only sound, as the rest of the room was silent.

Noah looked down, before meeting the gaze of everyone in the room. When he reached Adam, he paused, nodded, and continued.

"It took another woman, my son's ex-girlfriend, to make me see the error of my ways. In the process, she provided proof—proof I should have found myself— Adam is completely innocent. His accuser made up the story in order to try to get another man in this firm the promotion, and hopefully, to get him interested in her."

Adam staggered and reached behind him to hold onto the wall. His father admitted his mistake to everyone in this room.

"Prior to the accusations, both Adam and James were considered for junior partner. The accusation, and

Adam's subsequent dismissal, removed my son from consideration. The accuser's retaliation included poisoning other firms against my son, making it impossible for him to find another job."

Everyone turned to look at each other, shock on their faces. A few, who noticed him, looked sympathetic. Some, like Paul and John, who avoided him, looked embarrassed.

"As of today, we are suing Ashley Peters for slander. We took out a full-page ad in all the major law publications refuting the charges, standing behind Adam and restoring his reputation. I will ask Adam for a list of all the firms he's submitted résumés to and will personally call their managing partners to explain the situation. Then Adam will have a choice. He can return to work here as a junior partner—James, you will keep your new title as well, since you had no knowledge of her actions—or he can work for any other firm he chooses. The choice will be his. But should he choose to rejoin us, we will welcome him with open arms."

One by one, everyone in the room clapped, until the sound of hands together was deafening. Those who were seated, rose. Those who knew Adam was in the room turned toward him and eventually, everyone clapped. He bowed his head until the room silenced. Then, he walked to his father.

"You and I have had our differences over the years," he said, "and I suspect we will continue to have them. But it takes an honorable man to publicly admit when he's wrong. I appreciate what you've said, and I'd be happy to accept the position of junior partner here." He turned toward the rest of the room. "However, as much as I owe my father respect for what he has said today, I would not be here if it weren't for Dina Jacobs. She believed in me from the very beginning, when our relationship was new, and she could have easily walked away and assumed the worst. But she didn't. And after we broke up, which was completely my fault, she had a choice. She could have kept her knowledge to herself, written me off, and forgotten all about me. But instead, she went to my father. Now, as I'm sure all of you have figured out, my father isn't the easiest man to confront."

A smattering of laughter met Adam's remark, and he nodded.

"But she didn't let him intimidate her. She went to him and told him of his error, and she did it in a way to make him listen to her and believe her. I'm sure most of you will agree with me when I say it's not an easy thing to do. But she did it." He looked at his father and for the first time saw admiration—for him.

"My father's biggest regret might be not believing in me, but mine is not believing in Dina. You all gave me a standing ovation welcoming me back. My wish for my time here is not only do I continue to remain worthy of your welcome, but I also continue to learn from you all and from Dina—to believe in people and to give them second chances. Thank you."

En mass, people crowded around him, shook his hand, and congratulated him. Everyone said he had guts to make the speech. Most said they'd always believed in him, though he knew they lied. The people he valued most in the office apologized. But the one person he wished more than anything could have heard him wasn't here.

And she was the only one who mattered.

****

Dina sat in the waiting room of her doctor's office, passing the time on her phone while waiting for her physical. She scrolled through Twitter, updated Goodreads, and moved onto Instagram. With the waiting room packed, the doctor was already behind, and Dina moved onto Reddit.

And stopped.

One of the highlighted videos caught her eye. Adam spoke to a crowd. She stared at it. His father sat next to him. The video was liked several hundred times.

She should ignore it. Who cared what it was about?

She did.

She pressed play, lowered the volume, and held her phone to her ear.

Tears streamed down her face.

This man who was concerned about his image confessed to everyone he worked with what a horrible person he was to her. She wasn't there, he wasn't doing it for affect. He simply owned up to his mistake publicly.

And nothing about it was simple.

She replayed it two more times, trying to find something to dislike. But there was nothing. Of all his gestures—the texts, the phone calls, and the ridiculous number of flowers and herbs—this was the one that got her.

And she could no longer ignore him.

Chapter Twenty-Seven

Adam sank onto the sofa after work and turned on the baseball game. Outside, noise from the street below was muted, but he heard the low bass of passing cars and the higher tones of the commuter train as it slowed on its way from Manhattan. If he worked for a big Manhattan firm, he might be riding it, but he wasn't. He worked for his father again, and this time, he was happy about it.

Opening a diet soda with a pop and a fizz, he gulped the carbonated liquid and leaned his head on the leather cushion. He'd put in a twelve-hour day at the office, worked through lunch and didn't leave before seven. After everyone gave him that warm welcome the other day in the conference room, his friends at work accepted him once again. In fact, everyone did, even the paralegals. Kim talked to him again. Sure, some people still kept their distance, including James, but they were in the minority now. And professionally, he was satisfied.

As the game went to commercial, an ad for a Manhattan law firm appeared, and he thought about where he might have ended up if things were different. For once, he didn't have some deep desire to be in the city. Now, looking at the commercial, the law firm appeared cold and impersonal, whereas it used to seem to be the embodiment of his professional dreams. But everything changed once his father backed him up.

Was he really desperate for his father's approval? They still had a lot to work out, but knowing his father supported him meant a lot. Now if only he could fix the hole in his heart.

He looked to the side. If he had his way, the other part of the couch would not be empty. Dina would sit there. Of course, if she were, they probably wouldn't watch baseball…or maybe they would? She was never selfish enough to prevent him from doing what he liked, and she'd always tried to join in. He remembered the books she'd given him on superheroes and how he'd initially reacted. He'd been so consumed with what others thought, he didn't recognize the gesture for what it was—someone who thought only of others.

God, he missed her. He'd spent weeks trying to get her back, to show her he was sorry, to demonstrate how much he cared. And she'd refused all of his overtures. His hands chilled, and sweat beaded his brow. If he thought he'd been afraid of her leaving him, it was nothing to knowing she wasn't coming back.

His efforts weren't good enough. He'd lost her.

He took deep breaths, trying to control his heartbeat. He would be okay.

The knock at the door startled him, and soda splashed out of the can as he rose. He took a peek through the peephole, blinked, and looked again.

He opened the door.

"Dina." The sight of her, here on his doorstep, left him speechless. Her beautiful frizzy hair was pulled into a low ponytail. A pink scarf gave her cheeks a rosy glow. And the scent of coconuts filled the air, making him want to fold her into his arms and inhale her.

"Adam. I hope you don't mind my showing up…"

"Never. I'm glad you're here." Her expression was wary. She'd never looked wary when she looked at him, and his chest ached. After everything he'd done to show her how much she meant to him, she still had doubts? If only she'd been in his father's office to hear his speech.

He stepped out of the doorway and motioned her inside. She followed, not touching him, leaving a margin of space around her, like a personal "Do Not Touch" zone. The Dina he remembered never did that before.

Leading her into the living room, he pointed to the couch he'd vacated, imagining his wish of her sitting next to him coming true. But she sat across the coffee table from him, as if she needed the physical barrier between them. Bands of pressure tightened around his chest.

"Would you like something to drink? Eat?"

She shook her head, making her curls bounce, making Adam's fingers itch to touch them. He sat on his couch on top of his hands and stared at her, drinking her in. There were so many things he wanted to say to her, and he didn't know what to say first. It was as if all the words he wanted to say rushed from his brain toward his mouth at once, couldn't all fit, and sat behind his lips, trying to jam forward and getting stuck.

"I heard what you said." She twined her fingers together until her knuckles turned white.

What he'd said? When? Where? He wracked his brain trying to figure out what she meant. Oh, his phone calls.

"You mean the messages I left on your voice

mail."

She bit her lip. "No. I deleted those."

The bands around his chest grew tighter. He cleared his throat. "Oh. The texts?"

"No, I still have those, but I meant the video."

Oh God, there's a video? Images of Kardashian sex tapes filtered through his mind. What the hell did he do? "What video?"

She pulled out her phone, tapped on the screen and held it out. His breath expelled in a whoosh of relief, before he inhaled sharply, making himself choke. Dina half rose as if to help him, but he waved her away, rubbed his streaming eyes, and sat back on the couch. "Where did this come from?"

"I found it on Reddit."

Only now did her earlier words sink in. *I heard what you said.* Never mind where the video came from, she'd watched it.

Admitting he was wrong was the right thing to do. It was honorable and honest and some might say, brave. And although he'd chosen to do it in a roomful of people he worked with, it was easier than one would think because Dina wasn't there. He only had to say his side of the story. She wasn't there to respond or reject him.

But she was here now. He should be thrilled because he'd tried to talk to her for weeks without success. He'd even wished she'd been in the office to hear his speech. Her unexpected appearance at his apartment meant she wanted to talk to him too, and now he was scared of what she'd say. His heart pounded, and his throat went dry. He reached for his soda and took a long swallow. God, what he'd give for a beer right now. But he'd overdone it lately, and the last thing he wanted was to blow this time with Dina. He focused on her and tried to calm the bouncing ball of fear in his chest.

"It was quite an apology you gave," she said.

"I meant every word, and more."

"Why did you tell them? They don't know me."

He leaned forward, resting his elbows on his knees. "My dad made this big speech. About how I was innocent. And about how you proved it. He was honest, and I needed to be too. Including about how badly I'd treated you and how sorry I was. Because I wanted a fresh start. And I couldn't have one unless I told them everything."

She rose, and he opened his mouth to stop her from leaving. But she was only pacing, and he kept his gaze trained on her, ready to jump up and block the door if she left, or better yet, fall to his knees and beg her to stay.

"But you couldn't tell me. I don't understand what happened the night of my reunion. One moment, those women pulled me away, the next moment you shut down, and you accused me of being in collusion with them."

Collusion. God, he loved her. Even if she didn't love him back. "I was afraid of what they'd told you and what you'd believe." At her look of surprise, he held up his hand. "I'd finally found someone I wanted to be with, and I blew it. Before you, I never committed to anyone."

"I know."

His jaw dropped.

She reached for his hand. "Come on, Adam, your

personality, at first glance, screams player. I'm sure you've done plenty of things with plenty of women before me. I don't care about any of it, as long as it happened *before* me."

He swallowed, afraid if he spoke, he'd pop whatever bubble supported this fantasy and fall splat into reality.

"What I do care about is everything else," she said.

He ran a hand over his head. How could he possibly explain this to her? He'd show all his insecurities at once. Taking a deep breath, he took the plunge. "We were dancing, and I told you I loved you, and you didn't reply." A squeak made him look up, and he held up a hand. "No, don't. It's fine. You didn't have to say it then, or at all. I didn't tell you because I wanted you to say anything. I told you because it's what was in my heart and I wanted you to know. But the accusations started, and I saw you with them and I didn't know what they'd told you. And knowing my reputation, I was afraid you'd believe them. Especially because I hadn't told you first."

"I never knew Ashley, never liked any of her friends, and no reunion will change it. I'd never believe them over you. They mean nothing to me."

"I know, but I panicked."

"Why?"

"Because I was afraid you'd leave me because I hadn't told you the truth. My dad's firing twisted me up inside and I let it bleed into our relationship. I'm sorry."

"You should have had faith in me. You should have been the one to tell me about losing your job. And if you had doubts about me, you should have told me that, too."

He nodded. "I know. I knew you weren't really with them. I accused you of being on their side in order to leave you first."

"Why?"

"You're the first person I've ever fallen in love with. I mean, really fallen in love with. Dina, I love everything about you—your hair, your smile, the way you don't take me too seriously, your vocabulary and the crazy facts you know. All of it. And it terrified me. Because I was afraid when you knew the whole story about Ashley, you'd realize how unworthy I was and leave. It was okay you didn't tell me you loved me—I had time to change that—but if you'd walked out on me, you would be the third person I'd loved who'd left, and I couldn't have lived with it. So I left first."

"You didn't think I'd believe you if you told me the truth?"

"My father didn't."

"Your father is an ass."

Adam laughed. "I used to think so, too. Now I'm not sure."

"And I'm not your mother."

Adam froze. "What?"

Dina moved onto the couch next to him, exactly where he'd wanted her to sit when she'd first entered. Only now he wished she were anywhere else. His heart pounded in his chest, and the bands of pressure squeezed so hard, spots flickered in front of his eyes. He didn't want to talk about his mother.

His hand grew cool and he looked to see Dina's hand covering it, her thumb stroking across his knuckles.

"I'm not your mother. And her leaving had nothing

to do with you."

"You don't know for sure."

"No, I don't. Only your father does, and he could probably give you the answers you're looking for. But I do know children are never the cause of their parents' problems. Whatever her reasons for leaving, it was not a lack of love for you."

Adam gripped Dina's hand. "I have this irrational fear if I let go, you'll disappear." Her mouth was serious, her gaze somber. She cupped his cheek with her free hand. Her skin was soft, smooth and cool, providing another touch point he didn't want to lose, and he covered it with his other hand. "You can hold on for as long as you'd like. I'm not going anywhere, even when you let go."

The bands of pressure in his chest loosened, and calm settled over him for the first time in as long as he could remember. He let go of the hand on his cheek and pulled her close, inhaling the coconut scent of her hair as he tried to keep his breathing steady.

"I love you," she whispered against his ear.

He pulled away. "You don't have to say it. I don't deserve it."

She stroked the side of his face. "I've wanted to say it for weeks, but I was scared. And when you said it to me at the reunion, I didn't want to prattle it to you like some talking parrot. My feelings mean too much for me to do it."

"Why?" When she frowned, he hurried to continue, "No, not why do your feelings mean something. Why would you possibly love me after the way I treated you?"

"Because I can see through you. I see who you are

inside." She touched his chest, and he wished for her skin to touch his. "I don't care about the rest of this—your money, your looks, your job, although I'm glad you have one because it makes you happy and everyone needs to make a living. But it's not why I love you. I'd love you if you were a janitor on a bicycle."

The image made Adam exhale and he hugged her to him, kissing the part in her hair. After a moment, he grew serious again. "But after the way I've treated you?"

She pulled away, and he tamped down the automatic tremor of fear. She was still here. She said she wouldn't leave. He needed to believe her.

"I hate the way you treated me. You forgot who I am and what about me makes you love me, and while you're very good at apologizing, it can't happen again. I can't be with someone who doesn't trust me, and I won't be with someone who thinks so little of me they'll drop me anytime something gets hard."

"How do I fix this? Because you mean more to me than anyone, and I don't ever want to let you go."

Dina bit her lip and Adam wanted to draw her into his arms and hold her close. But he'd learned he had to give her freedom, to trust her to come back to him, even on the little things, like pulling away from him to think. He sat, and he waited.

"Your calls and your texts and the flowers and herbs with meanings behind them showed me how sorry you are and what I mean to you."

"I'm glad you understood it."

She bit her lip. "Tracy helped at first. I caught on. It was impressive. A little over the top, but impressive."

He nodded.

"And you showed me with your speech to your co-workers I don't embarrass you."

"I never expected it to go online," he said.

"You've given me more than enough reasons to forgive you, and I do. I think I need us to take things slow, to talk and to see how things go from here."

He nodded, and they sat in silence for several minutes. Their only contact was the touch of their hands. Adam concentrated on the texture of her skin against his. Although her hands were perpetually cold, her touch sent a path of warmth up his arm straight to his heart. The apartment was silent, except for the sounds of their breathing and the hum of the refrigerator in the background, and the urge to mingle more than the sound of their breath washed over him.

"Would kissing you be moving too fast?" He glanced sideways at her.

Her hair swung as she shook her head. A ghost of a smile peeked through the strands, and it was all the encouragement he needed. Wrapping his arm around her shoulder, he threaded his fingers through her hair as he drew her toward him. Their lips touched, their breath mingled, and, at last, he was where he belonged.

When they finally pulled apart, she whispered, "You know, I might be willing to compromise on the speed."

He bent his forehead until it touched hers. "Whatever you want, for as long as you want, I will be yours and you can be mine."

And it was enough.

A word about the author…

Jennifer started telling herself stories as a little girl when she couldn't fall asleep at night. Pretty soon, her head was filled with these stories and the characters that populated them. Even as an adult, she thinks about the characters and stories at night before she falls asleep, or in the car on her way to or from her daughters' numerous activities (anything that will drown out their music is a good thing). Eventually, she started writing things down. Her favorite stories to write are those with smart, sassy, independent heroines; handsome, strong and slightly vulnerable heroes; and her stories always end with happily ever after.

In the real world, she's the mother of two amazing daughters and wife of one of the smartest men she knows. When she's not writing, she loves to laugh with her family and friends. She believes humor is the only way to get through the day, mornings are evil and she does not believe in sharing her chocolate.

She writes contemporary romance, some of which are mainstream and some of which involve Jewish characters. All are available through Amazon and Barnes & Noble.

She can be reached at:

http://www.jenniferwilck.com

http://www.facebook.com/pages/Jennifer-Wilck/201342863240160.

She tweets at @JWilck. Her blog (Fried Oreos) is http://www.jenniferwilck.blogspot.com.

And she contributes to Heroines With Hearts blog monthly http://www.heroineswithhearts.blogspot.com.

33848427R00163